Acknowledgements

My wife, my muse, my inspiratic Mary, for being you.

Our kids and their spouses, Hal & Stephanie, Jennifer & Barry, Melissa & Chris, Kevin & Felisha, Brooke & Pat, Mary & Derek.

Fifteen grandkids, Chris, Derrick, CJ, Elizabeth, Isabelle, Kevin Jr, Alexandria, Zane, Addison, Truett, Eli, Dexter, Emi, Logan, Elli. This story is for you guys.

My brothers, sisters, nieces and nephews, all of you left something in my story.

So many former students were inspiration for characters. Thanks for just being there and encouraging me.

My Uncle, Charlie Lake, 90 years young. Thanks for helping me understand myself.

Illustrations: Devin Begay, lives in Kayenta, Arizona and is a member of the Navajo Nation.

He is an extremely talented high school artist. I sent him the story and he produced 8 drawings in a short period of time. Each illustration captures part of the story.

Questions and thoughts before you read the story.

Flip thru the next few pages, and then spend some time contemplating, thinking about how you feel about issues threatening mankind's existence.

I hold multiple degrees; business administration, liberal arts, education and it simple makes me a student of these disciplines. I can read the Bible, Koran, a study on Social Sciences and have an informed opinion, so can you.

Use your skills, research, use Wikipedia and the CIA factbook online and form your own opinions. Jump deep down into the rabbit hole and search for facts. Remember, evidence is not proof of guilt. Do not believe as fact everything you read in textbooks and teachers spout during lecture, everybody has an agenda.

This is my story. I'm not an alarmist, a survivalist or an end of times conspiracy fan. Neither am I a religious zealot or a hater of religion, or other non-Christian religions. I am a Christian, unashamed and proud that God has blessed me in life.

I have faith that something I can't see or prove beyond a reasonable doubt exists.

I'm not a theologian, so when I deal with the subject of God I keep it simple. KISS for short, Keep it simple stupid.

I believe humans are resilient and adaptable. The ability for mankind to overcome a crisis and defeat obstacles is astounding.

I also worry that mankind is greedy and always wanting the dollar and asset belonging to his neighbor. Hate in the form of bigotry, nationalism, race, and religion comes easy to humans. People tend to show too little compassion for neighbors separated by borders, oceans, Gods, race, gender, and religion.

We continually abuse the environment and expect nature to repair our careless acts.

Lake   Doomsday Clock 11:59:59

If you are a teacher, it's a great time for class discussion. If you're a parent, start discussing these issues with your kids.

The world is in a crisis. The threat of a nuclear holocaust is real as more countries acquire nuclear weapons and then proceed to test ICBM missiles to launch and at the same time miniaturize the payloads. Bitter rivals such as India and Pakistan stare each other down. What happens if a nuclear bomb is accidently detonated? Which world leader will be the voice of reason? What if nobody steps forward to stop the escalation and ultimate destruction?

The world's population is exploding. 200 years ago, there were less than an estimated 1 billion people. Between 1900 and 2000 the population increased from 1.5 billion to 6.1 billion.

In 1962 the annual population increase peaked at 2.1%. Today that increase has slowed to less than 1% and by 2100 is expected to go down to 0.1%.

It took 45 years, (1972-2017) to double from 3.05 billion to 7.1 billion. Even at 0.1 of a percent growth, the population is still increasing at an enormous rate.

How many people is too many? Where do we cross the line and run short our food supply chain or clean water? What about air pollution?

Biological warfare sits on an evil shelf ready to be released on purpose or accidentally.

A pandemic flu strain could easily wipe out a large percentage of the population. An asteroid, a super volcanic eruption…on and on.

Artificial Intelligence is rapidly taking over the decision-making part in many industries. Robots are making human labor obsolete.

Cars are becoming self-driving. One-day, soon, commercial trucks will deliver goods without a driver.

Lake   Doomsday Clock 11:59:59

Why do we need 7 billion people? How do we reduce the population? Who decides the perfect population for the world and what methods do we use to reduce?

World Health Organization? UN? G20?

Entrepreneurs are already suggesting a universal income. An example of a question to ask and debate would be: Why should Tech giants pay 7 billion people to sit around and live self-fulfilling creative lives when they only need 10 million to work the robots and produce the goods wealthy people expect?

Nobody is without biases or prejudices…I've tried to limit my opinions. If you disagree with me, write me and tell me. If you feel strongly against my version, write your own story.

I'm a one man show. I'm sure I've made mistakes in the book. Please forgive me and show a little toleration for my lapses.

I've not tried to match up topography and towns with real geography. If I need a hill, presto, one appears. I'm simply inadequate as a writer to make everything match up.

Enjoy my story.

Prologue:

1 In the beginning, when God created the
heavens and the earth

2 and the earth was without form or shape,
with darkness over the abyss and a mighty
wind sweeping over the waters

3 Then God said: Let there be light, and there
was light.

4 God saw that the light was good. God then
separated the light from the darkness.

5 God called the light "day," and the darkness
he called "night." Evening came, and morning
followed—the first day.

6 Then God said: Let there be a dome in the
middle of the waters, to separate one body of
water from the other.

7 God made the dome, and it separated the
water below the dome from the water above the
dome. And so it happened.

8 God called the dome "sky." Evening came,
and morning followed—the second day.

9 Then God said: Let the water under the sky be
gathered into a single basin, so that the dry land
may appear. And so it happened: the water
under the sky was gathered into its basin, and
the dry land appeared.

10 God called the dry land "earth," and the
basin of water he called "sea." God saw that it
was good.

11 Then God said: Let the earth bring forth
vegetation: every kind of plant that bears seed

and every kind of fruit tree on earth that bears fruit with its seed in it. And so it happened:

12 the earth brought forth vegetation: every kind of plant that bears seed and every kind of fruit tree that bears fruit with its seed in it. God saw that it was good.

13 Evening came, and morning followed—the third day.

14 Then God said: Let there be lights in the dome of the sky, to separate day from night. Let them mark the seasons, the days and the years,

15 and serve as lights in the dome of the sky, to illuminate the earth. And so it happened:

16 God made the two great lights, the greater one to govern the day, and the lesser one to govern the night, and the stars.

17 God set them in the dome of the sky, to illuminate the earth,

18 to govern the day and the night, and to separate the light from the darkness. God saw that it was good.

19 Evening came, and morning followed—the fourth day.

20 Then God said: Let the water teem with an abundance of living creatures, and on the earth let birds fly beneath the dome of the sky.

21 God created the great sea monsters and all kinds of crawling living creatures with which the water teems, and all kinds of winged birds. God saw that it was good,

22 and God blessed them, saying: Be fertile, multiply, and fill the water of the seas; and let the birds multiply on the earth.

23 Evening came, and morning followed—the fifth day.

24 Then God said: Let the earth bring forth every kind of living creature: tame animals, crawling things, and every kind of wild animal. And so it happened:

25 God made every kind of wild animal, every kind of tame animal, and every kind of thing that crawls on the ground. God saw that it was good.

26 Then God said: Let us make* human beings in our image, after our likeness. Let them have dominion over the fish of the sea, the birds of the air, the tame animals, all the wild animals, and all the creatures that crawl on the earth.

27 God created mankind in his image; in the image of God he created them;

male and female he created them.

28 God blessed them and God said to them: Be fertile and multiply; fill the earth and subdue it. Have dominion over the fish of the sea, the birds of the air, and all the living things that crawl on the earth.

29 God also said: See, I give you every seed-bearing plant on all the earth and every tree that has seed-bearing fruit on it to be your food;

30 and to all the wild animals, all the birds of the air, and all the living creatures that crawl on the earth, I give all the green plants for food. And so it happened.

31 God looked at everything he had made, and found it very good. Evening came, and morning followed—the sixth day.

NaNa softly sighed, closed the Bible, the story of creation was one of her favorite parts. She closed her wrinkly eyelids, they fluttered once…twice…stopped…closed and dreamed.

The world is on edge as the story begins.

Numerous regional conflicts have sprung up. The middle east is still sucking resources from America. Manpower and money seems to flow one way.

North Korea is threatening to launch an ICBM at the mainland of the US monthly. Japan and South Korea are on edge. China and Russia are staying neutral.

Brownouts have become common in many parts of the United States. Wind Power and Solar Power versus Coal and Nuclear power are at a tipping point.

Coal plants are closing at a rapid pace and nuclear plants are no longer being built. Wind and solar can't be stored long term. When large cloud producing storms prevent solar from producing energy and the winds die down, the existing nuclear and coal power plants can't keep up during a crisis.

These brownouts have created a worldwide financial crisis. Credit and debit cards often can't be used for days at a time. Cash and barter has become king around the world. Debts are being called in and countries are defaulting on foreign loans.

Lake   Doomsday Clock 11:59:59

Joy and Steven's Story

Chapter 1

July 3, A year in the not too distant future

14:00 Hours

Day 1 0:00

Southeast Oklahoma

Joy's phone chirped signaling a text message as she glided thru the S-curve on the sparsely traveled two lane country road...seconds later her children's phones went off one by one. First Ned, 17, then Gail 15 and finally Chip 12.

Chip the youngest read it first and said nonchalantly, "Strange, a message from Dad; Operation Overlord. What does that mean?"

Joy's heart plunged from her chest to her stomach and she gulped...fought the urge to vomit, swallowed the bile in the Lake   Doomsday Clock 11:59:59

back of her throat and said, "We have an emergency. All of you please no talking and follow my lead, no questions. I'll explain as we go along!"

"But Mom.", said Gail.

Ned glared at his two siblings. He was the sibling family leader and scheduled to join the Air Force Reserves after high school next year, go to college on an ROTC scholarship.

The other two reluctantly stopped talking, Chip rolled his eyes, he was 12.

She slowed the Jeep Wrangler down and looked for an opening in the trees along the road; a driveway, cow path, anything leading away from traffic and people. Thirty long seconds ticked off the clock and she found an almost hidden dirt trail leading off the two-lane farm to market road.

She followed the rutted dirt driveway back about 400 yards and that took 45 more seconds. An old abandoned farmhouse leaning to one side sat alone and she thought what a blessing. She tapped the brakes a bit too hard and the Jeep veered a little to one side and stopped. She looked around at her kids.

This wasn't the way her and Steven drew up their emergency plans. In theory, they were together as a family, not 135 miles apart and her with the three kids.

"Everybody out", she said in a voice quavering and all three kids opened their doors and followed her to the rear of the jeep. Gail and Chip still showing a stunned look on their faces.

Joy continued, "Ned, help me get the emergency supplies out; Chip and Gail go check out the house, be careful!"

"But Mom…", her daughter protested again.

Ned cut her off, "Just do what your told, please!", his voice softened at the end. He has natural leadership skills she thought. Smart enough to invite cooperation and throw his sister a bone at the end of a command.

She checked the survival kit. Four gallons of water, a Sig Sauer M400 with 4 extra magazines and 200 rounds of 5.56 NATO ammo, assorted antibiotics from Mexico, first aid kit, plastic gloves, several light weight blankets, a quart of bleach, dehydrated packets of veggies and fruits, extra clothing, feminine products, several knives, a basic tool kit, a jump box, folding shovel, flashlight, extra batteries, hand crank charger, lighter, NOAA radio, and several maps.

At home, they had an even more extensive survival kit, the car was a backup plan. Thank goodness, they had a plan B.

Almost 3 minutes had passed since the original text message. She looked at the atlas, did a few quick calculations with her phone calculator. Then using a small plastic dollar store protractor/ruler, fired off a response that only her husband would understand, "47 degrees N, approx. 55.4 miles, BF&R."

She had done all she could do for her husband. If he could drive a few miles before gas gave out it would help. 135-mile hike at 15 miles per day, he'd be here in 9-14 days. If not…maybe never. She dismissed that line of thought. She had to stay positive and work on surviving right now…for her…for their three kids.

Chip bounded out of the house with the enthusiasm that only a 12-year-old can have in a crisis, "There's an old couple living here. The man really seems sick mom!"

She closed her eyes and tried to soak up everything that had happened in the last 5 minutes. She pinched the bridge of her nose and let out a shallow breath, slowly.

"Okay", she said. "I'll be there in a minute. Tell your sister to do a walk about and see about food and water. You look around outside and check the out buildings for, well anything we might use."

Lake   Doomsday Clock 11:59:59

Chip looked at her, obviously perplexed. She thought about it for a second. "Pretend we need to survive on our own. Weapons, tools, food, storage." She wanted to give him a sense of urgency without setting off a full panic with her youngest child.

"Okay Mom, got it." Off he ran, full of energy like this was just a game.

An old couple. That wasn't in any of the scenarios they talked about or planned for. Things kept going from worse to a total disaster. And she still didn't know what Armageddon event had tripped their emergency plan and sent the code word Operation Overlord from Steven, her husband. 8 minutes had passed.

Chapter 2

Day One 0:00

Dallas, Texas

Steven sent the text to Joy and the kids knowing their life would probably never be the same.

The G20 Summit was happening in Hamburg, Germany and a terrorist group or rogue state detonated an atomic bomb of approximately 15 kilotons of TNT killing all if not most of the summit participants. Heads of state, Presidents, Prime Ministers, high ranking cabinet members, banking and business leaders controlling 85% of the world's gross nation product, 80% of world trade, 66% of the world's population and 50% of the land mass.

Left wing groups and anarchist regularly stage protests at the summits. Intellectuals criticize the elite symbolism of the group and countries left out feel disenfranchised. So, plenty of enemies and motivation to shock the world and say, "I'm important too!"

Steven worked for a large worldwide financial institution, with fingers, ears and voices everywhere. A backdoor email message had been sent confirming the source of the explosion by a low level nuclear monitoring official in India and his office was inadvertently included.

The mushroom cloud should have been a great lead, unfortunately the explosion knocked out all electricity and data lines so the public would be in the dark for about 10 minutes. It wouldn't take long for somebody to post a picture on Facebook, Twitter, Instagram or one of the other social media sites and then hell and chaos would break lose as 7.1 billon people slowly learned the world they knew was ending.

He headed down the back hall to the stairwell and Jack, his boss, poked his ashen face out and said, "Where are you going buddy?"

He glanced back, "Out...got an errand to run!"

Lake   Doomsday Clock 11:59:59

Jack said in a loud voice, standing out in the hallway now, hands and feet spread out wide "No way…we have the crisis of the century, clients to look after, you leave, you're done Steve!"

Steven kept walking. His boss was still thinking about money and Steven was trying to survive and live the next 30 days.

He made it down the two flights of stairs and out to his car in a record 90 seconds. He walked passed a group of people in the lobby, all clustered around a blank TV screen. Two minutes had passed since he'd texted Joy and the kids. He took 20 seconds to change into running shoes and started their 20-year-old Acura TL. Cursed silently because he only had a quarter tank of gas. His rule, always fill up at half a tank just in case of an emergency, like today!

It took him a minute to get to I-635 and, pushing the car furiously, drove 5 miles in 3 minutes. 8 minutes had now passed since the beginning of the end.

Chapter 3

Southeast Oklahoma

0:08 Day One

Ned came jogging up the driveway, under control.

He said, "I covered the driveway entrance with some brush and a small log I found. The best I could do in a hurry, not going to fool anybody for long.", He said, panting, a little out of breath.

Joy replied, "Okay. What next Ned?" Leadership changes in a crisis. Her son was a more natural leader of people, like his dad. She on the other hand could organize and make long term plans.

Ned thought for about 2 seconds, and replied, "Inventory what we have, make a list of what we need, make a plan. We can't stay here for more than a day or two. Too close to the road." He said facing his mom, hands on hips.

"I agree", she said and continued, "Chip says an elderly couple live in the house and the man is pretty sick."

Ned, an Eagle Scout, star athlete, honor student, shrugged nonchalantly, "We'll adapt the plan, got to survive until Dad catches up to us. We can't leave anybody to face a disaster alone."

Five minutes passed and everybody was inside the house. Thirteen minutes had passed since the text from their Dad. The lights flickered once…twice…three times and then died. No electric, no lights, no charging electronics, no microwave, no A/C, no refrigerator, no…

Ned took charge with one powerful word, "Status?"

Chip responded first, still brimming with an adventurous spirit, "An old tractor, a big ATV, old looking thing, an old looking like muscle car, Shelby something, welder, garden tools, gas cans, Dodge ¾ ton pickup, machine tools, we could survive right here."

Lake   Doomsday Clock 11:59:59

Gail, 15, 6 feet tall, athletic build, long legs, high jumper prototype, brunette hair, dark skin tone, Nordic facial features, her genes looked like a Heinz 57 mix; she was the sensitive one and a nurturer. She said, "The old guy, Elmer, he's really sick. I know you don't care...but I"

Her Mom responded, laying a hand on her slender shoulder "We do care, and we need to talk about that. First tell us what you found? Please."

Gail said, "The usual stuff. They eat mostly frozen dinners, cereal, sandwiches. They don't have much extra. I asked Marilyn if they had a root cellar or a large pantry. She looked at me funny and said to talk to Elmer, but he was sleeping. Lots of blankets and clothes, a few guns in a cabinet, mostly rifles."

Ned looked at Chip and said, "We need to know the caliber of the rifles and ammo amounts."

Chip gave a mocking and playful salute and barked, "Yes Sir El Capitan!" Turned and strolled out of the room with a purpose. Chip was 12, going on 21 it seems. Big for his age, 6 feet tall, 180 pounds, blonde hair, blue eyes, farmer hands and huge feet, even his ears stuck out. He was always smiling, like he knew something the rest of us didn't. Puberty smacked him early in 5th grade.

"What else Mom?" Ned said, looking for confirmation he wasn't missing something obvious.

Joy said, "Somebody needs to monitor the news. We really need to know what's happened to set Dad off enough to send an emergency message. I'll monitor the radio, try to find PRN. Why don't you go have a man to man talk with Elmer?"

"I can do that. Mom, we'll be okay. I promise. There isn't anything Dad hasn't prepared me for." He started to walk away.

Joy responded, "Remember, God has a plan for each of our lives. Dying is part of that plan."

Lake   Doomsday Clock 11:59:59

He just turned his head back and with a slight smile said, "I know Mom. But, I'm going to give the devil a run for his money and use all the resources and knowledge God has placed in my head and path to live each day and fulfill God's plan for me and this family." It was a statement made without boasting, but full of youthful confidence.

Elmer was awake and ready to talk. He was old at 89, but not quite ready for death, just having a bad day. Kidneys were giving out on him and without dialysis he wouldn't last too long. Slightly built, 5'1", 130 pounds, wisps of white hair covered his forehead, a raspy voice from living life fully; smoking an occasional cigar and tossing back a few shots of Kentucky's finest bourbon to celebrate the good times.

Him and Marilyn had been married 70 years, raised 3 girls and a boy. The girls had given them 5 grandkids and the boy had died on 9/11 working as a stock trader in the One World Trade Center.

Elmer joined the army at 18. Army Corp of Engineers 44 years, served in Korea, Vietnam and finished with a slam dunk on the Kuwait oil field fires in Gulf I. The war that should have toppled Sadam Hussein and his cronies.

Ned was respectful, he'd noticed the army memorabilia and awards on the living room wall.

He introduced himself and said, "How are you doing Sir?"

The old man replied, "Fine. What's happening?" A simple question, getting right to the point.

Ned responded, "My Dad sent an emergency message. A code. My Mom is listening to the news and trying to figure out what's happening, Sir."

Elmer asked, "Is your Dad a cautious man?"

Ned said, "If you mean did he panic, no. My Dad is cautious, but a planner. If he sent up a red flag we'd better expect something bad to happen soon. We already lost power."

Elmer hesitated, "I can appreciate a planner. I noticed we lost power a few minutes ago, seems like a regular occurrence lately. What would you do son?" A simple test for the boy.

Ned thought for about 15 seconds at a time when every second counted, "We can't stay here for long. A day or two at the most. We need to move further away from people, isolate ourselves in case of a pandemic epidemic, biological attack, civil war, nuclear explosion. Probably something I've failed to mention." He shrugged his shoulders.

Elmer grinned just a little. The boy had passed with flying colors. "I agree with you. I have a bug out site, a hidey hole. I was Army Corp of Engineer for 40 plus years. I retired after Gulf I and we had a succession of centrist Presidents. Clinton couldn't keep his pants zipped, Bush 43 deferred to his VP, Obama turned his back on Israel and Trump ran a zoo. So, I planned for dooms day. I lived thru the Cuban Missile crisis in the early 60's."

He continued, "The shelter is 5 miles away as a crow flies, isolated and hidden. Fully stocked for 6 months, 10 people. Food, water, weapons, shelter, medicine, if you need it, it's there. My kids and grandkids all live on Kodiak Island in Alaska, they should be okay. Nothing I can do for them right now. Why don't we join forces and ride this one out together son?"

Ned smiled, sometimes life, luck and fate seemed fickle, "Yes Sir! I think my family just caught a huge break. God is good!"

The old man, wrinkles and all, smiled slightly and said, "God is always good!" He reached out with his frail right hand and Ned shook it warmly. Sealed, a pact, a partnership, an agreement between two men.

They ended the handshake just as Joy strode into the bedroom with Marilyn beside her.

Lake   Doomsday Clock 11:59:59

Joy said with some emotion, "Suspected atomic blast at the G20 convention in Hamburg, Germany, according to PBS, BBC, Instagram, Twitter and Facebook."

The old man cracked a slight smile, "Then it's official if Facebook says so!" And he continued, "Okay, serious and I think your husband was correct in running up the red flag. Marilyn, what next?"

Joy's opinion of the man quickly skyrocketed. 70 years of marriage, plus a 40-year successful career in the Army; he'd learned something about teamwork and who to consult and trust during a crisis.

Marilyn, frail looking frame, sharp angular weather beaten facial features, smaller than her husband, short cropped straight white hair, but loaded with Michigan farmer DNA. Raised four kids largely alone and followed her husband around the world as an Army wife while earning a Master's Degree in Political Science.

Marilyn said, "Load up what we need to take to the camp and burn the farm, make it look like looters came here first. The sooner we leave the better. Geopolitically this can only end in a disaster. North Korea, India, Pakistan, Israel, somebody with more weapons than brains will pop off a nuke and then somebody bigger will retaliate. It will be interesting where the uranium was produced. Pardon my French, but the shit will hit the fan in a hurry." Concise, honest, nothing held back, a career soldier's wife vocabulary.

50 precious minutes had passed since the alarm from Steven.

Chapter 4

0:08 Day One

Near Mesquite, Texas on I-30

The Acura speedometer hit 90 and Steven prayed silently for safety and more speed. This felt like a bad B movie and he was the villain everybody hated.

The Acura shot across the Lake Ray Hubbard bridge and he noticed increased traffic. All lanes were slowing down to a crawl. He turned on the radio and the news from Hamburg was everywhere.

Speculation as always ruled the day. Opinion makers and liars were trying to get ahead of the PR nightmare and set the tone. Fake news was everywhere in the electronic age. Honest people spread fake news by trusting any source. People don't verify a story they just find a reflection of their beliefs and hit share.

40 minutes had passed since he texted Joy and the kids. His sole focus was on finding them right now. What a terrible time to have a crisis, 135 miles apart. Electricity was obviously out because the traffic lights next to I-30 exits weren't working and lines of vehicles were waiting to fill up with gas which created a backup of trucks and cars on the exit ramp and ultimately stopped traffic on I-30. Somebody is always special and wants to cut in line at the last second and inevitable a fender bender happened.

He saw two guys at exit 87 arguing next to a fender bender on the right shoulder and one pulled a gun. He whipped by in the left emergency shoulder, heard a shot and a loud bang like a rock hit the back of his car as he passed, but didn't dare stop.

He finally got off on 380 just short of Greenville and headed to Farmersville. He knew there was a rail for trails entrance there and he was headed to Roxton because the trail led right thru the tiny town.

Five miles from Farmersville and a warning ding sounded. He checked the dash, the fuel light was on.

Two miles later, three miles from the trailhead and the 2.5 Liter engine sputtered and died. He pulled over to the right, onto a grass shoulder, coasted to a stop. Popped the trunk latch and got out. Put the keys in his right front pants pocket, which a moment later seemed a bit stupid and pointless, kept them anyhow out of habit. Went to the trunk and took out his rainy-day backpack.

Typical stuff, a handgun, extra ammo, 2 liters of water, minimal first aid kit, flash drives with important survival information stored on them. Nobody knows everything and if the world falls apart you'd better be able to become a hunter and gatherer. If enough people survive we can rebuild.

He noticed an exit gunshot hole next to the fuel lid. He assumed the gas tank was punctured by an errant bullet from the argument on I-30 and that's why he ran out of fuel. He thought, six feet to the right and it might have hit me. Life is short and unpredictable.

He took a minute and hydrated with partial water bottles found in the car. Steven can be messy at times and today it worked in his favor. He adjusted the backpack and took off at a slow 10 minute a mile jog. 45 years old, not in triathlete training, but 10K shape on any given weekend.

50 minutes after the text, July weather in Texas, 92 degrees and he was already sweating like a pig. Two miles to go to the trailhead. A little girls voice disrupts his family reunion vision.

She said, in a squeaky voice, "Mister...please help!"

He stopped jogging and turned. She was standing on the front porch of an old frame house, very little faded green paint left on the walls, yard was nothing but weeds. Several blue tarps served as a roof.

An old Cadillac from the 90's sat in the front yard, tires and wheels missing, cinderblocks holding it up.

Lake   Doomsday Clock 11:59:59

The little girl looked maybe 6 years old, dirty and torn light yellow sleeveless dress, dirt streaks dried on her face, tiny waif frame, black hair, dark eyes, red from crying. She was pointing inside the house.

He walked over and she lightly took his hand; intertwined his large fingers with her tiny fingers and led him into the front room, just off the porch.

The room was a mess, dirty clothes, plates with cockroaches as a cheering section, trash piled high.

Two adults laying on the floor, side by side, needles sticking out of their arms, obviously deceased and next to the couch lay a small infant, softly cooing as if everything was okay.

Chapter 5

Southeast Oklahoma

00:50

They wasted 15 minutes debating the benefits of sleeping now, packing and then leaving or packing now, leaving, and sleeping when they arrived at the shelter.

Marilyn and Joy convinced the men to see the light and start packing. They needed to leave, the sooner the better.

The news was flooded with contradictory information. Groups were claiming responsibility for the G20 explosion. ISIS, Al-Qaeda, and several fringe groups boasted of success. A few experts were pointing the finger at North Korea.

Power failed because several nuclear power plants shut down after the federal government warned of impending terrorist attacks. The federal government, Department of Energy, denied the report. Brown outs started in the northeast and quickly spread across the country except for Texas which has its own power grid.

Texas lost power when the Governor ordered the National Guard to surround the states four nuclear power plants and protect them from any terrorist threat. The plants felt in imminent danger and started emergency shut down procedures. What a mess.

Elmer was a sneaky old man. His ATV was modified with a diesel engine and could pull all the equipment the group were loading.

Elmer had 7 rifles, all different calibers, from pellet to 50 calibers, plus 1,000 rounds of ammo per gun.

He had animal traps and nets for fishing. He was the ultimate survivalist and seemed thrilled to have a chance to use his knowledge and equipment in his lifetime. Men are like boys, mankind is on the brink of an unprecedented disaster, Armageddon, and they treat it like a game.

Lake   Doomsday Clock 11:59:59

The old man sat in a chair giving directions. Occasionally he'd look at his wife for affirmation, making sure his decision-making process made sense.

Gail, Chip and Ned quietly carried out each request, occasionally asking questions for clarification. All of them were running scenarios in the minds, trying to make sense of what had been reported and what might happen next.

One minute they were enjoying a four-day road trip to St. Louis and the next a text from their Dad changed the future.

They had been lucky to be in this place now. Fortunate to find a man prepared for dooms day and willing to share his foresight with total strangers. Ten miles either way and something totally different might have happened. A fellow believer, God works behind the scenes in mysterious ways.

The last thing Ned did was use a chainsaw and cut away part of the front living room, push the jeep inside, douse the structure with diesel fuel, set a delayed fuse using a bag of ice and then everybody climbed on the ATV. Elmer promised they had 45-60 minutes before the house burned.

Ned drove, Elmer beside him, Marilyn, and Joy in the backseat, Chip and Gail on the trailer. Elmer's two hunting dogs trotted up front.

90 minutes had passed since Steven texted. Life was fragile, too short. You'd better hug and say I love you to those who care about you. Tomorrow isn't guaranteed.

Chapter 6

00:50

"What happened to your mom and dad?" Steven asked and just as quickly realized it was a stupid question.

She looked up at me, her eyes big and round, "They scared. Momma said the world was ending. No more drugs. Don't do drugs. She said a man would come get us. You!"

He said, "She didn't mean me sweetheart. I don't know you. Do you have an Aunt, Uncle, Grandparent we can call?"

She looked at him like he was a simpleton, "She said you would come. A man with a backpack."

Steven frowned, "Sweety…"

She said, "My name is Maria and my sister is Isabelle."

"Okay. Maria, I can't take care of you. I don't know what to do." Steven said, totally confused.

"That's okay mister." She smiled.

"My name is Steven." I said.

"Mr. Steven, my mom said you'd have help." Maria said.

He thought for a few seconds, and said, "My wife is 90 miles away. I have no car. I can walk 90 miles but you can't and your baby sister…"

"Mister Steven, you'll have help. My sister has a case of formula. You change diapers when they are wet or poopy and give her a bottle every few hours. I've been doing it for a long time. I'm 6…you're old compared to me." She stopped and her lower lip trembled.

She continued, "You need to help save us…"

Steven knelt next to her and hugged her. She cried a little and melted into his chest. She was right. He had no choice. He'd made a pact with his wife to join her, but he

Lake   Doomsday Clock 11:59:59

could never forgive himself if he walked out of this house and left two helpless kids to die.

He gathered up formula and diapers. There were 12 cans of formula and a box of diapers. It was enough for 3-4 days. What would he do after that? He found several changes of clothes for both girls.

He wasn't a strong believer like Joy and Ned. He had doubts and questions. He believed in God, but didn't fully trust Him to watch over him.

They took off 15 minutes later, headed to the trailhead.

They'd walked ½ mile with Maria asking 100 questions a minute.

50 yards ahead an old black lady sat in a one-piece white plastic chair. She sat straight up as if this was her throne and she was the Queen. As they approached she stood up and faced them. Her skin shined, her face rounded, a large dress draped over her shapeless figure. Steven couldn't tell if she was thin or overweight.

She said in a smooth voice, "I've been waiting. I'm Momma Wafer."

Steven was speechless. Finally, his tongue came unglued and he responded, "I'm Steven, this is Maria and her sister Isabelle."

She said, "Let's go. Daylight is burning and night brings out the devil."

He said, "Who told you to wait? Marie's Mom?"

She said, "God told me a man with two children needed my help and I was to travel with them without any questions."

90 minutes had passed since the text was sent.

Lake   Doomsday Clock 11:59:59

Chapter 7

Southeast Oklahoma

00:90

It took 5 hours to go 5 miles as a crow flies. Come on math wizards, how fast did they travel?

The shortest distance between two points is a straight line. They didn't travel in a straight line. If you traced their path on a map it would have looked like a drunk two-year-old scribbling on a menu. It felt like they must have travelled 15 miles.

Started north, turned west, turned south, then west again, mostly followed property lines, opening and closing gates and crossing pastures and streams. Mosquitoes the size of Chihuahua's sucked their blood as evening arrived. Gnats buzzed around their faces causing them to flap their hands and blow to prevent from sucking them into their mouths. The group was quiet. Reality was settling in and the fallout from this disaster was serious.

Each of them sat quietly with their own thoughts and questions. Finally, Elmer indicated to Ned to cut the engine.

Joy's knees and feet ached from being bounced around, her kidneys screamed from being pressed against the seat, her head hurt from stress and her heart thought about Steven and their kids. What would the future hold for them? For anybody?

Elmer crawled off the ATV and with a sweep of his hand and removing an OKC Thunder cap from his head, announced, "We have arrived. My rainy-day fortress, home sweet home, my sweet abode. Welcome!"

Joy looked around and didn't see anything except shadows dancing against a small hill, a few lightening bugs, and a cluster of evergreen bushes.

It didn't look like much of a home to me or a bug out site.

Lake   Doomsday Clock 11:59:59

6 ½ hours had passed since Steven's text.

Lake   Doomsday Clock 11:59:59

Chapter 8

Farmersville, Texas trail head

01:30

They walked beside the road, Steven carrying Maria piggyback. Mamma Wafer holding Isabelle, softly singing lullabies and spiritual songs from the south. 20 minutes per mile pace.

Cars sped past in a hurry to get somewhere. Several gas stations with long lines. Nobody pulling a gun because in small town Texas, people tend to be polite. Give it a little more pressure and the good manners would fade. A few more days of July heat with no A/C, no electricity, no gas, no running water and people would forget about being gracious.

They passed several grocery stores with signs stating, "Cash Only". People were scurrying in and out with bags of groceries and bottles of water. Heads down, no eye contact and Steven realized it was fear they felt. Fear of the unknown, the direction the world was going, what would happen next.

Word of the bomb in Hamburg must have spread by now; or at least rumors.

Steven suggested maybe buying some food was a good idea. Mamma Wafer looked at him like he was a bit touched in the head.

She finally said, "Trust in the Lord Mr. Steven. He will provide food for us."

He didn't share her deep loyalty and trust in God. He dealt in numbers, facts, and maybe a little skepticism.

He said, "I'm a little like Ronald Reagan, trust but verify. I trust God, but I'd like to verify food in my backpack…"

She didn't respond, they kept walking and found the trailhead, turned north and headed out of town.

Lake   Doomsday Clock 11:59:59

They rounded a bend and saw a man sitting beside the trail, leaning up against a tree.

He waved and said, "I've been waiting for you guys."

Steven took a chance and said, "God sent you?"

He said, "Nope, Momma Wafer's neighbor drove past 15 minutes ago and said you guys were walking this way. My name is Jonah." He stuck out his large hand and they shook.

Jonah wasn't tall, average height, but he was as wide as he was tall. At least it seemed that way. He looked strong like an ox, but possessed a gentle aura.

Jonah liked to talk and told them all about himself in the first few miles. He had failed to finish high school and joined the Navy. He was trained as a barber and had served 10 years in the Navy and then cut hair in Farmersville for 20 years.

His hard luck story was about how a girl on vacation in Hawaii had convinced him to come to Texas. She loved him and so he parted amicable from the Navy.

He arrived in Farmersville only to discover her husband lived there as well. So, he set up a barber shop, cut hair six days a week and went to Church every Sunday. He never talked to the girl again.

The group walked on and came upon a table beside the trail loaded with bread, peanut butter, jam, water, cookies and a whole sweet potato pie.

A simple sign said, "Take what you need, give thanks to God. There is a barn 50 yards south if you need lodging for the night."

Steven was famished. Mamma Wafer insisted they say a blessing and so they did. It seemed like a long prayer, but maybe it was because he was hungry. Her blessing made him feel better and they fixed sandwiches, took the gallon of water, 8 cookies, 2 apiece and the whole pie. He loved sweet potato pie.

Lake   Doomsday Clock 11:59:59

They made their way to the barn just off the trail. It was at least 100 years old. Sturdy, peeling red paint, tin roof, open in the middle, stalls on the side for animals and a loft with fresh hay and a pile of blankets. It was July in Texas. He didn't think they'd need the blankets.

They ate in silence. The blueberry jam was delicious and the pie out of this world. If they had a scoop of Blue Bell vanilla ice cream on top of the pie, Steven's world would be complete.

Thinking about pie and ice cream made him a bit sad. So, he thought about his wife and kids. How were they doing? Was Joy okay? How about Ned, Gail and Chip? Each of his kids were different and unique. He loved his wife and each of his kids.

Steven talked to God. Asked Him some questions. What would he do with the two girls, Maria and Isabelle? Thanked Him for Mamma Wafer. She was taking care of the baby and talking to Marie. What was his role?

Jonah was good at talking and eating sweet potato pie. They spread out the hay and blankets, laid down for the night. 15 minutes later the first flash of lightning and thunder shook the barn and both kids began to cry. The rain pounded down on the metal roof, fast, soft, hard; like a drum played by a novice in a junior high band.

Momma Wafer fixed a bottle for Isabelle and said to Steven and Jonah, "Entertain the girl, make yourself useful."

Steven didn't know what to do. So, he said, "Jonah, what do you suggest?"

Jonah said, "How about we tell scary stories?"

Mamma Wafer quickly barked, "How about you don't…"

Steven thought back to camping trips with his kids and remembered a game they played. He dug in his backpack and found a small Maglite.

He told Jonah, "Bring a blanket."

Lake   Doomsday Clock 11:59:59

He whispered to Maria, "Under the blanket." Then he turned on the light.

He said, "We're safe in here. This is our shelter. Nothing can penetrate our shield. This is like God's love for us."

They didn't tell scary stories, but talked and made each other feel safe and secure. The thunderstorm drifted towards the northeast and they finally started to doze off.

6 ½ hours since he sent the text to his wife.

Chapter 9

06:30

Southeast Oklahoma

The sun was starting to dip in the Oklahoma sky when her son Ned turned off the ATV. A short debate followed and they agreed to pitch some blankets on the ground and rest the best they could until daylight.

Sleep didn't come easy for many reasons. The kids wanted to know about their Dad. What was his plan? How would he find them? Phone service was dead so it wasn't like she could send him an update.

Joy did her best to answer their questions. She had done her part to implement the Armageddon plan.

Elmer gave a great top 6 main points about D Day and Operation Overlord.

1. Occurred June 6, 1944 Normandy, France
2. Largest Amphibious landing in history
3. General Dwight Eisenhower US Army Commanded the invasion (later became our President)
4. Five beaches were Juno, Gold, Sword, Omaha, Utah
5. 13,000 aircraft and 5,000 ships supported the operation
6. 10,000 Allied troops killed, wounded or missing on D-Day, 2/3 of those were Americans

Elmer was good at summarizing complicated concepts.

She talked with Ned for a bit. He was in a "Go Mode."

He said, "Mom…it's all about clean water, food and shelter."

She said, "What about our children, my kids, you? What about the bad guys who did this? How do we stop vigilantes who want to take from us? How do we predict what's going to happen next?"

Lake   Doomsday Clock 11:59:59

Joy continued, "Right now we have no power, no cell phone service. That's survivable. What if somebody drops a nuke or two on the US?"

Her son answered, "We adapt and overcome. I can't guarantee anything Mom. Maybe nothing happens and we all go home in a week, a little embarrassed, but alive. Dad knew something big had happened and we needed to bug out now. He'll find us. We left a few clues along the way."

Joy said, "I know...Dad can handle himself."

Ned drifted over to his siblings to talk with them. Elmer and Marilyn were already sleeping.

Joy listened to NPR radio and it was just a rehash of earlier news. "This is former VP Joe Blow and now President Blow telling everybody to stay calm. We're working on finding who is responsible for this horrible act and we will strike back with a vengeance. Freedom cannot be threatened in this manner. Our labs are working on where the uranium was produced to provide raw material for this dastardly and cowardly act. When we know who is responsible, even if they only provided materials we will respond in kind. Scientist can look at the ratio of Plutonium 239 and 240 isotopes and determine which nuclear reactor produced the fissile material for the bomb detonated in Hamburg, Germany."

After three news cycles with nothing new to offer she clicked off the radio and finally drifted off to a restless sleep.

12 hours had passed since Steven sent the text.

Chapter 10

06:30 Northeast of Farmersville.

The storms passed, the wind subsided and the night sky cleared, turned black, and full of stars. Nothing beats a clear moonless night packed with a billion sparkling stars. Steven laid on his back and watched, saw an occasional shooting star and a satellite glide past his field of view.

Thought about communication. Cell phones were down, but satellite phones still worked. What about short wave radio's and CB's? IDK…need to think about that.

Thought about his wife Joy and the kids. Nothing more he could do for them. His priority was to stay safe and find them. He also had a new priority, two orphans and a caregiver to think about. He not only needed to care for himself, but also those three.

Water, food and shelter in that order. Jonah needed to pull his own weight or move on. He knew that sounded harsh, but his life was already complicated by the responsibility of three new lives.

Again, he thought about Joy. Where was she right now? What was she thinking about? It made him sad so he dismissed the thought and focused on the here and now.

Where were they going tomorrow? How many miles a day could they walk? What immediate problems did they face? What about in the next few days or week?

Steven thought about feet. They needed to make sure their feet were in good shape. Check for blisters, cuts, raw spots, shoes; they couldn't walk far with damaged feet.

The two young kids had drifted off to sleep. Steven was exhausted and checked outside one more time. It seemed the barn housed a few feral pigs, some racoons, possums and a skunk at night. He told all the animals to get along, the world had changed. He felt a bit melancholy.

Momma Wafer was sleeping when he climbed back up the ladder.

Lake   Doomsday Clock 11:59:59

He told Jonah, "Night."

Jonah said, "Night."

He fell asleep immediately. exhausted.

12:00 hours after he sent the text.

Chapter 11

Southeast Oklahoma

5:00 AM and the sound of thumping woke Joy up. She could hear and feel the blades from the helicopter slice thru the air…far away and then closer and closer. Thump…thump…thump…

She looked over and saw Elmer and Ned standing, looking up in the sky. The helicopter flew passed them and circled back.

It was a Sikorsky twin engine, four bladed, UH-60 Black Hawk. The name came from the Native American Chief, Black Hawk.

A spot light came on and the Sikorsky slowly dropped down, settling in a flat part of a field about 200 yards away from their camp. Since they were in a pasture area, the grass wasn't very high. The few trees around them were gently swaying from the disturbed air.

The helicopter lightly settled, dark colored in the sparse morning light, and the engine spooled down. It took 10 seconds to see the blades were slowing as well. Finally, everything was quiet, the dirt kicked up by the landing fell silently back to earth, a new resting spot.

The door slid open and a big guy slid off the deck, onto the ground, and stood up.

She heard Elmer suck in a big breath of air and say, "JC. What the hell is he doing here?"

His wife quietly replied, "Watch your language around the kids Elmer."

He glared at her, but kept his mouth shut. It took 90 slow seconds for the man in desert fatigues and wearing a cap to cross the field. He carried a side arm on his right hip and a folder tucked under his left elbow. Trailing behind him was a man and a woman, also wearing desert fatigues, side arms, and black MP bands attached with velcro on their upper left arms.

Lake   Doomsday Clock 11:59:59

Joy thought to herself…what is going on here? Why would the military want to talk to an old engineer? Why would they bring MP's? The man is almost 90, bringing MP's seem like overkill. I mean a 5-year-old could outrun Elmer.

The old guy leading the group crossing the field had a serious look on his face, the MP's weren't in PR mode.

I watched Elmer straighten up just a little and his wife looked sad.

The soldier in front, the name Yazzie on his uniform, stopped 3 feet in front of Elmer, snapped a salute, which Elmer returned, but not with much enthusiasm.

Nobody said anything for about 5 seconds and finally the man in charge opened the folder and took out a sheet of paper.

Cleared his voice and said, "The President of the United States and Congress have declared a national emergency. The Secretary of Defense; Under US code Title 10, Subchapter A, Part II, Chapter 39, Code 688. Elmer Franklin Begay, you are returned to active duty effective immediately upon this notice being served. Sir, you will need to come with us. What do you need to bring with you? I can give you about 10 minutes Sir. You have a teleconference scheduled in 60 minutes General Begay."

Elmer quietly replied, "Thank you Major Yazzie."

I can't imagine what Elmer was feeling. Being recalled to active military service at age 89? Having to leave his wife of 70 years. His health wasn't the best.

Marilyn had a stoic look on her face. She dug in the wagon we pulled with the ATV and came out with a shaving kit and an overnight bag.

She said, "This has what he needs. A few clothes and heart medicine."

She looked at the Major and added, "You take care of him. He's almost 90 years old."

Lake   Doomsday Clock 11:59:59

He said, "The country needs what he knows, his brain, not his body Ma'am."

Elmer looked at her and quietly whispered, "I'm sorry Marilyn."

She hugged her husband, gave a quick peck on the cheek and said, "I know, duty before family. It's okay Elmer. Do what you've got to do and come back home."

He turned to Ned, put his hand on his shoulder and said, "It's your camp now son. Marilyn knows where everything is located and how to open the bunker. Keep everybody safe."

Joy looked around and didn't see a bunker anywhere.

Marilyn asked Major Yazzie, "How did you find him?"

Joy quickly realized it was a great question.

The Major cracked a small smile, "He's wearing a Fitbit...the NSA used the GPS from the device and it's been stationary for 5 hours now. So, we lifted off 30 minutes ago and came here."

Elmer slipped off his Fitbit and handed it to Ned and said, "Destroy electronic devices we don't need using a hammer, burn-em, then bury them far away or put them in the faraday cage located in the bunker. Individuals in the government are your friend; the government is not your friend."

The group of 3 soldiers, now 4 started making their way slowly across the field. Joy heard the whine of the Sikorsky's two General Electric T700 Turboshaft engines, the blades slowly started to turn and gain speed. Dirt kicked up as the group disappeared into the helicopter. Within a few seconds it lifted off, gained some altitude and shot away like a dragon fly.

The General was gone, our leader, the man with the confidence.

Joy's daughter Gail asked, "What's for breakfast Mom?"

Lake   Doomsday Clock 11:59:59

Chip pitched in, "What's a faraday cage?"

Marilyn said, "Damn Fitbit. He got that from one of the grandkids living on Kodiak Island in Alaska. Wear it grandpa, you can keep track of your steps, sleep and heartrate."

Joy watched a single tear slowly travel down Marilyn's cheek and fall to the ground. Joy's heart ached for her. Would she ever see her husband again?

Ned said, "Eat a granola bar Gail. Chip, a faraday cage blocks electronic signals from entering or leaving an enclosed space. It's not fool proof and part of it depends on the radio frequency. I think we protect the important electronics and destroy stuff that's not important and worthless...like your choice in music Gail..." He smiled at his sister. Joy was glad to see he still possessed a sense of humor even in a stressful situation.

Gail playfully slapped her brothers arm and walked over to the wagon in search of breakfast.

Marilyn said, "We need to uncover the bunker entrance. Help me boys." It was a statement, not a question.

The bunker was cleverly hidden. The fake evergreen bushes on the hillside was covering the entrance, almost undetectable. You twisted the bush trunk a quarter turn clockwise and they pulled off revealing a sealed door. Ingenious, simple, and amazing at the same time.

The vertical cement door looked like the top of a submarine. You turned the wheel counter clockwise and with a hiss the bunker was unsealed. The door probable weighed thousands of pounds at 5 feet thick, but with a special bearing in the hinge a single person could easily open the hatch.

Joy was the last one inside the door. She walked down a narrow hall about ten feet, made a 90% turn and walked ten more feet, one more 90% turn and walked ten more feet. The first room was, twenty by twenty feet lined with filled water containers, chairs, a table and two old couches.

Lake   Doomsday Clock 11:59:59

At the end of the room was a door leading into a long 10-foot-wide, 100 feet long hall. There were locked doors leading off on both sides, five on each side.

Joy asked Marilyn about the rooms and she said, "The rooms house sleeping quarters for males and females, a kitchen, food storage, weapons, medical station, library, mechanical room, spare parts and a jail. My Elmer always over engineered, over thought and over planned everything. It took him almost ten years to build."

Joy, at that moment, was thankful for Elmer's attention to detail.

They ate lunch consisting of WASA toast covered with peanut butter and honey, canned peaches and water. It wasn't a meal for royalty, but survivors, and this is how they would eat until they figured out what was happening.

In the weeks leading up to the terrorist attack in Germany commercial air travel had become scarce in part because of increased terrorist attacks worldwide. There were cyber-attacks on the Federal Aviation Administration site and hacking of all airlines booking and crew schedule software.

Fuel glitches had slowed freight to a crawl and trucks need diesel to deliver jet fuel to the planes. Crews ended up out of flying hours or in the wrong city and people showed up at the wrong time for flights that didn't even exist.

Looking back gives you 20/20 vision. Joy thought maybe her husband was seeing early signs because of the financial markets and backdoor contacts. He probably saw the nuclear attack at the G20 conference as a tipping point.

NPR reported all commercial and private air travel was suspended until further notice and that Congress and the President had declared a state of emergency. The sky was devoid of commercial planes and every couple of hours they'd noticed 2 Air Force F-22 Raptors streak across the sky. It reminded her of the days following 9/11.

9/11 memories led Joy to thoughts about Elmer and Marilyn's son dying…and that left her sad. She couldn't imagine her heart beating with a hole that size.

Marilyn explained that her and Elmer owned 100 acres of land. It looked like grazing land for the most part and Elmer ran a few head of cattle. But, it also housed several small fruit orchards, a stocked pond, a creek with a small hydro generator and a small landing strip for drones.

Joy grew to admire a man who in his 70's built this emergency camp. It was a long shot it would ever be needed. However, that miniscule odd arrived, and her family was in the right place at the right time to be the beneficiaries.

It seemed like her kids needed to explore Elmer's 100 acres to discover how they would find drinking water, and food. Shelter seemed to be in place. We could eat for a year with 5 people. That wouldn't allow us to survive long term.

God is good.

24:00 since Steven's text.

Chapter 12

Northeast of Farmersville

An obnoxious rooster woke them up at first light. Mamma Wafer folded the blankets while Jonah and Steven entertained Marie and Isabelle.

It turns out that Marie is 9 years old, but malnutrition and constant moving to stay away from CPS has contributed to her stunted growth. She has a good mind and a better memory. She could tell Steven in detail about the 15 schools she attended in her first 4 years of public education. Next year she would start 4th grade. He didn't have the heart to tell her it probably wouldn't happen.

She understood her parents were dead. It didn't seem to bother her, but Steven knew she would need to deal with the finality and forever trauma in a different way to ensure closure and possess the ability to move ahead. Right now, she was in denial that it even hurt, this was still a big adventure. He found himself drawn to her. She possessed a survivor's spirit and a fighter's heart. She loved to read and he needed to find some books to entertain her during times they weren't walking. She had taken lemons, added a bunch of water and her own natural sweetness to make lemonade.

Her sister Isabelle was almost 8 months old. Steven was trying to remember when his own kids went off formula and started drinking milk and eating solid food. Maybe they needed to try a few squished-up apples or wild pears today.

Steven mentioned the apples and pears to Mamma Wafer.

She looked at him, no nonsense, and said, "I thought we discussed this already? My responsibility is to the children; your job is to get us to wherever God needs us to be."

She continued, "I trust you Mr. Steven, now trust me please?"

Steven said, "Yes Ma'am, sorry Mamma Wafer."

Lake   Doomsday Clock 11:59:59

She said, "I was thinking this baby child needs some fresh fruit and vegetables. If you see some apples, pears, corn, just grab-em and we'll mix them up for the baby."

Yep…great minds think alike.

The table by the trail was filled with a gallon of water, a flask of fresh squeezed OJ, muffins and sweet rolls. They stuffed their faces, but not until Mamma Wafer blessed the food. As they prepared to leave they found a small bag under the table loaded with bottles of fresh fruits and vegetables and a simple note.

"For the baby. She is a special child and God will bless those who intercede on her behalf; God bless you on your journey."

Steven wasn't a deeply spiritual man. He simply didn't know what to think of the note or the gift of fruit. He folded the paper in half and stuck it in his back pants pocket.

They examined each other's feet for blisters and sore spots. Jonah had a spot on the ball of his left foot and Mamma Wafer had a scrape on her left heel. Steven told them we needed to examine each other's feet daily and take whatever precautions necessary to prevent a serious problem. Armies have been stopped due to foot problems.

Jonah had rigged a sling from a thin barn blanket for Mamma Wafer to carry Isabelle. He gained an important point in Steven's book by contributing in a positive way.

Jonah next suggested, as they moved out on the trail, that the two men take turns carrying Maria piggy back, so we could move faster. He was now plus two for the day.

They were moving at a 3 MPH clip. The trail was well maintained and fairly level. Railroads tend to have grades of less than 4% due to the weight of long trains and the problems created by weight when they stop.

9 miles, just about 12:00 noon and they noticed light colored smoke floating across the trail from west too east. Steven wasn't alarmed, because people in rural areas tend to burn brush as needed.
Lake   Doomsday Clock 11:59:59

Over the next 15 minutes the smoke became much thicker. This was a serious, fast moving, wildfire. Steven realized there had been no sirens indicating emergency crews were fighting the blaze.

He started to look at options, where to go, how to get away from the flames, when they showed up. The time to think in a crisis is before it becomes a life and death situation.

He looked off in the distance, maybe 500 yards away, a wall of flames 50 feet in the air were headed towards them.

Everything slowed up as his mind raced to find a way to survive. Steven remembered reading a book called, "Young Men and Fire" by Norman Mclean. It told the story about the Mann Gulch Fire that occurred on August 5, 1949 and cost 13 of 16 firefighters their lives. It happened in The Gates of the Mountain Wilderness in Montana.

One of the firefighters set an escape fire. He burned a circle around him as the flames approached and then laid down as the fire passed.

Steven quickly told the others what he planned to do as the flames raced towards them. He took out a lighter from his back pack and quickly started a circular fire with a diameter of 75 feet. It burned down and then started spreading out which was fine.

You could feel the heat as the flames were within 100 yards of them, next you could hear the crackling of the tree sap as small trees and large trees were quickly consumed. The fire sounded like a freight train approaching. Smoke clogged their lungs and Jonah quickly handed out swatches of cloth saturated with water and instructed everybody to cover their mouths and noses.

Steven told everybody to lay down in the middle of the still warm smoldering circle. He wasn't sure they could survive this fierce, raging fire.

Then the fire was on top of them. The heavy smoke made it difficult to breathe and the embers stung their exposed arms. They covered the kids with their bodies curled up on their side in a fetal position to shield them from the intense heat.

Just as quickly as it arrived, the crisis was over. You could feel the air heat dissipate and start too cool.

Steven checked everybody, no injuries, no major burns, it almost felt like a small miracle. God had watched over them and given the group what they needed to survive.

Jonah has earned the right to be part of the team, no question.

Two more miles of walking and they stopped for a break. An adrenaline rush, flight or fight response, is usually followed by fatigue.

Mamma Wafer had noticed an old homestead 200 yards off the trail. The barn offered some shelter and shade from the hot, Texas, July sun. The remnants from an old chimney still stood tall and seemed to say, "I'm a survivor"; and in the shadow of a withered pecan tree an old well with a pump that somebody maintained and still might be used to water cattle.

They drank the cool water and fixed PB and strawberry preserve sandwiches. They felt like royalty. They'd miraculously survived what mother nature had angrily thrown at them. A lightning strike from the storm the night before, fast moving brush fire today, and lived to tell the tale.

24 hours had passed since Steven texted Joy. Both survived day one. Took him less than a day to go from I too we. Life is unpredictable.

Lake   Doomsday Clock 11:59:59

Chonna and Clancy's Story

Chapter 13

Day 1

00:00

Silicon Valley, near San Jose, California.

Chonna Lin sat in her seat, quiet, but like most brilliant kids bored. She attended a small prestigious, invitation only, private science and math college close to her home. The old geezer teacher, he had to be 60, rambled on about the history of analog machines and electronics. Why did she need to learn this part? Computers were digital, electronics ran the world, 0-1, on or off.

Analog was old school, slide rules, nomographs, naval gunfire control computers, ancient history. Cams, pulleys, rods, wheels, gears, the dark age before digital. A line that curved gently up and down.

Digital was yes or no, the line looked like small rectangles. Digital didn't retrograde over time like analog.

The Antikythera mechanism was an orrery, a mechanical model of the solar system, rediscovered in 1901, in a shipwreck, off the island of Antikythera, between the islands of Crete and Kythera. It dated back to 100 B.C. and nothing close to its sophistication would be discovered being used for 1000 years.

She thought, to herself, so there was some smart dude or dudes, probable a woman 2100 years ago and it took 1000 years for somebody else to duplicate the idea. What's the big deal?

The lecture was a small part of the class. Students came to learn and be challenged. Learning took place by doing. The main grade; her group was assigned a tidal machine attributed to Lord Sir Kelvin in 1872-3. They used some early research by Al Jazeera who wrote a book in 1206, *"The Book of Knowledge of Ingenious Mechanical Devices"*.

She wanted to poke herself in the eye, go to the nurse, go home. Even spending time with her knuckle dragging bodyguard Clancy was better than a 100-minute-long history block. Her parents were in Hamburg, Germany attending a big G20 conference. Her dad owned a big research firm a few miles away. Her mom was the brains behind the science. The company seemed focused on battery storage and solar cells. She wasn't sure at times. Everybody was involved in the race to store renewable energy efficiently.

She thought about the weekend coming up. What should she do? She was 18, almost 19 and not very social. Her physical appearance mimicked her parents, petite, slim, black hair, dark skin, narrow face. She was ordinary, born in America, but both parents were natives of Thailand. First generation immigrants.

Lake   Doomsday Clock 11:59:59

She knew learning came easy for her. She could understand how systems worked, and how to match up seemingly incompatible programs. She got that from her mom.

Her Apple watch buzzed indicating a critical message. She only received emergency information during school hours. She glanced at the message, "10-55 U-235 GER".

Her parents were dead. Both parents confided in her the dangerous path the world was taking. How do you process the unthinkable? She knew her life depended on getting out of the classroom, the school, Silicon Valley.

She maintained focus by listening to what her teacher was saying across the room. Her mind kept bouncing back to U-235, which meant a nuclear blast. How?

She knew help would arrive shorty. Somebody would show up and give the emergency signal.

Chapter 14

00:00

The Bat Cave, Silicon Valley, California

Clancy was sitting in a high back leather chair, feet up on the table, contemplating. He did that quite often since the death of his wife and daughter.

Suddenly the light that never blinked started blinking. The bell that never clanked started clanking. The whistle that never sang started whistling.

The emergency plan constantly practiced, but always on the sideline was now in play. He was trained as a soldier, conditioned to follow orders. His feet hit the floor. No time to think, just execute the exit strategy for Google.

He punched in his acknowledgement code. Everything went quiet in the room, the bell, the whistle, the light, once again back too normal.

He jogged from the monitoring room to the garage. Voice commands opened the garage door and started the armored car, a modified Hummer H2.

30 seconds had passed since the alarm. He drove straight out of the garage. Squealed the tires just a little pulling out on the side street. There was a fine line between being in a hurry and being careless.

His smart phone buzzed once, twice, three times. Three messages. Two miles of driving at 40 mph, 3 minutes to get to the school and grab Google.

He quickly scanned the messages, glancing down and then up, always under control. First message was brief, "Little Boy, Hamburg, Germany, 0 probability of survivors, execute exit plan."

Second message also short, "Chonna is a VIP. Support will be provided if possible. Take her to site O."

Third message, "No backup available. Just two for travel. God speed. Good luck."

Clancy had three minutes to read and digest the news. 30 seconds to read.

First message, a nuclear blast in Hamburg had ended the lives of Chonna's parents.

Second message, the girl possessed skills and or information Clancy's second boss found important.

Last message, nobody available to help. Clancy was part of a 6-man team hired to protect the Lin family. Half the team was in Hamburg and the other three rotated 12-hour shifts in California. Whatever happened in the next few days would happen with just Clancy and Google, his nickname for Chonna.

90 seconds from the school. What would he tell Chonna? Her parents were dead. Was it his job to say anything? He quickly decided he'd answer her questions, volunteer nothing.

Arriving at the school he parked in front, ignoring the "no parking" signs. He bypassed the office and walked straight to her room. He had the master code to unlock all the school doors.

He opened the door to the history room, nodded at Mr. Pellet, the teacher. Quickly located Chonna and made eye contact. He brushed at his left ear, a signal, family emergency. She responded back with a brush on the right ear, I'm safe nobody is threatening me. Message sent, message received, simple and effective safeguard.

She got up and grabbed her purse and backpack off a chair. No words were spoken, kids kept working, teacher kept talking to a group working on an early Apple computer. They strolled out of the room without speaking.

They passed the office, turned left, and headed to the vehicle. Two large guys emerged from the office as they closed the doors to the Hummer. Military type haircuts, khaki pants, polo shirts, one wearing a solid blue and the Lake   Doomsday Clock 11:59:59

other red. Clancy new they had company and a potential conflict. It didn't take long for news to travel in the digital world.

Ten minutes since the alarm sounded.

He drove under control for three minutes, two miles. Back to the Lin's house, a fortress, a compound, almost impregnatable by normal standards.

The garage door opened and this time he drove straight in without backing up. No time, a black colored Dodge Challenger wasn't far behind.

He spoke for the first time, "We have company right behind us. Are you expecting anybody?"

Chonna replied, "No. Probably knuckle draggers from some competitor. I saw them leave the office at school. What's happening Clancy?"

He replied, honestly. "I'm not sure, but I think we should activate the safe room. It's just me and you kid."

She said, "Okay. You're scaring me just a little."

Clancy spoke softly, "Don't mean to alarm you, but I've got serious messages about your parents and your safety. Better to be safe and find out they just want to sell Encyclopedia's."

They walked thru the garage with the big door closing smoothly behind them, into the house and crossed the kitchen and living room to the entrance to the safe room. Both entered the activation key and the elevator door opened. A huge crash indicated somebody kicked in the front door.

They entered the elevator and pressed their right thumbs on a pad. The door closed with a swoosh. The sound of gunfire harmlessly hitting the bullet proof outer doors made Chonna jump.

She said, "I don't think they were selling encyclopedias."

Lake   Doomsday Clock 11:59:59

The elevator, with a soft hum, descended five floors below the ground. It settled and the doors opened. They walked down a short hall to a vault door standing open.

The two unlikely partners walked into a large 30 by 30-foot room, 10 feet of concrete, almost impregnatable.

Almost. Two guys with resources and time could blow up anything.

The vault door shut with a hiss. Sealed, they were trapped, but safe for now.

They worked as a team to activate the life support and communication systems. No small talk, just being efficient. Alarms began to sound immediately. No communications anywhere. 911 down, cell phone signal down, internet not connected.

Chonna ran troubleshooting on the communication systems to no avail. They had food, water, air, and shelter for a year. Provided nobody dropped a huge bomb on them. The two Neanderthals upstairs could either be stopped by Clancy or bought off in her opinion.

She told Clancy her thoughts and he disagreed.

He said, "I don't think so. Those two are professionals. They were dispatched before whatever happened in Germany..." And he stopped. He'd screwed up.

Chonna quickly asked the obvious, "What happened in Germany?"

Clancy remembered his promise, don't lie, don't volunteer. "I don't know what happened with certainty. Your parents have sensors on their bodies that trigger alarms, safeguards if anything interferes with the signals."

He paused, "Something triggered the emergency plan here and somebody knew it was going to happen. That's all I know Chonna."

She glared at him, "You'd better tell me the truth."

It was a statement and not a question.

Lake   Doomsday Clock 11:59:59

Their nose to nose standoff was interrupted by a large explosion upstairs. Now the video monitors were operating and a dust cloud appeared near the elevator shaft. The doors remained undamaged. The two guys were giving it their best shot. Clancy felt a little better about their immediate safety. Plus, the question about the death of her parents was avoided for now.

The video system showed four official military looking vehicles pull up outside, no markings. Four guys popped out of each one, everybody armed and moving with precision. Trained, not weekend warrior wannabes, not a rent a cop operation.

The two guys inside took cover. A brief, but fierce fire fight ensued. 16 against 2, out gunned, out flanked, equals 2 guys dead inside the house and 3 guys dead outside the house.

Clancy thought, our odds are better, 13 against 2. It didn't make him feel better.

He said, "Can we hack a satellite? Maybe tap into a low priority military communication system?"

She liked Clancy. If she had to be in a safe room with a knuckle dragger he's the one she'd choose. He treated her like a grownup, was polite and could carry on a conversation about most subjects.

She said, "I'm already working on it. I wish I had my thumb drives."

Clancy responded, "They're in my backpack right there." Pointing across the room.

She started digging thru the pack and found the one she needed. It gave her the ability to hack most low-level password security programs. Not the big NSA ones.

A light blinked on in the bank of monitors.

Clancy said, "Seems our friends upstairs want to talk."

He flipped the switch, "Welcome to McDonald's, order when you're ready?"

The voice from above let out a small frustrated breath, "A funny man."

Clancy smiled, he'd scored a small victory by aggravating the enemy. Him and the girl were screwed. A safe room only works if you can hold out until help arrives. No communication access meant the situation around the world was dire. No help was arriving, plan B needed implemented.

Clancy answered, "Do you want fries with that?"

The voice replied, "We want the girl and the thumb drives. You may walk away Sergeant Clancy."

Clancy thought for a second and responded, "You have me at a disadvantage Sir. Whom am I speaking with?"

The voice responded, "You have five minutes before we start blowing this place up."

Clancy thought, good, blow it up, we're 75 feet underground. He checked the console and realized his defensive options were disabled. The builder of the bug out room had added a few remote-control devices, guns, teargas, explosives. None of that did him any good now.

Chonna seemed to sense his anxiety. She said, "I can bypass the disable button. Dad gave me complete control of everything in an emergency."

Clancy smiled, head cocked to one side, "Now might be a good time to consider this an emergency."

Chonna took a tablet out of her backpack and it started up immediately. She entered a code, pressed her right thumb to the screen and tapped a few buttons.

She said, "There! It's all under your control again. I can get us out of here whenever you're ready Clancy."

He laughed, "Let me fight the bad guys. If I need your help I'll let you know."

Lake   Doomsday Clock 11:59:59

She raised her eyebrows at him and rolled her eyes, as if to say, moron, have it your way, "Okay. Just saying. I know everything about this shelter."

He looked back at the screens and noticed 3 of the bad guys were in the field of fire of the remote-controlled guns.

He sighted them in with a joy stick, aimed at knees and ankles and fired a 3-round burst from the three guns…pop…scream…pop…scream…pop scream…100% efficient.

She looked at him. "You wounded them, why? Those animals are trying to kill me…and you mister."

He stopped, "I wounded three…pretty severe. Each of them will require one person to help take care of their wounds. I took out 6 bad guys. Now it's 7 against 2. The odds are improving."

Chonna thought about it for a few seconds. "Okay, I see your logic. Pretty smart old man."

Clancy was 25 years old. A veteran in more ways than one. He'd fought for his country, killed for men and women with unknown motives. And sacrificed, losing his wife and daughter. Just for a moment he felt a connection to Chonna. Both had lost people they loved. Just as quickly the feeling left, duty first.

The odds quickly changed as the leader calmly walked to each of the wounded men and ended their suffering with a bullet to the head. Cold, calloused, calculating. The odds were now 10 bad guys against 2 good guys.

The speaker light flashed again. Clancy considered not answering, but if they were talking there was hope they could get out alive. Right now, it was a Mexican standoff.

Clancy tapped the button, "Yes Adolph Hitler?"

The voice gave a small laugh, "Hey, somebody has to pay for being careless. I believe you knew one of them Rusty. Tom from your time in Algeria? You caused this Sergeant."

It's hard to separate your feelings when you feel a certain amount of responsibility for a person's death. Clancy knew Tom Green quite well from his time in the military. It also confused the issue of who they were fighting. Tom and Clancy worked for the same boss in the private sector. All contract people, ex-military. They were the puppets called upon when the government wanted a certain amount of plausible deniability.

Clancy answered, "No sir Chief. You pulled the trigger. I'm following orders to save my client."

The voice quickly answered, "Stand down Sergeant. You are relived of this mission. Release the girl and turn over the flash drives now! It's not a request, it is an order! Mission number G03CA is terminated. New mission is G03A"

Clancy knew that everything felt wrong about the order. The numbers and letters were correct. He should turn over the girl and the flash drives, duty told him to follow protocol. His heart told him evil was running the show.

He said, "Give me 5 minutes to confer with the client and explain what is happening."

The voice said, "5 minutes is all I can give you Mister. We have a daisy cutter coming this way. It's 15 minutes out."

Clancy looked at Chonna. Her eyes glistened with tears and registered that look that said, you've betrayed me. His heart sunk just a little. It had been a long time since a woman had touched his heart with her eyes.

He took a deep breath and said, "I'm not giving you up. You said you knew of a way out. Don't hold anything back."

Her lower lip trembled and she threw her arms around his neck and sobbed for about 10 seconds. He wasn't sure what to do, so he lightly pulled her closer and kissed the top of her head and said, "I'm not letting anybody hurt you Chonna. I promise."

Lake   Doomsday Clock 11:59:59

She stepped back and wiped her eyes and nose with her hand and straightened up just a tad.

She said, "There's a back way out, hidden. My dad showed me this passage years ago. The only problem is it takes 10 minutes to activate the drill to finish drilling thru the last 10 feet of soft dirt."

Clancy said, "Activate and we'll make a plan. We need to buy some time."

Chonna stepped into a small closet filled with pipes and wires, flipped a screen down and used a triple identification process consisting of a password, iris scan and thumb print. She tapped the screen and a whirl could be heard instantly, far away, deep down in the earth às the tunnel boring machine engaged, a ten-minute life span.

Clancy knew they needed to buy some time. A daisy cutter was one of the largest bombs in the Air Forces arsenal from the Vietnam War. Who could possible order up a bomb of any size to be dropped on United States soil? Who would fly such a mission? Certainly, it must be a private air force doing the unofficial bidding of someone in the US government. Clancy had questions but no time.

He looked at Chonna and said, "In for a penny, in for a pound. We're partners in crime."

She said, "Have you noticed what we've not heard?"

He responded, "EMS! No firetrucks, police, paramedics, nothing."

She thought, sometimes silence can be deafening.

Clancy asked her, "How does this escape plan work? Tell me every detail."

She told him, "Simple last resort plan. The boring machine was put in place 10 years ago, reverse planning. It was added by a contractor that owed my Dad a huge favor. He imported temporary workers who dug straight down about 100 yards out and then they dug back 90 yards and out 50 yards. My Dad hired a separate crew to dig the down

Lake   Doomsday Clock 11:59:59

tunnel connecting to the 140-yard tunnel. The main tunnel is 10 feet from a small creek that runs near our property."

She stopped and then continued, glanced at Clancy to make sure he was still paying attention, "This is the weird part. There is a robot in the tunnel that I call Mr. B. It's programmed to defend my family with lethal force. My parents were working on a DARPA (Defense Advanced Research Projects Agency) contract about 12 years ago and what they developed scared my Dad. He could see the good, but also the bad if an army of these robots were unleashed. I remember several demonstrations for DARPA and they were super excited. My mom planted a virus in the test model and DARPA was disappointed in the results, so they dropped the program."

Clancy thought, sounds like Science Fiction, but he kept those thoughts to himself.

He thought for a minute and replied. "We need to climb down 15 feet, run 140 yards and then make it 2 miles or so away. A daisy cutter creates a mushroom cloud Chonna. That will take us 20 minutes, give or take. We don't..."

She cut him off, "No...no...no, Mr. B will be at the tunnel 15 feet below. He can move for short distances up to 20 mph. So, we need 8 minutes to get two miles away."

He added time up in his head. They talked for two minutes before activating the drilling machine, ten minutes to drill, twelve minutes' total. That left 3 minutes to get away if Ronnie "the clown" McDonald up top was telling the truth about their time line before a bomb was dropped.

This was going to end badly for some or all of them. What was the group up top going to do? Run and jump in their cars with two minutes' left? Fall on their boss's sword? Take one for the team and pay with their life?

They were mercenaries just like him. They might be Americans, but money trumped all allegiances. Was the same true for him? He didn't want to believe that was true.

The light on the console started blinking, time to talk.

Lake   Doomsday Clock 11:59:59

Clancy spoke first, "We've talked. The girl would like to live. We'd send up the backpack with the flash drives. I'd like your word the bombing run is cancelled. You drive off and we wait for the cavalry. Deal?"

Mr. Hemorrhoid said, "Let me make a quick call. I'll call you back in exactly one minute."

Clancy knew he must be using a satellite phone because cell towers were off line everywhere. Either that, or he was the one making all the decisions, which was not impossible, but highly unlikely. He sounded and acted like Clancy, a foot soldier.

He asked Chonna, "Take the remote guns and line up on their vehicles, full automatic. Set the timer on our Hummer to self-destruct in 10 minutes. I don't want their vehicles to be drivable."

She said, "You're going to kill all of them. They'll panic and climb in the Hummer and a mile down the road it will explode."

He said, "Yes. I didn't make the rules. I'm trying to save your life and mine. They decided to be on the losing side today, not me."

She smiled sadly, shook her head slowly, and said, "I'm glad you're on my side Clancy."

Clancy said, "I'm sending up my backpack with flashbangs and tear gas set to go off 15 seconds after the elevator door closes. I hope that will buy us a minute or so, cause a little confusion."

He called Clancy back in exactly one minute. He was abrupt, "Deal, send the backpack up now, no delays."

This was it. No turning back. When that elevator closed the clock was ticking. They would either live or die depending on their plan, and how the group up top reacted.

Clancy told Chonna to turn on the microphones so they could hear what was happening upstairs in the panic to follow.

Lake   Doomsday Clock 11:59:59

He opened the elevator door, armed the flashbangs and tear gas and quickly walked back to the shelter. He was counting in his head and listening with his ears. He heard somebody up top mumble here it is and a second later a huge explosion, followed by voices yelling.

Chapter 15

Rusty turned to Chonna and said, "Let's go!"

The door opened and down the chute they went, 15 feet to the bottom of the main tunnel. Waiting for them was a large matte black robot.

About 5 feet tall, propelled by triangular tracks powered by powerful batteries. The robot was pulling small encased trailer 3 feet, by 2 feet.

Mr. B's (originally Chonna had called him Beep Beep Bop Bop as a child) design might have been 10 years old, but his artificial intelligence software and defensive counter measures were 2 generations ahead of most countries and 1 generation ahead of the most modern army.

Mr. B said, "Hi Chonna. Hi Rusty. Climb on, let's go."

They quickly scrambled aboard the trailer. Side by side, hips touching, hands gripping side rails. Clancy felt the comfort of his 9 mm Barretta in a concealed waist holster.

Mr. B took off hitting top speed almost immediately. Clancy did the math in his head. A mile was 1,760 yards at 20 mph it would take 3 minutes to do a mile. 140 yards' times 3 = 420 divided by 1,760 equaled 23.86 seconds to the end of the tunnel.

Chonna took a different route to the answer, "Mr. B, how long until we exit the tunnel?"

Mr. B, "24.2781 seconds Chonna."

Down the tunnel they flew, 140 yards felt like forever, bounce, bounce, thud, thud. The tunnel opening to the creek grew larger and they passed the boring machine pressed against the side, power off.

Mr. B said, "So long schmuck…you one dimensional bot! Drill your ten-feet and die man."

Lake   Doomsday Clock 11:59:59

Chonna replied between jolts and bounces, "My dad was a big comedy fan, slapstick, stand-up, he loved to laugh. Mr. B uses humor inappropriately."

Clancy thought, but didn't speak. I'm in a life or death situation with a young lady and a robot who thinks he's a cross between Charlie Chan, Bob Hope and Richard Pryor.

They exited the tunnel and Mr. B said, "Lean right, hard right, 110 degrees." And the robot and trailer swung violently to the right.

Clancy held on with one hand and grabbed Chonna's waist with the other, pulling her close and she stayed pressed up against him.

The sound of automatic gunfire filled the air along with shouts from the distance. Mr. B climbed the creek bank and found a bike trail, empty, middle of the day. Now speed was everything. Putting distance between them and the Lin house.

Three and a half minutes since Mr. B had told them to hop on and a tremendous explosion ripped the air 300 yards away. They felt a slight concussion wave and a few pieces of plastic ended up falling nearby.

Clancy wondered if he knew any of the ten men jammed into the Hummer that just exploded. On an intellectual level, he knew all were dead and it didn't really bother him because they started the fight and tried to kill the girl. The thought quickly went away. The mission was a priority and of course the dedication and loyalty to country and men he didn't know is what contributed to the loss of his wife and child 2 years ago.

Maybe it was time for Clancy to do what was best for him instead of saving the world. And that thought went away as well. Clancy was a warrior, a fighter, for the underdog and down trodden. Women and children would seek him out in a crisis because he was a natural protector. An alpha male in the truest sense.

They covered 2 miles in 7 minutes. Clancy kept waiting for an explosion. One big enough to knock over Mr. B and send Chonna and him tumbling into forever.

Mr. B seemed to read his mind and said, "Rusty, the threat is over."

Clancy responded, mildly aggravated, "Nobody calls me Rusty. Please stop."

Mr. B, would have smiled, but because he was a robot, just said, "Don't have a cow man!"

Chonna intervened, "Mr. B, please refer too Rusty as Clancy from now on."

Mr. B said, "Okay, as you wish Chonna. Clancy, please remove your arm from Chonna's waist. The threat is over. Remember, I'm here to protect her from all threats."

Clancy felt embarrassment running up his chest, his neck, his face. He started to pull his arm back, but Chonna grabbed his wrist and pulled his arm back around her waist.

Chonna said, "Mr. B, protecting me doesn't give you the right to intrude on my personal space. If I want Clancy's arm around my waist, I will. Please mind your own business."

Clancy thought, wow, she told him, that meddler.

Clancy said, "How do you like those apples tin man!"

Mr. B said, "Mr. B not made of tin, Mr. B a top-secret alloy Clancy. Chonna, Mr. B simply noticed your vital signs running high when Clancy pulled you close. Increased pulse…breathing…blood pressure spiked."

Chonna said, "Okay Mr. B, enough." She felt the same redness Clancy felt creep up her torso. "Next time you're concerned about my vitals send a message to my Apple wrist computer."

Lake   Doomsday Clock 11:59:59

Silence followed, Chonna said, "Clancy you may remove your arm now. I feel safe. Thank you." And she leaned over and kissed him on the cheek.

Clancy rubbed his cheek. He felt calm in the middle of a storm.

Chonna felt her watch buzz and ignored the message, it buzzed twice more. Mr. B was incorrigible.

Mr. B said, "Did you get the private message Mr. B sent you Missy?"

Chonna, "I did, thank you!"

Clancy spoke to Mr. B, "We need to head to site O. Do you know where…"

Mr. B, "Change of plans. Site Y is now the destination."

Clancy, a little bit aggravated said, "I'm in charge of Chonna's safe arrival."

Mr. B, "And you are. Mr. B has access to information you don't Major. We need to work together. My job is to protect her. Remember Mr. B can kill you 10 different ways. That's a joke."

Clancy, "I mustered out a Sergeant."

Mr. B, gave a metallic chuckle, "My Lady should marry an officer. I'm so funny!"

Clancy, "We need to move ahead, quickly, leave Silicon Valley."

Mr. B, said, "Agreed. Mr. B can travel about 35 miles a day, recharging with solar and wind as we go. Mr., B also have a hydro generator if we're close to water. If you two ride me, Mr. B can only travel 20 miles a day. You weigh 165 pounds and Chonna…"

Chonna said, "You don't tell a man how much a woman weights."

Mr. B, "We can maximize our travel time by you two walking for 10 miles and riding for 15 miles. 25 miles a day. Camp Y is in southeastern Oklahoma."

Clancy glanced at his watch, 35 minutes had passed since the alarm sounded. It seemed like hours ago.

Chonna said, "Mr. B, how can we help you do your job. Please protect Clancy as well as me. You may consider that order an amendment to your prime directive."

Mr. B., "Yes Ma'am. Mr. B not sure that's a wise decision on your part. Never the less; release the four drones to gather information and do a threat assessment. This will help Mr. B make recommendations to Clancy."

Chonna asked, "What about me?"

Mr. B, said, "Mr. B will communicate with you by private message. Mr. B has several private concerns to discuss and some troubling information to pass along."

Mr. B continued, "Clancy before you get your panties in a wad, none of this is about you personally. It concerns Mr. and Mrs. Lin's company and what happened in Germany. Plus, some irregularities in security personnel, rotations and roster changes."

The drones with just a tiny buzz were tossed in the air and lifted off, headed in different directions, east, south, west, north.

Both humans were off the trailer and moving at a quick pace, southeast, away from San Jose.

Chapter 16

Mr. B gave a report 20 minutes and almost 2 miles later. Traffic snarls to the west and north, lack of electricity has reduced roads to parking lots. EMS not able to respond and cell towers are down. East of us is a large body of water and going back would cost us most of the day. South is a group of five juvenile males, mugging people along this path."

Clancy thought for a moment, and asked, "Threat level on the group south and proposed solution?"

Mr. B quickly responded, "Mr. B says we smoke them with a hellfire missile, just kidding. Mr. B doesn't have one anyhow, but give him 4 hours and one can be called up.

Their threat value on a scale of 1-10 is a 3. They don't have guns, just knives, chains, brass knuckles, and a baseball bat. Don't worry about the bat. It's a 2009 Mark Reynolds, Arizona Diamondback edition, whatever they swing at will be missed."

Mr. B was a jokester and continued, "In my bag of weapons is a quick acting chemical agent, delivered by dart, accurate from 20 yards.

As a group, we should approach casually and deliver the dart loaded with a chemical solution and within 5 seconds they'll be incapacitated, lights out. 45 minutes later they'll wake up with a big headache. Plan approved?"

Clancy couldn't think of any downside to the concept, simple, minimal risk and so he said, "Okay! Let's execute."

Mr. B said, "The two of you move ahead of me about 20 yards. Distract them, act casual, be an easy target. They're about 200 yards away right now."

Chonna asked a good question, "How do you know this group has been mugging people?"

Mr. B replied, "Mr. B's software is connected to Police Department reports. GPS has shown a gang operating within 400 yards of light rail stops. Quick off, mug, hop Lake   Doomsday Clock 11:59:59

back on and their gone. Before the cell towers went down there was several 911 calls to police. Unfortunately, they were low priority and officers never responded."

Clancy and the girl started walking ahead and Chonna slipped her hand into Clancy's.

She said, "Just pretend we're lovers out for an afternoon stroll. Tell me about yourself Clancy?"

Her touch made him nervous and his hands sweaty.

He said, "Not much to tell. Raised by a single Mom in Massachusetts, joined the army at 19, left at 22 with the rank of Sergeant. Hired by a private firm 12 months ago and assigned to your family 6 months ago. Can we talk about something else? Please?"

She turned and faced him. Dropped his hand and wrapped her arms around his neck and kissed him on the mouth. He tried to pull away and she placed one hand behind his head and refused to submit to his feeble effort. Her watch buzzed numerous times. He finally kissed her back and was surprised at how comfortable her body felt melted into his.

Her watch kept buzzing. She didn't care. Whatever was happening between them felt natural and good. If this was love she'd waited too long.

The embrace was shattered by laughter. The gang of five had arrived for an easy meal. A bi-racial couple, an Oriental chick and a Hispanic guy.

The leader, always the biggest guy with thugs was 6'2" and almost 300 pounds. The rest were smaller stair steps with the smallest kid being 5'7" and 140 pounds, all white.

Big guy said, "Well…well a taco and a chink. What's a cute slant eye like you spending time with a greaser?"

The cavalry arrived. Mr. B calmly said, "5 slow white guys, what's the punch line?"

Lake   Doomsday Clock 11:59:59

The middle kid said, "What the hell; R2D2." And laughed, which was a mistake.

A tranquilizing dart traveling faster than the eye can see struck him in the arm. He yelped, tried to brush it off. Lost his balance, stumbled, bounced off the tree next to him and slid to the ground.

Mr. B said, "Insulting, R2D2 indeed."

Chonna said, "We know you're more the terminator type Mr. B.; Arnold Schwarzenegger has nothing on you!"

Four more darts shot out with blinding speed. 5 seconds later all the bad guys were sprawled on the ground, unconscious, the threat neutralized.

Mr. B calmly said, "Missy, Mr. B needs to talk to you about your conduct."

Clancy could still feel her lips on his, her hands rubbing his chest and upper arms. He wanted to remember this feeling, but like most men he didn't want to talk about feelings.

Chonna was confused in many ways. Hormones her mother would have said to her. Female hormones are a curse and a blessing.

So much had happened in the span of 90 minutes. One minute she'd been sitting with a group of kids her age, received a life changing message about her parent's death, and the next moment she'd been whisked off by her knight in shining armor.

Clancy had caught her eye from the moment he'd started working for the family. Her father told her he was a complicated one and someday he'd answer the questions she had about him.

Where did he come from? His history? He seemed smart. He asked intelligent questions about her projects. He asked questions for understanding and clarification.

She'd come home from class today, watched men being shot for the first time. Then watched a monster execute them in cold blood because they were excess baggage to a mission. The mission to kidnap her and take the information in her head or on the flash drives.

She'd willingly programmed guns to shoot up cars and force men into a vehicle that would explode and kill them all. Was she any better than a monster who executed wounded men to move along a mission?

Now…she'd all but mauled Clancy to set up five guys just to help Mr. B tranquilize them with darts.

It was all too much and she began to sob…slowly at first and then completely dissolved, uncontrollable tears and sat down.

She got up this morning and went to college…and now the world seemed to be collapsing around her. Why?

Clancy had no idea what to do. He knew they had to keep moving.

Mr. B said," Chonna, you're suffering from Post-Traumatic-Stress Disorder symptoms. You've witnessed and been part of several horrific incidents in a short period of time."

Chonna sat and didn't speak for a few minutes.

Clancy finally broke the ice, "Chonna, I know you've seen a bunch of stuff today. I'd like to sit here and talk about what happened and why, but we've got to keep moving or else."

He knelt next to her and took her hand, gently. She slowly stood up. Clancy's presence calmed her. She didn't know why, it just did.

They started walking down the bike path. Clancy held her hand and Mr. B followed.

Mr. B suggested Chonna ride for a bit and so she climbed on the trailer and off they went at a brisk pace.

Chonna listened to the sound of Clancy's shoes hitting the gravel path. A steady rhythm after a few minutes,

Lake   Doomsday Clock 11:59:59

thump...thump...thump, constant. His breathing slowly deepened, not distressed, just consistent, sucking air in and slowly blowing it out.

After 3 miles Clancy called for a break. He needed water.

Mr. B had two gallons of water in the trailer. Water wasn't the only item in the trailer. Mr. B had a full arsenal of handguns and rifles plus ammunition. In addition, a complete survival kit was included. Clancy felt just a little better about his resources to do the job. And the job was protecting Chonna, not falling in love with her.

He was confused about his feelings for Chonna. Taking this assignment was just part of the healing process, losing his wife and infant daughter two and a half years ago still stung.

It had become more than a job. He enjoyed spending time with her. She was smart. Clancy was smart, but in different ways. Clancy held a degree in applied mathematics from MIT. Started college when he was 16 and finished at 19. Didn't know what he wanted to do in life, so he drifted for two years and finally joined the army at 20 years of age.

He rarely dated. Never in college because of his age. Only a few dates after college, a long dry run. A bit of a social misfit, he met a girl, also a social misfit, at a bar one night after boot camp was over. They had a one-night stand, too much alcohol was involved. She ended up pregnant, they talked, they got married. It seemed like the right thing to do at the time. Family and friends criticized their decision and said it wouldn't last, it did.

Then he was recruited for a special operation because of his math background, low risk they told him. All he had to do was enter a foreign country, illegally, talk to the scientist who wanted to defect, make sure the guy knew what he was talking about and slip back out.

It went smooth. The guy knew his stuff and what he'd figured out for a software program using an algorithm was valuable to the guys at the DOD (Department of Defense). Enough value that Clancy figured the guy had probably won a travel VISA and eventual citizenship for him and his family to the USA.

And it should have ended right there. All he had to do was walk out of the Internet/coffee cafe, cross the street and climb in a car with a driver. The rest was easy, go to a private airfield and fly to a neutral country, go to the US embassy, pick up his true travel documents and go home to his wife and kid. Done.

But as he exited the cafe he noticed a toddler wander into the street. Clancy ran over and snatched her up just as a car ran a red light. The mother of the child ran over in tears upon discovering what had happened and thanked Clancy profusely. That should have been the end of a White Christmas moment.

A documentary crew was nearby filming and heard the commotion, then the camera guy realized he'd filmed the entire rescue. Including Clancy walking out of the cafe and 30 seconds later the scientist leaving as well.

Clancy was a hero in a 3rd world country starving for every morsel of good news. He couldn't leave because the police had shown up and were celebrating as well. Everybody wanted to talk to Clancy and have their picture taken. He was a hero, until somebody asked for his name and he drew a blank. His forged documents didn't hold up very well.

It didn't end well for anybody. The scientist was taken into custody after police viewed the film shot be the documentary crew. He was questioned, tortured, confessed to meeting Clancy. Dr. Who and his family were never seen again.

Clancy, because he was American, was declared persona non-gratis and expelled. Canada claimed him, because the US didn't have an embassy there. God bless the Canucks to the north.

A Facebook friend, soon after the incident, commented on the photo of Clancy that went viral on social media. "Is that our friend Rusty Clancy? I thought he was back from

Lake   Doomsday Clock 11:59:59

deployment and living in Killen, Texas with Barbara and their daughter?" And it was shared 10,000 times and garnered well over 1 million views.

Which allowed the embarrassed 3rd world country to, know his identity, and order the execution of Clancy's wife and child in retaliation. Nobody likes to be embarrassed. Which of course caused outrage that nobody thought to protect them after he rescued a child from certain death. Which caused Clancy's cover to be blown.

The CIA who trained him for the mission knew he could never be used again because of his picture and identity being broadcast worldwide. They washed their hands of him. The army wasn't the best place for a reluctant celebrity like Clancy. He was politely refused a chance to re-enlist and serve additional time. Clancy mustered out 6 months after his family was murdered.

He spent 6 months in New Mexico. He thought about teaching, but his name was flagged in the FBI background check as a security risk because of his family's murder.

He bought 10 acres of high desert land, north of Albuquerque, built a metal shed, bought a 1970 Torino and worked on it every day. Slowly taking it apart, media blasting, painting it Lotus green with a wide yellow stripe, interior redone, buying new and refurbished parts. Making something new out of something old. Trying to fix himself. The car, (nicknamed the beast) totally restored, sat in the garage waiting for its master to come home.

His CIA handler retired and started a security firm. He contacted Clancy and offered him a chance to work security. Trained him for 6 months and assigned him to the Lin family. Clancy accepted the job; which is how he ended up here, screwed again.

He slowly withdrew from his pity party. Chonna was sitting next to him.

She asked, "What are you thinking about?"

Lake   Doomsday Clock 11:59:59

He smiled, "Life, and how it's conspired to bring the two of us together fleeing evil."

She said, "I believe God has a plan."

He interrupted, "Really? Did God's plan include somebody detonating an atomic bomb in Germany?"

She asked in return, "Clancy, do you believe in God?"

Did he believe in God? He thought about it for a few seconds, pinched the bridge of his nose, blinked his eyes a few times, and said, "Yes, but me and God have a complicated relationship."

She thought about correcting his English for a nanosecond. She'd always swore she wouldn't be an English Nazi. If a man was trying to express himself, she could handle a small faux in his syntax.

Mr. B said, "The two of you need to talk while you move. You need to cover 15 more miles as quickly as possible before we stop for the night."

Clancy asked, "Where are we headed?"

Mr. B, "Eastern foothills."

Clancy said, "Let's roll." And off they went.

Water food and shelter. Clancy thought about each of them and then realized he owed Chonna the truth about her parents. They had done more than just survive today. They had bonded as only two people can in a crisis. It wasn't about her being a female that made the bond, it was the experience.

Clancy said, using a soft voice, "Chonna, I need to talk to you about something."

She said, "Okay."

He said, "Your parents in Germany..."

She said, "I know Clancy. I know they're dead. I received a message."

Lake   Doomsday Clock 11:59:59

He said, "I'm sorry Chonna." And he meant it.

She replied, "I am too. Right now, I can't mourn or feel sorry for myself. Somebody is trying to start World War III."

He said, "Okay. When and if you need to talk, I'm here. I lost my wife and daughter in a terrorist attack. I understand how you feel."

She said, "I knew you'd been thru stuff. I didn't want to ask. Maybe later when we stop we can talk?"

They easily covered 15 miles in the next 5 hours. Both were young adults; their bodies were in peak condition. Jog and walk, jog and walk, easy breezy…

Mr. B carried a week of emergency rations so food wasn't an issue today, but Clancy knew he had to solve that problem before too long.

The robot also carried a small two-person tent and several light weight blankets in his trailer. Clancy wasn't sure how he felt about sleeping in the same tent as a beautiful woman. He was obviously attracted to her. They'd cross that bridge tonight.

They made the foothills and Mr. B found a hidden spot free from prying eyes. The propeller drones were recalled and a small tethered blimp released to gather information and be the eye in the sky.

They were tucked away between two hills with a distant view of the California shoreline. Early July and the sun set late, fiery orange ball slowly settling down on the water and then rapidly sinking. Chonna never tired of the view. The end of daylight, one more day down in her life.

Would she see many more? Was today the beginning of the end? Would she live to be an old lady? Enjoy grandkids? Have kids? Get married?

Her parent's dead. No more conversations with her mom about boys. No more talking about important stuff and frivolous things. That was taken away from her, by somebody or something. She moved her mind passed her parents.

Today. She'd never seen people hurt before. Never. She'd lived a sheltered life. No street beatings, school fights, no siblings to beat on her... All her news was digital. Pictures and videos combined with words to explain how cruel people could be to each other.

She thought about Mr. B and the Three Laws of Robotics or Asimov's Laws.

1. A robot may not injure a human being, or thru inaction allow a human being to come to harm.
2. A robot must obey orders given it by human beings except when such orders would conflict with the First law.
3. A robot must protect its own existence if such protection does not conflict with the First or Second laws.

Bullshit. Ambiguous at best she thought.

Her Mom programmed Mr. B with his AI capability. She used an algorithm to find information. Original source was best. Wikipedia was high on the list. News organization such as FOX and CNN were almost never considered trustworthy.

Old print was of greater value than new print. The sophistication to plant ideas and thoughts had evolved at a tremendous pace. What was the truth? What was a planted lie?

Ty Cobb, a great baseball player in the early 1900's had his reputation ruined by several biographies published after his death. Al Stump a sportswriter wrote a book painting Cobb in a dark light. Only many years later were the stories found to be sensationalized and in part fictionalized. Cobb was a drinker, a fighter, a southern bigot, but a hell of a baseball player.

Notes of Debates in the Federal Convention of 1787 by James Madison is valuable to historians. What if Mr.

Lake   Doomsday Clock 11:59:59

Madison projected his own views onto the debate notes? Possible, Mr. B cross references each piece of second hand information and assigns a value designed to give a best guess choice. Is the author avoiding biases?

Emails can be planted. People share information that supports their shallow point of view. Conservatives, liberals, Republicans, Democrats, hard core supporters, deeply invested groups all need to be treated with suspicion.

The sun was completely down and the sky streaked with the remaining light slowly filtering out and falling gentle to the ground. Clancy felt morose and wasn't sure why. Maybe it was the depth and width of emotions he'd been thru today.

Mr. B asked if they'd enjoyed the fine dinner of protein, carbohydrates, and fat paste, in the correct proportion; reconstituted with water of course. No response received.

The small talk between them resumed with the setting sun.

Chonna started, "What do you mean your relationship with God is complicated?"

Clancy tried to deflect, "Mr. B, she asked a question."

Mr. B replied, "Answer the question soldier. Mr. B's learning all the time, but not much from your strategies..." And he laughed for the first time...a Joker laugh.

Clancy said, "That was stupid."

Chonna said, "Clancy, you're arguing with a machine."

Clancy took a deep breath, "I like control over my life. I don't feel comfortable saying, what next God?"

Mr. B suggested, "It's been a long day. Both of you are showing PTSD symptoms. Go to bed, sleep, tomorrow will be a long day. We need to cover 40 miles and that means the two of you need to walk 30 miles."

They pitched the tent and Chonna turned off some of Mr. B's functions. He was not happy.

Lake   Doomsday Clock 11:59:59

They laid down in the tent. The wind blew softly and made the night air seem cool.

Chonna was turned away from Clancy, on her side and moved back so she was snuggled against him, spooning. Neither of them said a word for 10 minutes or so.

Both were processing the day's events in their head. Different brains, many of the same conclusions.   A man and a woman, so close to death multiple times today.

Clancy had wrapped both his arms around Chonna. Her right arm was pulling his neck closer. She pressed her head back against his chest.

He responded and said, "I want you Chonna." It wasn't a question, but a statement and she understood.

Mr. B's functions returned during the early morning hours. He was programmed to ensure Chonna's safety. Her vital signs were steady, surprisingly low after such a stressed filled day. He decided Clancy was good for her.

The morning light, lifted from the ground, slowly woke up the sleeping couple. Entwined arms and legs were unwound. A final embrace, awkward smiles of new lovers, but a shared commitment to the mission and making sure mankind survived in the chaos to follow. A kiss, clothes casually rearranged and they emerged from the tiny tent.

Mr. B was always awake. His tiny wind turbine had recharged battery packs all night, his solar panels tilted to maximum sun exposure kicked in as well.

A hasty breakfast of reconstituted paste consumed. Rehydrate with water and Mr. B led the way into the hills.

Mr. B explained a search was under way for them. Their pictures were being circulated by law enforcement via computer. An effort was under way to track their electronics so everything was turned off, and stored in a faraday cage inside the trailer.

They walked and jogged at a 4mph pace for 5 hours, 20 miles and Chonna realized it had been 24 hours since she received her text message and Clancy's alarms had sounded.

They were alive. The end of Day 1.

Jamal's Story

Chapter 17

Day 1, 00:00 Detroit, Michigan

Jamal sensed his alarm going off before it buzzed. Spending 8 years in the army had tweaked his senses into the subtlest of sounds.

He had detached from Army life; simply grown tired of taking seemingly senseless orders, working long days, family moving around every few years.

The Army was famous for hurry up and wait. Get up at 4:30 am, load the trucks, move out at 5:30. Drive for an hour and wait for two hours baking or freezing in a field because a C130 had engine trouble the night before and was being fixed. Nobody thought to tell the ground guys.

Working 6 days in a row from 6:00 am until midnight because the mechanic unit was down 3 bodies.

Lake   Doomsday Clock 11:59:59

The family would settle into adequate base housing and he'd get transfer papers or a12 month deployment.

Gone for 38 months total in 96 months. Afghanistan once, Iraq twice. Dumps. The conflicts were political in nature with no clear exit strategy. Frustrating at best, a damn shame for every American life lost in his opinion.

"Look Sharp, Be Sharp, Go Army" "Todays Army Wants to Join You" "Be All You Can Be" "Army of One" "Army Strong", every slogan from 1950 until now. He's joined under Army Strong. Finally mustered out as a Staff Sergeant after discussing it with his wife Janet.

They had two kids, Genet 8 and Curtis 6, both in primary school now. Good kids, made his life complete. Holding his newborn daughter at 19 years old, nothing like it, still brings tears to his eyes.

He went in as an E1 and left as an E6, earning $37,000 a year, knew he'd never be wealthy or even be a home owner earning that kind of money.

So, he left, mustered out. Came back to the old neighborhood and found a rundown rent house for $600 a month. Took a job in a small garage for $15 an hour. Not much, even by Army pay. $600 gross if he billed out 40 hours a week. Jamal did each job right, not fast.

The shop had software that estimated how long each repair should take. Some guys were fast and could do 50 hours of billable repairs in 40 hours of actual work. Jamal wasn't one of those guys. He was thorough, detail oriented. The Army didn't want a tank or a 3-ton truck breaking down the day after being fixed. Take your time and do it right the first time.

It was hard to make ends meet. Work 50 hours a week and only get paid for 40, some weeks 35 hours. Taxes, and the $600 became $500. Rent, utilities, food, gas, health insurance, internet, cell phones, not much left. The 1996 Ford Taurus barely ran and always needed something replaced. He couldn't afford new parts, so he went to a salvage yard.

Lake   Doomsday Clock 11:59:59

He was thankful the kids were healthy. Life was a challenge. He embraced the suck that came each Monday. No other choice. Fold up and quit?

Janet went to school. She dreamed of being a nurse, a RN. Because they moved so often she'd have to find a different college in a different state every few years and start a new degree plan.

Janet and Jamal were trying to break the poverty cycle. Both were raised by 3rd generation single black women. Welfare moms some called them.

When you have a child at 15 and drop out of school. What's left to dream about? You put your life and future on hold. Work odd jobs when possible. Join training programs that prepare you for nonexistent careers. Automation sucks up so many low-level jobs. Not everybody in the hood can cut hair.

No dependable babysitting available. Jobs lost due to a kid being sick or a sitter quitting at the last minute. Everybody seems to give up at some point. You don't start this way. The American dream seems a nightmare in low income and minority neighborhoods.

She'd married Jamal right after high school graduation eight years ago. Both were the first and only one of their siblings to graduate 12th grade. They were the hope and rising stars of their respective families.

Jamal had joined the Army to learn a trade. She'd gotten pregnant right away. 18 months after Genet was born Curtis arrived. They'd moved every few years across the country. Her and the kids would follow Jamal. He was a good husband and Dad. He also followed Christ.

They were Christians. Even in tough times they'd gone to Church, offered money and talent to help others.

They didn't have much. Lots of times clothes were from a no pay pantry or Salvation Army. Both kids liked to play sports and it was hard to find money for name brand shoes. Sports camps and travel teams weren't part of their world.

Grocery shopping was a challenge. Janet knew enough from her courses on developmental psychology, biology and nutrition about what they should eat.

How made in a production plant was bad, but made by natures plant was best. Plant protein was best. Most of the biggest and strongest mammals were herbivores. Elephants, bison, all ate a plant based diet. Meat was recycled protein from plants.

A liter of soda was $1. A quart of OJ was $3. Sugary cereal was cheap. She made tough choices every week at the store. Fresh fruit and vegetables were costly. Carbs were cheap. She often bought marked down meats and produce. Still they ate healthy compared to most low-income families.

Jamal had planted a garden at the beginning of the summer. Her and the kids tended to the weeds and the watering. They collected rain water using IBC totes which supplemented the garden during short droughts. Rows of corn, tomatoes, squash and a few pumpkins were starting to ripen.

Janet had swapped some homemade banana bread for 5 laying chickens and now they enjoyed 2-3 fresh eggs a day. The chickens free ranged in the back yard, crickets and other insects vacuumed up.

They had a computer to share at home, dial-up service for Internet. Her and Jamal had pre-pay cell phones, nothing fancy, phone calls, texts, a little Facebook. The kids had old tablets handed down from others, church and family friends. The screens were cracked, head phones and chargers were patched with electric tape and solder.

Janet had been accepted into a community college RN program just last week. The letter arrived and she'd been scared to open it. She waited until her husband arrived home and asked him to open and read it to her. They both danced and wept with joy over the news. It seemed like her dream of becoming a nurse might finally happen.

Lake   Doomsday Clock 11:59:59

Chapter 18

She nudged Jamal when the alarm went off. He rolled over and tried to go back to sleep, covered his head with the blanket.

She said, "Come on sleepy head. Rise and shine. Go to work, make some money."

He mumbled, "No electricity. The shop won't be open, again! How do we pay the bills when money is so unpredictable?"

She said, "God has always provided for this family. What makes you believe today is the day He stops? Now…get up, go to work, see what you can do to help out."

It's hard to argue against somebody who is right. Janet, his wife, was 5'2" tall. Beautiful facial features, coal black skin, a few pounds on her backside which made her even more attractive to him. He was 6' even, 200 pounds, lifted weights. And he feared her wrath. So, he got up.

Summer time, so the kids were still asleep, he glanced into their rooms. It did his heart good to watch them sleep, still innocent. He would do whatever it took to keep them safe.

Janet fixed Jamal a breakfast of scrambled eggs, toast, and coffee. He poured a little half and half into the coffee, a luxury. Life was tough, but fair in his opinion. You worked hard, lived a moral life, went to Church, obeyed most laws. A man could make something for himself and family.

He finished his breakfast, drained the last bit of coffee and kissed his wife goodbye.

The car was broken again so he rode his old, salvaged, one speed bike 3 miles to work. Past the large section of poor housing, the ones who were way down on their luck.

Across the railroad track and finally past several strip malls. Everything looked tired.

The asphalt roads, cracked and repaired a hundred times. The buildings, some windows boarded up, some with

Lake   Doomsday Clock 11:59:59

empty tenant spaces; even the signs in the shop windows were faded. He noticed a small group of people at a pawn shop that had a television set playing in the window.

He turned down the street where the repair shop was located and peddled into the parking lot. It was filled with vehicles waiting to be fixed or fixed and waiting for owners to scrape together the cash to pay the bill. Life was complicated at times. You owned a car which made you wealthy to some people. Car ownership came with costs, maintenance, repairs, gas, insurance. A game to elevate you in life and then take away your gains.

Housing was the same. Total welfare recipients got access to housing, job training, public transportation, food, medical, daycare, utilities. Get a job and things were taken away. Each dollar you made seemed like they wanted to take away $2. Where was the motivation to rise out of poverty for his people?

You voted liberals into office because they understood people needed a helping hand. The conservatives seemed to think if you handed a man a fishing pole and pointed towards the water; well that was enough. One side benefited by you staying poor and the other side thought nothing was enough. Life is complicated at times.

Even education was a mystery for the poor. Rise out of poverty with a college degree. Jamal knew 50 people with Bachelor degrees in Social Science, unemployed or under employed. Not only did they have a degree in a saturated field, but $80K in student loans to suck them dry on payday for the next 20 years.

Food stamps were a sore subject in his house. Three times they'd applied, twice they were turned down and one time they'd been approved for $18 a month. A person serving their country shouldn't need food stamps to feed their family. They'd used the card for 3 months and his wife had torn it up in frustration.

Unemployment was at 8.4% in Detroit, down from a high in 2009 of 28.4%. The steel belt of the 1900's became the rust belt of the 2000's.

Steel and iron manufacturing dwindled. Companies globalized and sent jobs to other countries, manufacturing moved to the south where labor was cheaper and weather caused fewer delays. Automation and robotics didn't help. Unemployment, crime and drugs, high taxes. These problems were a deadly combination for a major metropolitan area. Life is complicated at times.

His boss yelled, "Hey Jamal, what's happening?"

Jamal answered, "Just checking in and seeing if there's anything I can do to help."

The boss answered, "No electricity. Second day in a row."

Jamal said, "No electricity at my house either, but the pawn shop around the corner had a TV playing."

The boss said, a big smile on his face, "They have a generator. The guy who owns the shop always has CNN and FOX on two TV's. It's like they cancel each other out."

Jamal asked, "Anything I can do?"

His boss, eyebrows raised, "Not right now. I've heard other parts of Detroit has electricity. I wonder if we're being singled out?"

Jamal sighed, "I don't know. You see enough crap after a while. It seems like our grocery stores get the poorest cuts of meat. You go into a grocery store other places and the meat is red; here it's white, poor nutritional cuts, lots of fat. The vegetables and fruits come out of a box and onto the shelf almost rotted. I don't think big corporations really care about poor people. They come to the grand opening, make a bunch of promises and then look at the lower income neighborhood as a tax deduction and tax break for 10 years."

Lake   Doomsday Clock 11:59:59

Jamal rode his old bike back towards the main shopping section, where the grocery store, pawn shop, bank, electronic store, all were in two small shopping centers.

The crowd was large in front of the pawn shop. Shouts of anger could be heard echoing across the still empty parking lot.

Jamal approached and tried to figure out what was happening by reading the news feed at the bottom of the 52-inch screen. A bomb, a nuclear explosion suspected in Hamburg, Germany. He remembered something about a summit of world leaders. It didn't mean much to him. His life in Detroit wasn't changing because a bunch of honkies, wealthy dudes, were meeting in a foreign country.

Suddenly, out of the corner of his eye, he saw a brick fly thru the air and smash the plate glass window at the pawn shop. Nobody moved for a minute. Then a kid about 13 years old reached in and grabbed the FOX news TV. A second kid silenced CNN and grabbed that TV. The rout was quickly on, grab electronics and run. The easily carried items, bikes, tools, electronics were being snatched up and carried off by looters.

Smoke and fire were next. Somebody with a lighter who wanted to see if stuff burns. An old couch was set on fire. The owner was awake by now and screaming and yelling in a language not familiar to Jamal. Most of the owners in run down neighborhoods were first generation immigrants. They were willing to make less than minimum wage just to get a chance for a piece of the American dream.

The man shouting at the looters was brandishing a handgun. By now the crowd was in a frenzy and the shop owner was knocked down and several kids started to beat him with fists and feet, and then somebody produced a hammer. Jamal watched, shocked. Wishing and wanting to do more, but knowing if he intervened it meant the same fate awaited him. The shop owner was obviously dead in just a few minutes. Brains splattered on the sidewalk in front of his American dream. The sound of breaking glass and yells signaled the hooligans had found the jewelry and guns.

Jamal edged back from the crowd. He wasn't afraid for himself. He could handle physical confrontations, one on one. He couldn't defeat a mob.

Jamal noticed something else missing. No sirens. No EMS, no police, no firefighters. Had his neighborhood been abandoned by city officials?

The crowd moved on to the drug store. Now a few had weapons from the pawn shop.

The drug store was no match for the anger swelling in young people who were frustrated, without jobs or a future. They went straight for the pharmacy and demanded the narcotics.

In ten minutes pills were being dispended by the handful. Liquor and beer was next on the list. Those bottles and cans were grabbed, chugged, the crowd grew stronger and seemingly wiser. They knew what they wanted and how they'd been deprived. Clothes were set on fire and smoke poured out of the broken windows.

Still no sirens. The bank was next. Inside the bank was a security guard, a rent a cop. The doors were smashed and as they entered the lobby the guard shot each looter point blank. 9 dead. It stopped the looting. The remainder of the kids just stared at the lifeless eyes of brothers, cousins, sisters, aunts, looking up from the marble floor. A few isolated wails of regret. A mob has no conscience.

Somebody quickly yelled, "Let's do the grocery store!" Off they flew across the street to burn the grocery store. No sirens.

Jamal was sick to his stomach. This was out of hand. Where were the police?

He turned away. His people were burning buildings, looting inventory, and killing each other.

Lake   Doomsday Clock 11:59:59

Herd mentality where people imitate behavior of others from a higher social status. Nike, Adidas, Under Armor, all pay athletes to wear their brand. Mob mentality helps explain how people are influenced by peers to adopt certain behaviors or beliefs. Globalism, nationalism, stock market, home décor, all can be tied back to group intelligence, crown wisdom and decentralized decision-making practices.

Intelligent investors can join in ludicrous buying and selling practices to create bubbles and crashes in financial markets. Pyramid schemes, Ponzi schemes, same concept. Rear view reflection makes one scratch their head and wonder what were they thinking? How could they be so stupid. 5% of the people acting like they know what they're doing can lead the other 95% down a seemingly smart, but dead-end path.

No sirens, no help on the way.

Jamal circled back around to the bank, just to make sure he'd really seen 9 people shot in the head. Now there was 10 as the guard had joined them with a self-inflicted wound. Regret?

Enough blood ran to flow out of the lobby and onto the sidewalk. Who was responsible? Policy makers? Politicians? Activists? Voters?

Jamal didn't know. It seemed there was blame enough to go around and convict everybody who profited from the plight of the poor.

The drug store, pawn shop, grocery store, all were still burning. The few cars in the parking lot and on the street, in flames. The crowd seemed to settle down just a little. Swigging alcohol and popping pills, the leaders seemed powerful and sure of themselves.

Chapter 19

The sound of a car stereo getting louder echoed against the strip mall walls. The Jamaican drug dealers pulled up in a low rider. They were pissed because somebody started the revolution without consulting and inviting them.

Somebody fired a shot and a fierce firefight ensued between the mob leaders and the drug dealers. Bullets were flying everywhere. The sound of metal, glass, cement being hit was deafening. Dust filled the air, smoke followed, primeval screams and shouts. Nobody got hit, a few cuts from flying glass and cement chips. No muzzle or fire control. No training. Firefights in the movies aren't real. Rambo didn't join either side.

Highly ineffective to duck down low, raise your MAC-10 above your head and blindly pull the trigger. The MAC series is very inaccurate when aimed. It once was described by the International Association of Police Chiefs weapons researcher, David Steele as, "Only fit for combat in a telephone booth." But it looks intimidating and dealers like to look cool, be a badass. Image is everything when you're doing public service. Dealing drugs keeps the miserable poor happy and content.

Jamal was tucked next to an abandoned car wash wall watching the fiasco unfold. A pebble hit the top of his shoe, 15 seconds later a second pebble hit next to his shoe. He looked up and saw an old guy wearing a Navy ball cap leaning over the roof.

The old guy said, "Are you, "Army Strong", "The Few, The Proud, The Marines", "I'm a Navy Guy, We Don't Have a Slogan", "Aim High", "Be Part of the Action?"

Jamal had to low key chuckle, "Army Strong Sir!"

The Old guy, "I'm Walter. Retired Marine. I need your help Army."

Jamal said, "What? Stopping them?" He pointed to the two groups facing each other, a lull in the action.

Lake   Doomsday Clock 11:59:59

Walter said, "Yes Sir. When they finish shooting at each other they'll start going after women, children, the elderly. Somebody has to stand up to them, take away their guns."

Jamal realized the entire time the mob was organizing he didn't do a thing to stop them. Was it fear? His voice was silent, his actions neutral. Silence is consent. What about his obligation to his family?

Jamal said, "Where is law enforcement?"

Walter sighed, "We're on our own. This country is one step away from total chaos. We already have martial law. Two miles away the National Guard is blocking intersections. Nobody comes into our neighborhood, nobody leaves. In 5 minutes, a car will pull up with a group of White Skinheads. Three hate groups with guns. So, are you on our side? You don't get to sit this one out Army."

Jamal said, "I'm Jamal. What do you need me to do? How do you know about the National Guard and the Skinheads?"

Walter pointed to his ear, a bud sticking out, "Low tech, walkie talkies. Cell phones don't work."

Jamal asked, "How many of us are there?"

Walter smiled, "Four now including you. I need you to open the back door of the old car lot across the intersection and climb the stairs up to the roof. Hurry, you have four and a half minutes. Take a walkie talkie with you. No unnecessary communication."

Walter lowered a bucket by rope containing, a walkie talkie, three bottles of water, two power bars, 4 smoke grenades, 3 tear gas bombs and thirty 50 caliber bullets.

Jamal held up a cartridge, "Am I supposed to throw these big babies at them?"

Walter, "No...there's a rifle on the roof. You know how to use one, right?"

Jamal, "Yes Sir. I'm not a big fan of guns, but I own a few."

Lake   Doomsday Clock 11:59:59

Walter responded, "This is for your family Jamal, women, children who just want to leave this neighborhood alive. Innocents."

Jamal responded sternly, "I got it."

Off he went at a quick jog. Circling the two groups, opening the back door and climbing the stairs. Setting up a nest. Drinking a bottle of water and eating a power bar. Hydrate and eat before a fight, "Army Strong".

Have you ever watched a group of guys with more money than brains? A jacked up 1995 Dodge Ram 4X4 pickup came roaring up Main Street. The 8.0L Magnum V-10 roaring, two huge Rebel flags sticking up in the air and "Dixie" playing on the 8-track tape deck. I'm not making any of this up.

Jamal thought, how did God allow these people to be born? How do you take people with inbred social norms seriously?

The truck slid sideways, cross from the others, a triangle now. The miscreants piled out and ducked behind the tires. The dust slowly settled back to the earth. The media would call this a Mexican standoff. Each side was now exposed to at least one enemy.

A few shots were fired, tires slowly deflated, a few more yelp from glass cuts. Morons thought Jamal.

A few shouts, limited vocabulary was a problem. Mostly cuss words about each groups heritage, moms and absent fathers. Still, a bullet kills. This needed to end.

Walter used a bullhorn to talk to the groups. "I'm offering you a onetime deal. All of you put down your weapons, put up your hands up and walk into the bank."

Mr. White Supremacist leader said, "I don't think so. Why should we give up when we just got here?"

Walter said, "Have it your way."

Jamaican drug dealer leader spoke next, "Wait a minute. Can I ask a question?"

Walter said, "Sure. Talking is better than shooting."

Jamaican, "What are you going to do man, if we don't do what you say?"

Walter, "That's a good question. All of you are facing each other. I have a man behind each of you with a 50-caliber rifle ready, able and willing to shoot each of your sorry asses. All with military training."

Mr. Mob, "Prove it."

Walter spoke into his mike, "On the count of 3 ladies and gentlemen, put a bullet in the engine block of the vehicle they are hiding behind. Ready, 1, 2, 3..."

The sound made when a 50-caliber rifle fires is unique and impressive. Will a 50-caliber bullet stop a running engine? Yes.

Everybody jumped when the guns discharged, except the trigger guys/gals and Walter of course.

Mr. White Supremacist complained first, "That's a $7,000 engine MF."

Mr. Drug Dealer voiced similar sentiments, "You owe me and my boss a bunch of dollars old man."

Walter said, with a touch of sarcasm "Send me a bill. Do we have a deal?"

Jamal decided he liked the old man's style.

The mob decided to throw down their weapons. Not a surprise as several moms and aunts were beating them with shovels anyhow.

Walter finally talked the Jamaicans into give up their weapons up by convincing them he was with the CIA. He told them he knew Bob Marley and Marley would have wanted them to avoid violence. Sang a few bars of "Don't Worry Be Happy." Funnier in person than me telling you.

Lake   Doomsday Clock 11:59:59

The White Supremacist were a bit tougher. Walter told them all the gold in the vault was just for them, a mini Ft. Knox. It took them a while of searching to discover the vault held no gold. Dealing with KKK types was a little like telling a toddler to go sit in the corner of a round room.

The standoff finally ended. The bank president set the timer for 24 hours, we closed the vault and walked out of the bank. Jamal don't know how many would be alive in 24 hours and really didn't care.

Jamal knew he needed to get home to his family. He said a quick goodbye to Walter.

He would have ridden his bike 2 miles in 10 minutes. The bike was a victim of mob mentality and part of a bonfire. So, he jogged 2 miles in 18 minutes. It had been 4 hours since he left home.

Running gave him time to think. If Walter was correct and the country was on the verge of martial law they needed a plan. They needed to get out of the neighborhood. It was simply too dangerous. Not just their neighborhood, the city of Detroit. Bullies were everywhere.

People who will take from the weak, children, elderly, exist in the most affluent subdivision.

Where to go? How to get there? What to take with them?

They were in Detroit. Lake Erie and Ontario blocking travel to the east. Lake Huron ending the path to the north. South or West? West had Lake Michigan eventually, south had Lake Erie again. Damn great Lakes.

Jamal decided to defer any decision until he got home and talked to the real boss, his wife.

He arrived home and found his wife gathering eggs in the backyard. He explained what had happened since he had left the house 4 hours earlier. Janet had a different take on possible solutions.

She said, "We heard gunfire. Saw the smoke, but because I didn't hear or see any police or firetrucks, I just assumed it was a drill or something…" She let those words tail off.

She continued, "How many were killed?"

Jamal said, "At least 10. Maybe more. It was awful Honey."

Curtis 6 and Genet 8, listened to their parents. Like most kids they were wiser in the realities of life then adults cared to believe. Despite their parent's brave attempt to shield them from the ways of the world, they still attended a public school reflective of their neighborhood.

Some believe drug addicts and drunks only live in the ghetto's. The truth is they are in every township, every zip code. Parent's commit suicide, abuse their children and each other, across social circles, poor, middle class and wealthy. Cheaters, thieves, robbers, all live in houses that are worth $10,000 and $1 million.

Maybe the difference is poor people don't or can't hide their weakness or shame. Your dumb brother got shot by the police last night. Go to school. Your dad is in jail again, what a loser. Your mom is too strung out to fix you breakfast, get a pop tart, catch the bus, have a good day. Middle and upper class tend to sweep the unpleasantness under the rug to be dealt with at a different time and place. Usually as an adult and with a counselor.

Jamal asked, "Where do we go? We can't stay here. We've got to get away from people."

Janet raised her eyebrows, thinking, "Northwest or southwest. How long will we be gone?"

Jamal was thankful both of their parents passed away at an early age. "Forever Baby. Martial Law has been declared across the United States. Reports are that our President died in the summit in Germany."

Janet asked, "Let me make sure I understand what we're facing, as a family. You need us to grab what we need, travel fast, move to a different place and put down roots, start again? No services, self-sufficient?"

Lake   Doomsday Clock 11:59:59

Jamal realized what he was asking. "Yes. We have no choice. If we stay here violence will eventually come to our house. People who are stronger, or have guns and no work ethic will take from those who do have something. It might be canned goods, water, gasoline, a radio?"

She understood, "It's a family deal. We need the kids to help and be part of this solution." It was a statement and not a question.

Jamal looked at the kids and said, "Yes. If the two of you have something to say, add, question, whatever, speak up."

Janet said, "What do we need first?"

Jamal, "Water and food."

Genet said, "We got a bunch of empty plastic gallon jugs in the garage. I was saving them for a project."

Janet said, "Fill them up. Hopefully we have enough water pressure."

The water pressure still worked fine and within 15 minutes 8 gallons of water were placed next to the garage.

Curtis and Jamal worked on food next. Canned fruit, tuna fish, a loaf of bread, vegetables, cereal was dumped into plastic bags to save space. Pillow cases and backpacks held the food.

They all had bikes, except for Jamal who lost his to the mob. It worked out okay because they had a cart pulled behind a bike, used when the kids were small. Jamal loaded everything up in the cart.

He suggested they bring several changes of clothes, including jackets because fall hits early in Michigan.

They were ready to roll in 45 minutes. Reality was setting in and it scared all of them. This morning they'd woken up and complained about lack of electricity and 5 hours later they were making a run thru the streets of Detroit trying to make it to a rural area. Life was complicated at times thought Jamal.

It hit both Jamal and Janet at the same time. They were not prepared. So, they put their heads together and made a different plan.

Jamal said, "We need the jump box. Plus a few tools, wrenches, screw drivers, a hatchet for chopping wood."

Janet added, "We need a first aid kit, medical supplies, aspirin, so on. Pots and pans, silverware, spoons, spices. What were we thinking? And a can opener."

Curtis said, "We need a few games. Cards and stuff to be entertained around the campfire."

Genet said, "How about a hand crank charger for electrical devices? Charging cords?"

Jamal responded, "Good ideas from both of you. You have a hand crank charger?"

Genet smiled, "Lots of stuff you don't know about Daddy!"

Jamal smiles, raised his eyebrows and communicated silently to his daughter that they'd talk about that later.

Janet added, "Matches and lighters. A stove, we need to cook."

Jamal said, "We'll take the grill top from the Weber and two small pieces of rebar to balance it on a ring of rocks."

Curtis asked, "How about your guns Daddy?"

Jamal answered, "I got those and ammo."

Time for a new plan, how to carry all the extra supplies?

Genet thought about a Red Ryder wagon and pulled it over to the garage. Curtis found the wheelbarrow. They loaded everything up. If the circumstances weren't so dire Jamal would have cracked a joke or two. They looked like a two-bit circus as they moved out away from their house.

Lake   Doomsday Clock 11:59:59

Down the road, one house, two houses. Nobody outside, even with no electricity and July in Detroit, Michigan. Fear of the unknown drifted everywhere. A few dogs barked, bored, or wanting attention. Jamal wondered if their masters were in a body pile by the bank?

Janet was in survivor mode. She was a Mom first. She had a million questions and concerns but no real answers. What would happen when school started? Curtis barely knew how to read. Genet was doing good, but... Would she be able to teach them?

She yelled, "Stop! Kids, run back and get your summer school folder. The one with all the reading and math problems. Genet get a ream of paper from the office and a box of pencils."

The kids headed back three houses to pick up Moms order. Both a bit confused.

Jamal smiled and said, "We're not very good at this honey." More a statement then a question.

Janet responded, "We're not supposed to spend our time thinking about society melting down. We trust the government to keep society flowing smoothly and keep foreign affairs in check."

Jamal thought about that statement for a few seconds, "Maybe trusting the government was a mistake. Maybe every citizen should have a bug out plan?"

She replied, "Hindsight is 20/20. Go get the bleach from under the sink so we can treat water. We got to improve in a hurry. Our family is depending on us being moderately successful."

Jamal headed back to the house, he turned and said, "I'll get toilet paper as well and the family Bible." He laughed, which was better than crying.

20 minutes and 3 trips later they were ready to leave. Pictures...Janet needed the family picture album. Curtis wanted puzzles and Genet needed her American Girl doll

Lake   Doomsday Clock 11:59:59

bought with a bonus her Mom earned from a part time job two Christmas' before.

They restarted, moving down the street. The clanking of metal pots and silverware keeping an unsteady beat.

Genet said, "We look like the characters from "The Wizard of Oz". The wagon is Tin Man. Daddy is the Lion. I'm Dorothy of course. Curtis you're the Scarecrow."

Janet said, "Who am I?"

Jamal laughed and said, "I'm deaf and can't hear you Honey."

Genet said, with a mischievous smile, "You're either the wicked witch from the West or Glinda the good witch."

Curtis squirted a tiny stream of water from a water bottle on his mom. Then proudly announced, "She's Glinda the good witch from the West…look no smoke!"

The group broke into laughter. Anybody watching from inside their house would have decided all of them were crazy. Maybe having a sense of humor helps survive a nightmare.

They moved down the street at an unsteady pace. Stuff fell off, they readjusted or retied it. They were winging it as survivalist. Hoping the first wave could escape a total clampdown of the city.

They made several blocks. Things were starting to settle in until Curtis said, "I've got to pee momma."

Janet looked at Jamal as if to say, he's your son, take care of it.

Jamal said, "Go next to that abandoned house. Drop your pants and go."

Curtis stubbornly proclaimed, "I've never done that before. Momma always says only dogs and cats go in the yard."

Which was true.

Lake   Doomsday Clock 11:59:59

Janet said, "Honey. The rules have changed now. It's okay."

Curtis began to cry. He didn't like the new rules. Didn't know what had really changed. His world was different.

Jamal kneeled next to Curtis, placed a hand on his shoulder and spoke softly. "Little Man…you're right. The world just got scary. I can't lie to you. People are going a bit crazy right now in every neighborhood, every city. We must get away from people as quickly as possible. I need your help. Can you help me?"

Curtis wiped his eyes and nose with the back of his hand and softly said, "I can try, but I'm scared."

Jamal said, "I'm not asking you to not be scared. I want you to trust me. To lean on me when you're scared. Tell me what scares you?"

Curtis thought for a few seconds, "What's going to happen tonight? Where we going to sleep?"

Jamal said, "I don't know where. But I can tell you we will see stars. We will be together. We'll be okay tonight. Tomorrow we'll get up and travel further. Get away from Detroit. Find a safe place to live. Stick next to me."

Curtis was satisfied with those words. They began to walk again, after he peed against the house.

Chapter 20

They walked a few blocks south, then west, south again. Curtis had no idea where they were going. His feet hurt and his stomach was growling, but he kept quiet because it seemed important to act big right now.

A garage door to the left rumbled open, the springs groaning and the wheels on the rails squealing.

A big voice boomed, "Hot diggity dog. It's Army. Didn't think I'd ever see you again."

Jamal smiled at the old man, "Hey Marine. What's up?"

Walter laughed, "I could hear your band wagon coming from 6 blocks away. I thought somebody was running a car on just the rims."

Jamal looked inside the now open garage. An older looking black ATV cranked over with a gentle hum and then started purring.

Next to the funky looking ATV sat a small trailer. Maybe 3 feet by 5 feet, double axles, large wheels, solid steel, painted black.

Walter was a small, thin guy. Maybe 5' 6", 135 pounds soaking wet. He looked to be 65 years old.

The woman driving the ATV was big boned, red hair, same age, light black skin. She looked at the motley crew pulling the circus wagon and motioned them out of the way with her arms.

In less than 90 seconds the ATV was matched up with the trailer, connected with a ball hitch, safety chains attached and lights connected. Efficient.

The old woman jumped down and said, in a heavy Jamaican accent, "Hi, I'm Alvita. Walters better half!"

Walter said, "They knew that."

Alvita gave an easy smile, "What, my name is Alvita?"

Genet finished the joke, "No, she's your better half!"

Jamal introduced his family.

A large German Shepard appeared. Fang was playful, but serious. Walter and Fang went back 5 years, partners in crime and adventure as Edith explained. Fang tolerated her, but loved Walter the most.

Fang quickly licked and sniffed his way around the rag tag bunch. All seemed acceptable according to Walter's interpretation of Fangs actions. Jamal wasn't sure if that meant as a friend or a meal.

Walter spoke what was on everybody's mind, "Where you headed Army?"

Jamal answered, "Trying to find a greenbelt and head northwest. The streets won't be safe in a day or two. I figure to find an isolated patch and ride this one out. Hope for the best, but plan for the worst. Build a small house before winter hits hard. Lay up some wood for heating, shoot a few deer for meat, scrounge around for some roots and vegetables. Maybe find an apple orchard, make some cider. I'm not prepared Walter. I'm winging it as I go." The last sentence was the truth.

Janet asked Alvita, "What about you guys? You have a plan?"

Alvita laughed, a Jamaican nasal sound, "I married a fan of the Warrior Monk. He utters a General Mattis quote every day. His favorite, be polite, be professional, but have a plan to kill everybody you meet."

Genet at 8 years old, looking shocked, said, "You had a plan to kill us?"

Walter answered, "Yes, Fang was supposed to lick you to death. Damn dog must have had an Army mom."

Alvita spoke sharply, "No profanity around children."

Walter was chastised, "Yes Ma'am."

Lake   Doomsday Clock 11:59:59

Curtis giggled, but then changed his mind when he saw the look on Walter's face. He ducked behind his Daddy's legs.

Jamal said, "Walter is saying we should have had a plan to leave town. We practice our fire drill, always have two exits, our bad weather, hiding in the bathroom. We should have discussed a doomsday strategy."

Walter said, "Might of, Could of, Should of, Would of, too late now. We're headed east towards the Detroit River, travel up until we hit Lake St Clair, go north. Hit land, find a place up north near Port Huron. Fish, trap, farm a little. See if things cool off, blow over."

Janet said, "That sounds like a fantasy trip. How are you traveling on water? Do you have a boat stashed?"

Alvita answered, "The black avatar is water proof and so is the trailer. There's a jet pump on the ATV. It's not uber-fast, plus we'll be going against the current."

Genet asked, "How fast will it go on land and water?"

Alvita said, "Well...supposedly it will hit 50+ mph on land and almost 45 mph in water. This baby has a 1300 cc, BMW inline 4-cylinder engine. 175 HP available in the water."

Janet asked, "Who makes something like this?"

Walter answered, "Originally it was made by Gibbs and marketed as a quad ski amphibious vehicle. The first 1,000 prototypes were priced at 40K."

Jamal asked, because he wanted to know, "How did you get one. I'm mean come on, you don't look like the type to drop $40,000 on a toy. We all live in low income neighborhoods."

Walter laughed, "I borrowed it from the military. They requested a military prototype. Tested it, tore it down, didn't like something and told Gibbs to forget it and it sat in a warehouse for 3 years, in pieces. I have a friend who called me and asked if I wanted a project. I spent 6 months putting it back together and finding a few parts."

Curtis said, "You stole it!"

Walter looked at him, scowled, and said, "You want Fang to lick you again?"

Curtis gave a fake yell and ran behind his Daddy again.

Genet said, "So the Detroit River is 25 miles long. At 45 mph, you can get there in like 35 minutes," She did the calculations using mental math.

Walter said, "True, but the river flows at 3 meters per second and we're going upstream."

Genet did the mental math. 3 meters per second was about 7 mph. So, subtract 45-7 = 38 mph. Equivalent fraction, 38/60 = 25/X cross multiply 60 X 25 = 1500/38 = almost 40 minutes. "40 minutes!"

Alvita said, "Very good. Now, we must factor in the supplies we carry, the weight, the drag in the water."

Genet said, "I can't do that."

Alvita said, "That's okay. You'll learn."

Genet looked a little lost as she said, "What are we going to do if there's no more school?"

Curtis with a smile said, "Party like there's no tomorrow!"

Genet turned and quickly said, "Shut up Curtis!"

Janet with a sharp voice and a little irritated, said, "Enough, both of you!"

Both kids replied simultaneously, "Sorry Mom!"

Walter turned to Jamal and asked, "So, Army, you want to combine forces and make a run together?"

Jamal looked at Janet, she nodded. Husbands and wives come together in matters of protecting their children. Both knew their plan could succeed, but combining what they

Lake   Doomsday Clock 11:59:59

had with Walter and Alvita's resources and knowledge would only help their odds.

Jamal said, "Yes Sir! Where do we start?"

"I think we toss duplicate stuff. The hard part will be finding a way thru or around the National Guard road blocks. I'm hoping they're asking questions first and shooting as a last resort.", said Walter.

Jamal asked, "You think the fact both of us are military might help?"

Walter shrugged his shoulders, "Might. Might not. I'm willing to play any card in the deck."

Janet said, "What if they shoot first?"

Alvita sighed, "Oh Lord, I sense a Mattisism coming on..."

Walter smiled, "We're US citizens, We The People. The military exists because we say so. The government exists because we say so. There are some clowns in the world that just need to be shot! That's a Mattisism. Are you happy Ginger?"

Alvita laughed, "Oh boy. What got you riled up Walter?"

Walter looked like he was in pain, "Look what's happened in this country. People hate each other. Blacks versus whites. Republicans versus Democrats. Liberal versus Conservatives. We don't talk. We let the media influence our opinions and think for us. We never check out the facts. Social Media full time is a bad idea. We used to have news cycles. 24 hours for people to think about stuff, digest it, decide if they agreed or not. Now it's constant with no time to reflect. The world has been imploding since 9/11/01. I always said, not on my watch. Here we are, my watch and running for our lives and fearing the military. My group. Let's move out."

So, we did. Not as talkative.

We were within sight of the dead zone. No go. Off limits. Turn back. Do not pass go, do not collect $200.

Lake   Doomsday Clock 11:59:59

A military HUMVEE sat in the middle of the intersection, desert tan, low, squatty, menacing looking, big knobby tires, a machinegun barrel poking out the top. One soldier manning the M114 Minigun, 7.62 X 51mm NATO ammo, 6-barrel rotary fire, high rate of fire, 2,000 to 6,000 rounds per minute. 4 soldiers, each facing a different direction, north, east, south, west, M-16's pointed down. A freshly minted Second Lieutenant manning the radio, standing at the driver window.

They were just kids, National Guard. Doing their jobs, maybe on 2-week guard duty, just following orders. Even if the orders made no sense, duty first.

Marshall law declared. Military versus civilians? That thought chilled both Walter and Jamal. Walter was old enough to remember the debacle at Kent State.

May 4, 1970. The Kent State Shootings. 29 Ohio National Guardsman fired 67 rounds over 13 seconds at unarmed protestors. 4 dead and 9 wounded.

A tragedy. Nobody ever stood trial. Civil lawsuits were settled for the cost of defense lawyers. A gross overreaction by young men serving their country during the Vietnam War. Protestors refusing to disperse, destroying private and public property, burning the ROTC building. Plenty of blame and poor judgement to go around thought Walter.

Then, on May 8, four days later, 11 people were bayoneted at the University of New Mexico by New Mexico National Guard members.

Just 5 days after Kent State 100,000 protestors marched thru Washington DC destroying cars. They were against the Vietnam War and the killing of unarmed protestors.

The ragtag group stopped 50 yards short of the National Guard. Guardsman appeared relaxed.

Walter volunteered to approach the blockade. He casually closed the last 50 yards and spoke to the Second Lieutenant. He pointed in our direction and the soldier

Lake   Doomsday Clock 11:59:59

nodded her head. Walter started back towards the group at a slow jog.

Suddenly the roar of a loud engine filled the air and a World War 2 era Jeep swung around the corner, modified, jacked up, camouflage paint, a machine gun swinging wildly. The person manning the machine gun started shooting 3 round bursts at the guardsman. The second burst caught the Second Lieutenant across the chest. Red blood seeped out of two holes and she slowly slumped to the ground, fatally wounded.

The soldier manning the M114 minigun swiftly swung it around an unleashed an incredible number of shots at the Jeep. His aim was accurate. The jeep exploded into flames just as it passed the small group. The driver was almost cut in half and the gunner mortally wounded.

Jamal in the next instant had gathered everybody in the group and thrown them to the ground. His body lying across four people. His flesh and bones the first line of defense from bullets.

Nobody moved. Flames and smoke whipped the air, curling up and away; the fire quickly dying down. The smell of gunpowder blanketed the area.

Suddenly Alvita screamed, "Walter!"

He was lying on the ground, face up. A hole just above his right eye and an exit wound out the back of his head. Dead.

Alvita pried herself from under Jamal and ran to his body, kneeled and cradled her husband's lifeless torso in her arms, sobbing. Nothing anybody could do for him now, but pray for his soul.

One of the guardsman ran up and pointed to Jamal.

He screamed, "You! Get your family across this intersection now. You have 30 seconds or we will turn you back into the zone."

Jamal forced Alvita back on the black avatar and started it up. Walter's blood soaked her blouse and hands. In a few seconds, everybody was on board. All had tears in their eyes as they passed the HUMVEE.

Four soldiers gathered around their leader, making a fruitless, but valiant effort to save her. The soldier in the machinegun nest manning the M114, hyper vigilant now, eyes bouncing up and down, side to side, looking for any movement, adrenaline overload after the sudden, deadly, and quick firefight.

Chapter 21

The grieving group minus one moved towards the Detroit River.

Walters lifeless body slowly disappeared. The only sound was the steady hum of the Avatar's BMW engine and an occasional sob. Jamal thought, life was complicated at times. Unexpected leadership was a burden.

How would his kids respond to violence? As a couple, they'd tried to shield them from some of life's harsher elements. How about Alvita? Would she become a basket case, a burden on the group? Should he stop the ATV and push her off? Now?

No, he owed Walter for several favors, plus taking care of Alvita was the right thing to do. This morning Walter had helped him regain some self-esteem by standing up to the violent protestors. Then he'd invited him and his family to join them on this trip. Walter had given them much better equipment and an improved plan.

Janet was thinking about her family. What effect would first hand witnessing violence have on her children? The burden on Jamal. He was now the de facto leader of the clan. One more person added, a grieving widow who'd watched her spouse die violently and without warning.

Alvita wasn't thinking. She was mourning, she'd jumped down a dark hole where no light or hope existed. Walter was dead. Intellectually she knew that. Emotionally he still held her in his arms, chasing away all evil.

Genet could still sense the battle. The smell of gun smoke, the sting of concrete chips hitting her legs, the sound of bullets whizzing past her head. Seeing Walters eyes, open, empty. It sent shivers up and down her spine.

Curtis was still processing what had happened. Two lifeless bodies. The sudden attack by the men in the jeep. Why did they do that? It was stupid. It got Walter killed. His dad forcing him to the ground to help save him. He understood that as well.

Lake   Doomsday Clock 11:59:59

Jamal kept to side streets. Not much traffic. No sirens, no police. An occasional HUMVEE when they crossed the major roads. He wondered when they would hit the Detroit River. The Ryder came with a GPS and Walter had programmed it so Jamal was following the screen directions.

The ATV nicknamed the Black Avatar hummed along at 30 mph. The sun was beginning to set as they entered a park with several restaurants, day camping, and a boat ramp.

A HUMVEE was parked at the top of the ramp. These soldiers noticeably more relaxed than the ones at the first blockade. 6 of them again. Sitting around, some smoking cigarettes.

One of them signaled for Jamal to head over to them and stop. Which he did.

He said, "Please turn it off sir." Pointing to the ATV

Jamal shut it down.

The soldier said, "Detroit is under a curfew. The entire nation is under Martial Law. When the sun goes down you must be off the streets."

Jamal said, "Can I be on the water after dark?"

The soldier replied, "US waterways are already closed Sir! Did you serve Sir?"

Jamal said, "Yes Sir! Two tours in Iraq and one in Afghanistan, Army, Mechanic."

The soldier cracked a small smile. "Sir, the US waterways are closed, but the Canadian side is open."

Jamal said, "Permission to enter on the US side of the Detroit River to cross into Canada Sir?"

The Second Lieutenant said, "Permission granted this one time. Does this thing float?" He caressed the lines of the ATV with his fingers.

Lake   Doomsday Clock 11:59:59

Alvita answered, "We enter the water and the wheels on both the ATV and the trailer fold under. This thing floats just fine."

The soldier said, "Good luck Sir, it's real crap going down out there. Be careful Sir." He stepped back and saluted Jamal who quickly returned the gesture of respect.

The ATV turned, rolled down the boat ramp and without hardly a ripple, silently entered the water. Alvita was sitting up front with Jamal and pushed several buttons. The wheels folded under and the jet pump kicked in and off they went.

The six young soldiers waved. Curtis and Genet waved back, sorrow forgotten for just a minute. In a matter of minutes, they were going 25 mph and headed to the middle of the river.

Alvita asked Genet, "How long to get to the end of the river? We have 15 miles to go at 25 mph."

Genet thought for a few seconds, and said, "We are going 25 mph, but the river is flowing 7 mph. So, 25-7 = 18 mph. A little less than one hour to get to Lake St. Clair."

Alvita smiled, and said, "Very good Genet. Walter would be proud of you."

The mention of Walter's name made everybody a little sad.

Jamal said, "I'm going to slow it up a little so we make it to the Lake body after dark. I just think it's safer that way."

Janet asked, "When are we going to stop?"

Jamal said, "Not till we get out of the Lake. I'm guessing mid-morning or so. Then we'll find a place to sleep for a few hours and take off again."

Alvita said, "I've got snacks in my purse, energy bars, water bottles, granola bars, M&M Peanuts. Anybody hungry?" Four hands immediately shot up.

Darkness slowly crept across the river. No boats in sight. Quiet on the river. A few fish jumping. If they weren't

Lake   Doomsday Clock 11:59:59

running for their lives the group might have enjoyed the solitude.

Jamal had already decided to cross to the east of Belle Island. The sun slipped below the western horizon, now only soft shadows danced across the water.

Janet noticed several deer grazing near the water and the kids got excited. They begged their dad to move a little closer before the last twilight disappeared. Jamal obliged his family.

Janet knew the deer had to be European fallow deer and released from the Belle Park Nature Center. Legend has it the deer were a gift from the president of France in 1895. The deer were released to roam the island in 1930, but in 2002 because of illness and overpopulation they were rounded up and housed in the center. Now only a small number was left and somebody must have released the herd.

They were focused on the deer and didn't notice a man standing about 40 feet away.

He was waving his arms above his head, excited voice, "Hey. I need a ride off the island. Nobody is running boats. Help a brother?"

Jamal was instantly on alert. Experience told him the strangers body language was threatening. Jamal reached down and unsnapped his ankle holster that held a small caliber handgun. A Glock 26, 9 mm, 10 + 1 in the chamber.

The man had waded out to his knees and had closed to within 20 feet of the ATV. That was close enough for Jamal.

He pulled the Glock in one smooth motion and flipped the safety off. He said, "Sir, if you move one more inch I'm going to put a bullet between your eyes as a warning shot."

The man froze. He seemed to be mulling over the odds in his head. Go forward and close the gap, take a chance against a gun, or back away.

Lake   Doomsday Clock 11:59:59

Jamal said, with all the calmness he could muster, "8 years in the army, 11 chances to hit you. The odds are not in your favor Sir. Be smart, back up, live one more day."

The man slowly backed up. He said, "I'm stuck out here, out of beer!"

Jamal transferred power to the jet pump and they moved away from the threat.

In frustration, the man picked up a small round rock and hurled it at the water craft. It bounced harmlessly off the trailer. He yelled at the group, "You POS, you MF's..."

Curtis yelled, "Sticks and stones may break my bones, but names will never hurt me!"

The Black Avatar slipped back into the current, safely away from the threat.

They continued past Belle island and kept going north towards the open water of Lake St. Clair.

Genet said, "That man scared me Daddy."

Curtis said, "I liked the way you pulled that gun out Daddy."

Jamal said nothing.

Janet spoke up, "Your Daddy did what he had to do to protect us. I'm proud of him. I feel safe with him. What about you guys?"

They all agreed Daddy was the best. Jamal smiled inside. The open water of the Lake was within sight. Still, lots of miles to travel.

He turned to Alvita and said, "How much gas does this ATV carry?"

She said, "Walter swore we could go almost 400 miles plus the water miles. The trailer held a 40-gallon tank built into the bottom and the ATV 10 gallons."

They continued crossing the wide-open waterway, churning out the miles all night. The kids placed their Mom between them on the back seat, fell asleep leaning against Lake   Doomsday Clock 11:59:59

her. Janet slipped into a restless sleep around midnight, leaning back the best she could with two kids squeezing her.

Jamal had no choice. He had to keep the ATV pointed in the direction the map screen showed him. Alvita stayed awake as well. Silent, thinking about Walter.

The early morning hours saw the shoreline slowly come into view. A little fog obscured their approach. The seagulls squawking and divebombing for breakfast.

The ATV smoothly transitioned from a watercraft to a land vehicle. The wheels unfolded, touched bottom, power transferred to the transfer case and they rolled onto the beach. A narrow dirt road winding from the water to the high-water mark pointed away from shore.

Jamal followed the path and they headed inland. He was tired. His neck ached, shoulders, arms, all from being cramped up all night driving across open water. No place to step out and walk around or use the restroom.

They stopped at a day park near the beach, used the outhouses, saved their toilet paper. Janet had packed some sweet rolls and bananas. She passed them out and everybody ate at a picnic table. The trailer held 8 gallons of water, so they drank what they wanted, repacked the trailer and moved out.

Two more hours thought Jamal then he could rest, take a nap. They drove on and everybody was silent.

An hour later and many miles inland Jamal spotted a small shack. The path they'd taken was sparsely populated and they'd traveled on dirt roads and hunting paths. Walter had done a good job of planning the bug out path.

They stopped in front of the shack and Jamal said, "Let me check out the inside. See if anybody is here."

Which turned out to be a nobody here answer. The shack was used during hunting season as a place for hunters to sleep, eat meals and clean game.

Lake   Doomsday Clock 11:59:59

There were 3 bunkbeds and a queen-sized bed, a small kitchen with a green propane stove and a marine toilet. Alvita suggested they move the ATV around back and maybe cover it so nobody could see it from a distance or a plane flying over. Stealth seemed important right now.

It took maybe 15 minutes to get everything inside they needed and the Black Avatar hidden under a tarp. Jamal crawled into a lower bunkbed and within 30 seconds was fast asleep.

24 hours after he woke up the day before. Day 1 over.

Corderus' Story

Chapter 22

00:00 Kayenta, AZ Navajo Reservation

Corderus shut his eyes and counted slowly…1,2,3,4,5,6,7,8,9,10…and slowly opened them. He was still here. Still on the Rez.

He took a deep breath. Think, he thought to himself. There must be a way out of here. A way back to his mom.

He wasn't a child at 16. Why did the courts mandate a 30 day visit to his father's home? To learn about his culture?

I came, I saw, I conquered, he thought. It was a dead zone. High desert, red sandstone rock, dust everywhere, no sign of life and no green bushes. Yep, God took a day off on this landscape. Tossed some red dirt and a bunch of lizards out there and said, good luck, c'est la vie.

His dad was dead. Died in an auto accident 15 years ago. Corderus never remembered his father, or azhe'e as his mother referred to him.

As if being here wasn't bad enough. No electricity. The house and town was wired for electricity, but it was off. Nobody seemed bothered by that part. Just carry on his Grandmother told him. Find a balance without electricity. Probably Coyote playing a prank.

Find a balance? Are you kidding me. What planet did these people come from?

Coyote? Give me a gun he thought and I'll shoot Coyote.

He should have never asked what planet they came from?

My Shinálí asdzą́ą́ (Dad's Mom, Grandmother) has promised a lesson on the four worlds. Which interested Corderus just a bit because he had been raised a Christian and wanted to know how his belief system fit into his heritage.

There was no escape. He had to get up, face the day.

This was his third day here. He'd met some cool skaters at the Community skatepark. Keshawn, Nando, Jasian, Ryan, just to name a few. Cool dude's. Good jokes; who has the most expensive brain in the world? A skateboarder, never been used…funny stuff.

Walked over to the Kayenta Schools. One was a boarding school and the other a state of Arizona school. Shinali asdzaa told him she would explain the boarding school as well. That interested him, kids living in a dorm at such a young age.

He watched the Monument Valley high school kids play in a 7 on 7 football tournament. Met Coach Bryan Begay the winningest football coach on the Navajo reservation.

Corderus was missing summer football right now. Maybe he'd talk to Begay or one of the other coaches, Barnes or Franklin about playing a little or lifting weights. He'd spent 5 years preparing for football, lifting weights, practicing, camps, drills, and now he was away from his teammates. It just didn't seem right or fair.

He's met a middle school math teacher hiking "The Toes", Mr. Roberts. The guy was white and born in Maine. What the heck was he doing out here?

The hike was awesome, mostly slick rock and rough rock. The view was extraordinary. The town of Kayenta, K-Town to the east, one direction, Skeleton Mesa to the west, Laguna Creek to the north, Black Mesa to the south.

One night they'd driven out to Monument Valley to see the rock formations. He'd recognized a few from commercials and music videos. The west and east mittens are probably the best-known rock formations. We went to supper in Mexican Hat, ate steak at the Swinging Steak and drove back on highway 163 and saw the place where Forrest Gump stopped running. My grandfather said that was also where they took the cover photo for a Bob Seger album, "Ride Out", must be some old rocker.

Maybe, it wasn't being here that upset Corderus. It really was about a judge who had never met him deciding he'd go see people he'd never seen for 30 days. He'd always known he was Navajo. His mom didn't hide that part from him. She never stopped talking about his Dad. But, to him, the Rez was just a place and a person who existed in stories, fiction.

He felt a little like Alice going down the rabbit hole…

Corderus swung his feet out of bed, pulled on a pair of Wrangler pants, slipped a "Nirvana" t-shirt over his head, laced up his Adidas tennis shoes and walked out of his bedroom and into the kitchen.

His grandma had poured him a glass of orange juice and made him a breakfast burrito on the wood stove, eggs, cheese, sausage, delicious.

Lake   Doomsday Clock 11:59:59

She said, "Morning. Do you always sleep this late?"

He answered, "No Ma'am. We were just up late last night. I went to the skate park and hung around with a group of guys."

She said, "I know. Those guys aren't very motivated."

He responded, "Their cool. They just want to skate and be left alone."

Grandma smiled, "Yes…even the girls leave them alone. Your grandmother wants grandkids. Hang out with rodeo riders. They attract cute girls and make good kids."

He tried to change the subject, "Where's Grandpa?"

She said, "At the township, a meeting."

He said, "What about?"

Grandma smiled again, "They're trying to decide whether to shoot the skateboarders or ship them to Phoenix." Then she frowned just a little and continued, "No, they're discussing the power outage situation."

Corderus asked, "Oh…is this serious?"

Grandma said, "I don't know. We always have power outages. Our infrastructure isn't as good as other places. The reservation is always slow to modernize. Clean drinking water and even electricity is still not on parts of the Rez."

Corderus said, "Really. That sounds a bit odd. Even little towns have electricity."

She said, "Navajo's are proud and independent. We don't trust the federal government."

Corderus replied, "Why?"

Grandma said, "Eat your burrito and drink your juice. I'll tell you why the Dine' don't trust the government."

Corderus interrupted, "The People, Navajo's refer to themselves as Dine', which means "The People"."

Lake   Doomsday Clock 11:59:59

Grandma replied, "Yes my shinali. You are Dine' as well. My grandson from my son, my shinali."

Charlotte, her Christian name, Char to her friends, his grandmother, his Shinálí asdzą́ą́, started telling the story.

"The Long Walk is probable the best example of why the Dine' don't trust the federal government, white people in general."

Char continued, "A short history lesson is required. We speak a language called Na-Dene' Southern Athabaskan. The Apaches and Navajo's speak a similar language and both groups probable migrated from northeastern Canada and eastern Alaska in the 1400's.

We are hunters and gatherers. Plant a few crops, winter squash, maize (corn) and climbing beans, we call them the Three Sisters.

The men hunted game, rabbits, deer, antelope, and the women gathered nuts, fruits and herbs.

We traded with other tribes, we raided other tribes, we made peace with other tribes. We had our life and it worked, until the Spanish showed up with the concept of land ownership and superiority.

The Spanish introduced sheep, goats, cattle and horses. Which led to raiding and fighting because men want what other men possess. Navajo's are human with good, bad and indifferent people among us.

The Spanish also had rifles and handguns, revolvers. A fight with bow and arrows versus guns is never a fair fight. So, we made treaties and broke treaties, both sides.

The Americans showed up and kicked the Spanish out. Loose interpretation, but generally true. Then the Civil War breaks out which brings out the hate in men.

We'd had a series of treaties with the US. 1849, when our popular leader Narbona was killed. Some say he was scalped by soldiers. Another treaty in 1858 and then again in 1861.

Lake   Doomsday Clock 11:59:59

The Navajo's didn't have one leader, but local leaders. Men whose wealth and leadership were determined by the number of sheep and horses their family controlled. The amount of land they used for grazing. Central government like Washington DC was a foreign concept to our ancestors.

Maunuelito and Barboncito, two prominent leaders/chiefs reminded the Army they had reneged on feed agreements for animals and taken away the best grazing land to give to white settlers.

Everything came to a head when Kit Carson came sweeping thru Canyon de Chelly in January of 1864 and unleashed a scorched earth policy. Burn the crops, kill the animals and shoot anybody who resisted.

The plan was to force the Navajo to abandon their land, flee, extinguish the race of people. Kit Carson took away their homes, their food and their pride. Freezing temperatures and starvation forced the Dine' to surrender.

In the spring of 1864 the Long Walk began. From eastern Arizona Fort Sumner to Bosque Redondo 300 miles away. Men, women and children, no mercy shown. Stragglers were reportedly executed. They were never told where they were going or why they were being relocated and how long it would take to get there. Improperly clothed, under fed and dehydrated, many perished along the way. Nobody knows the exact number, 200 is given, but I believe it must be higher.

50 groups or more were marched over at least 7 known routes and when it finally ended more than 10,000 Dine' had been relocated and the resettlement camp hit a high population of 9,000 in the Spring of 1865. 40 square miles is all they were given for their new home.

Crops burned, animals shot, forced marched 300+ miles in freezing weather by a government promising to take care of you. Now you're placed in an area inhabited by 400 Mescalero Apaches, a bitter enemy. The benevolent US government provided rations for 5,000 people. Inept management of the 1.5 million dollars spent annually on food by the Army.

Fighting broke out between the Indians and the local population. That's a surprise?

By the end of 1865 Navajo's started leaving just to survive. You can't feed 10,000 people on rations for half that amount. The water was brackish and the grove of trees for firewood, heating and cooking was soon diminished.

We raided the non-natives for livestock and supplies and the Comanches raided the Dine'.

The 1886 corn crops were infested with worms and a total loss. The Pecos River flooded and washed away the head gates of the irrigation system. Humans and mother nature was sending us a clear message. We were in the wrong place, out of balance.

In 1867 the remaining Navajo's at Bosque Redondo refused to plant crops. Today we'd say they went on strike. The situation was indefensible and unsustainable. We were on the verge of becoming extinct as a group. Which was one of the goals in the first place by certain Indian haters in the United States government. Wipe out the indigenous population. Rewrite history as if you arrived on virgin land and because God blessed your people with modern tools of farming, hunting and war, you made the land productive.

The natives had been here for hundreds of years, living in balance with the land. Finding a way to exist with other indigenous groups. War between tribes existed, but we understood we couldn't wipe each other out. The federal government had no core values. It seemed to exist to satisfy a craving to populate the land, settle the frontier and exterminate the native population.

Even today you have a weasel Presidential candidate stand in front of a podium and proclaim the government owes the indigenous population for past wrongs. We just want the tools to create a sustainable economy so our children have jobs and a future. We want the shackles

Lake   Doomsday Clock 11:59:59

attached to the treaties removed so we have freedom of self-determination. Our land is owned by the Federal Government and we can co-manage what rightfully belongs to the Dine'.

My rant is over shinali. You might make a good Dine' yet. A man must do a bunch of listening to attract the right Navajo woman. After we find you the right wife then you'll listen to her the rest of your life."

Corderus smiled. His grandma was truly funny. She had a great sense of humor and even though they'd just met three days ago, she'd treated him like they'd been a family from the day he was born.

Grandma continued, "In 1868, the United States government tired from war between the states and needing to heal, abandoned the experiment, the reservation west of Indian territory. The nightmare was coming to an end and new challenges loomed ahead for the Dine'.

A nightmare almost as bad, maybe in some ways worst was on the horizon. Boarding schools. First let me finish my Long Walk history.

A treaty was proposed in early 1868 and signed on June 1st. On June 18th, "The "Long Walk Home" began.

The treaty established a reservation, provisions for the return trip, an Indian agent, military forts, compulsory education for children, railroads, agriculture implements, seed, and an annual amount not to exceed $5 per person on items the Navajo couldn't manufacture themselves.

Our reservation was the land inside our four sacred mountains, 3.5 million acres. Today our land has increased to 16 million acres."

Grandma and grandson were interrupted by the sound of grandpa Ran's diesel.

Grandma told Corderus, Grandpa Ran had lived on the reservation all his life except for an 8-year stretch from 18-26 years of age. He joined the Navy and did four years of service and then went to college, Northern Arizona

University Lumberjack and earned a teaching certificate. He came back to the reservation and had taught at the local Arizona public school ever since. A simple Dine'. A good Dine' husband and father, and now trying to be a grandfather.

Him and Charlotte were married his first year as a teacher. She was a bookkeeper for the Peabody Mining Company on Black Mesa. She went to most Aces High dances and that's where she met Ran at a Round Rock School community dance.

She remembered going into the gym that night and seeing the colorful murals on the walls, the big banner of the championship baseball team. Thirty-five years ago, but still the memories were like yesterday. He asked her to dance and swept her off her feet. They were married 6 months later and 9 months after that their son, their only child Treavore was born, Corderus' father.

Ran strode quickly into the house and spoke first, "We had a meeting. Serious stuff Char. An atomic bomb went off at the G20 summit in Germany. I guess it has killed all those world leaders. People are expecting the worst. Panic and such, food shortages, no electronics, that will kill half the millennials right there. The worthless…"

Char interrupted, "Ran, no rants. What do we need to do?"

Ran flashed a smile and said, "Take notes grandson. Don't ever marry a Dine' girl. You'll spend the rest of your life listening to them boss you around…"

Char looked at him, a little twinkle in her eyes and said, "Keep talking Ran. That bed can be big, lonely and cold."

Ran said, "See what I mean. Now I'm apologizing for speaking the truth. Sorry honey!"

He gave Char a hug and a kiss on the forehead. He obviously loved her. Corderus' mom had always been alone and affection between two adults was new to him.

Ran continued, "We were asked to spread out, go to summer camps and old grazing lands. We need to pack a
Lake   Doomsday Clock 11:59:59

few supplies and head to Tsegi canyon. End up near Keet Seel and Betatakin, set up a compound there, be self-sufficient."

Char said, "A return to the old ways?"

Ran spoke up, "Yes. Probably easier for us Dine' then any other group."

Char said, "What do I need to do, pack?"

Corderus said, "What about me?"

Ran said, "Life just handed you a lemon. Either add some sugar and make lemonade or be bitter. The ball is in your court sonny boy."

Corderus thought for a second and replied, "What about my Mom? Who will take care of her? That's my job."

Ran replied, "You're right shinali. You'll make a Dine' yet. Your mom is visiting friends up north, an isolated cattle ranch. She's in the best place possible and your 1,000 miles away from her. She'll be fine. I know the guy who owns the spread and him and his family are good people. When this storm is over and we figure out what's happening I'll take you to her myself. That's a promise. Now I need your help?" It was a question and not a statement.

Corderus said, "I'm all in, you can count on me."

Somehow all the anger he had felt was gone. In its place was a realization he was finding what he'd not even known was missing. His story, his heritage. Now he wanted to know and feel what it meant to be Dine'

Chapter 23

They were going to travel on ATV's. The kind every Navajo kid knows how to ride.

Navajo's round up sheep, cattle and goats with ATV's. If Bigfoot were out here they'd catch him with one as well.

The small herd of goats and sheep owned by the James family were turned loose. A neighbor would come collect them in a day or so and care for them, or bring them out to their new home.

Navajo's survive on cooperation, clans mean everything. It determines who you can date, kiss, marry, and loyalty. Every Dine' has four clans. Corderus knew about that part, but didn't know his clans. It hadn't seemed important until now. The Long Walk history lesson woke something up inside of him.

His grandfather asked him to check the ATV's, "Oil, gas, and air pressure, shinali. Hurry. I'm depending on you."

Those words uttered by a male meant everything to Corderus. He'd had coaches and teachers who'd influenced him, but not a male relative.

Grandmother packed food and medicine, lots of herbs, with names Corderus had never heard. Grandma told him the Dine' had herbs and compounds to cure or treat most anything. They were in synch with nature.

She called it hozho naasha, walking in beauty, the natural order of things.

The things they couldn't treat were introduced by whites. Such as a diet high in fats, which facilitated diabetes, kidney failure, heart disease. Things the Navajo never experienced until the White Father decided to take care of them like little children. Bitterness maybe. Justified, yes!

Grandmother didn't seem to hold any bitterness. She told Corderus if a person knew eating frybread was bad for you, don't eat it, or reduce the quantity or size. Personal responsibility shinali.

Lake   Doomsday Clock 11:59:59

They loaded three trailers with Char's stuff; plus, odds and ends from Ran's list. Some of it made sense to Corderus, and other items made no sense what so ever.

Finally, the group was ready to roll out. They made sure the animals left behind had water troughs filled and enough feed to last a few days.

Headed south on highway 163. Easy miles, "The Toes" on the right and past The Community Boarding School and Kayenta Unified School District with three schools in one location.

The family had three sheep dogs, took two dogs with them. Both running with the ATV's, still unhappy they'd left their sheep behind. The oldest dog had been left to tend the remaining flock.

Char had stopped and talked to her friend Arlene who lived next to the old Indian Health Services clinic. She'd promised to send her lazy bilaga'ana husband Brett to check on the animals. Everybody was laughing and smiling so Corderus assumed they were just making fun of Brett.

 They rode past the Skate park, with skaters practicing, the post office soon appeared and then Amigo's café. They arrived at the intersection of 163 and 160, turned right onto 160 and passed the Blue Coffee Pot and McDonalds.

Tsegi was about 8 miles from Kayenta and the dogs soon decided to jump on the ATV's with no end in sight. Highway 160, usually busy with tour buses taking guest out to Monument Valley, Moab, and other points of interest was empty. They had the road to themselves and an occasional Navajo truck. You knew it was owned by a Navajo because of the 275-330-gallon IBC tote in the back, straining the leaf springs. That's how ranchers hauled water to distance herds of sheep or cattle when windmills didn't work. It was one more way natives survived in a modern world slanted against them.

The population was increasing on the Rez and the best grazing and farming lands were spoken for by previous generations. Grazing and farming rights were inherited.

The new families had to move further back and adapt, overcome, no public complaining, shared responsibility. Dine'.

They came over a hill and saw a truck parked beside the road pulling a trailer loaded with three horses. They stopped and Grandfather asked what he could do to help? The tires were low and the driver was afraid to go forward and suffer a blowout, might hurt the horses.

Grandfather agreed it was good he'd stopped before blowing a tire. Ran had a portable air compressor and quickly started it up and filled the tires. Fifteen minutes later they all said goodbye, the truck started up and pulled away with the horses happy for the breeze to cool them off. The ATV group pulled back on highway 160 and quickly covered the remaining 2 miles to a dirt road leading to Tsegi canyon.

The started down the one lane dirt road which soon gave way to a deep rutted cow path. Life on the reservation. Most of the kids lived outside of Kayenta and rode the bus to and from school. Routes were measured in hours and not miles. The longest ride was from Forrest Lake on Black Mesa, almost 2 hours one way. You slept on the bus, told stupid jokes and listened to music. The life of a Dine' boy, but not Corderus.

The dogs were on the ATV's Ran and Char rode. The dogs sensed Corderus was a rookie and not to be trusted.

The narrow Tsegi canyon finally opened into pasture and farm land.

An old windmill came into view, the wheel slowly spinning, creaking and groaning as if to say, I'm old. Cows, sheep and wild horses gathered around the empty water trough.

Grandpa stopped his ATV, shut it off and climbed off. Roscoe and Sam, the sheepdogs, jumped down and started nipping at the cows and sheep. They left the horses alone.

Corderus asked, "What's wrong?"

Lake   Doomsday Clock 11:59:59

Char replied, "The animals are out of water."

Corderus responded, "How is that our problem? Who owns them?"

Grandma looked around, "Everybody owns them shinali. Our neighbor's problems are our problems. These animals are a shared responsibility. The land belongs to everybody and nobody."

Corderus looked around, thought about what was said and decided it all made sense. His mom always said, it takes a village to raise a knucklehead.

Grandpa called out, "Corderus, get me the tool kit. Bring me that jar of washers as well."

Corderus hustled to help his Grandfather. He watched as he took apart the pump attached to the windmill. There was a worn-out washer and a loose screw or two.

Corderus watched Ran put everything back together again, slow, and deliberate. The wild horses kept nipping at the cows and sheep, driving them back from the dry trough. The animals seemed to sense water would be flowing soon.

Grandpa turned the screwdriver clockwise twice more and indicated for Corderus to try the pump. A half dozen pumps and water started to flow.

Corderus pumped until his arm ached. The horses drank their fill and kicked up their heels and ran off into the distance. The sheep and cows were willing to share space and everybody drank their fill.

Grandma said, "Fill it back up so it's full for later shinali. Always take care of tomorrows problem today. The animals can't pump their own water, they depend on us to take care of them."

Corderus felt like he'd been part of something important. He felt just a little Dine' and it felt good.

Lake   Doomsday Clock 11:59:59

Grandpa told him to put the tool box back together. Make sure everything was in the right place and clean. A man never knew when he might need his tools, better to have them ready and organized then strewn about.

Chapter 24

They restarted the ATV's and chased the wild horses across the open pasture, headed in the direction of Keet Seel and Betatakin. Sam and Roscoe barked a bunch and led the convoy. It still seemed like an adventure to Corderus.

After an hour of riding hard the group came to a halt by a group of pinon trees. The dogs sniffed around a bunch, proclaimed everything seemed okay, drank from the bowl of water Grandmother placed on the ground, circled once or twice and laid down to nap.

Grandma started to make sandwiches. Sliced mutton, cheddar cheese and mayo. Grandfather stared off in the distance at a small cloud of dust swirling in the distance.

Char asked, "What do you see Ran?"

Granddad, one hand above his squinting eyes, replied "An ATV coming this way, one rider, moving really fast. The guy is big, looks like Royce Charley. I don't know how the shocks take the beating."

Grandma laughed, "Stop it Ran. You're still sore he hit you with a fastball in high school; the big game. The one you two still argue about 45 years later. He's not fat!"

Ran laughed, "He's not twiggy and it was 46 years ago. Plus, that fastball hurt."

The ATV bounced along the rutted ground and finally slowed to a stop. The guy driving cut the engine and climbed off the ATV which exposed a young girl sitting behind him. Small frame, 3 inches shorter than Corderus, full bloodied Navajo, dark hair, dark eyes.

Corderus turned three shades of red, he could feel his cheeks flush, the girl from the Skatepark. The one he tried to talk to and she asked him about his clans, which of course he had no idea. Then she refused to talk to him.

She climbed off the ATV and joined Royce.

Lake   Doomsday Clock 11:59:59

A round of "Yaateeh" a typical Navajo greeting was exchanged.

The girl with Royce said, "Oh, it's the boy with no clans." A little smirk smile at the end, arms folded across her chest.

Grandma said, "You've met my shinali." It wasn't a question and her tone contained an elders rebuke.

The girl said, "Yes Grandmother. But we were not formally introduced." Her arms now unfolded. The smile gone from her face, chin pointed down just a few degrees, acknowledging the rebuke.

Corderus was confused.

Char said, "Adrianna meet Corderus."

They were both 16, shy, teenagers and they smiled awkwardly at each other, but kept quiet.

After 10 seconds of strained silence and shuffling feet, eyes looking at the ground, Adrianna said, "You're a good skater Corderus. Do you ride bulls?"

Corderus replied, "Thanks, no bull riding yet, but maybe Grandfather will teach me. Grandma is going to teach me about my clans."

Adrianna said, "Good. It is something all Navajo's should know, clans and bull riding. You are Navajo, right?"

Corderus realized for the first time he was proud to be Dine'. "Yes Ma'am. I've not spent any time on the Rez. I've lived with my Mom in Phoenix my whole life."

Ran and Royce concluded their quiet talk and walked back to the group.

Royce and Adrianna climbed back on the ATV, started it up.

A round of "Hagooshii" meaning see you in a while followed and off the two went flying across the grazing land, thick dust, like a rooster tail, pointing them out.

Lake   Doomsday Clock 11:59:59

Ran said, "I hope he doesn't bottom out with all that weight."

Grandma shook her head from side to side and said, "Come, eat a sandwich incorrigible husband of mine."

Corderus asked, "Tell me about my clans Grandmother?"

Char said, "Okay, but eat while I talk so we're not delayed moving."

Corderus nodded and took a bite of the mutton sandwich, it tasted phenomenally delicious. He hadn't realized how hungry he was and how late in the afternoon it was becoming.

She started, "It starts with the creation story."

Corderus interrupted, "Like Adam and Eve, the apple, forbidden fruit. Noah's ark, the animals two-by-two, and the great flood?"

Ran said, "No. Navajo stories contain the oral history, passed down from generation to generation by Native storytellers. The Bible is a written history for mankind. The Navajo's didn't have a written language until the 1930's. Plus Christianity wasn't introduced to the Dine' until the Spanish with the Catholic Padres appeared in the 1700's. But you will see some clear parallelism in both versions."

Char restarted her lesson, glancing sternly at Ran for interrupting her, "The Dine' believe in two classes of people, Earth People and Holy People.

The Navajo's believe they passed thru three different worlds before arriving at the fourth world, or the Glittering world. As Earth People we, Dine', must do everything in our power to maintain a balance between mother earth and man.

The first, or dark world is where the four Diyin Dine' lived and where First Woman and First Man came into existence. Because this world was so dark they couldn't thrive and survive there so they moved on into the second world.

Lake   Doomsday Clock 11:59:59

The Second, or Blue World was occupied by some of the mammals we know today as well as the Swallow Chief, also known as Tashchozhii. The First World people offended him and were asked to leave. They headed south and arrived in the Third World.

The Third World, or Yellow World was where the four sacred mountains were found. However, due to a great flood, First Woman and First Man, along with the Holy People were forced to find a new home.

This time they stayed in the Fourth World, in the Glittering World, where true death came into existence, as well as the creation of the seasons, the moon, stars, and the sun.

The Holy People instructed the Earth People to stay within the boundaries of the four sacred mountains and never leave. Blanca Peak, Mount Taylor, San Francisco Peak and Hesperus Mountain define our territory. Times of day and colors are used to represent the four different mountains.

If you must travel outside of the four mountains many believe you should wear turquoise as a defense against outside influences." Grandmother paused.

Corderus fingered the necklace around his neck, it was turquoise. His mother had insisted he always wear it except playing sports and then she'd give him a small ankle bracelet to wear with a tiny turquoise nugget. Dine', protected, without even knowing he was one of "The People".

Ran said, "Break time is over Grandmother. Let's load up and finish this trip before dark."

They packed up the ATV's. Started back across the pasture.

The Canyon was starting to narrow, maybe ¼ of a mile wide now. The rock formations spiraling high on the sides. Conspicuous red, Wingate Sandstone and the red Navajo Sandstone forming prominent cliffs. These two sandstone units separated by variably colored siltstone, silty

Lake   Doomsday Clock 11:59:59

sandstone, and sandstone of the Kayenta and Moenave Formations.

Corderus saw her first, an elderly Navajo woman making a chopping motion with a hoe. He pointed towards her and the ATV's headed in her direction.

She was old, spine bent like a willow tree in a high wind. Thin arms, but hacking away at a mound of dirt that had fallen and clogged her irrigation head way. The corn, squash and beans in the field were looking a bit weathered and in need of a drink.

"Yaateeh", exchanged by everybody.

Ran asked, "You look tired Grandmother and in need of a drink."

The woman responded, "I am a bit thirsty my grandson. I've been swinging this hoe for two days trying to unclog the dirt so my crops can drink their fill."

Char gently said, "Come, sit with me and have a drink of cool water. Let the men swing the hoe and shovel for a bit."

The old woman laid the hoe on the ground and limped over to the ATV's where Char offered her a bottle of water and a seat to rest her weary bones.

Grandpa looked at Corderus and asked, "Hoe or shovel? Pick your poison."

Corderus looked at the pile of dirt and said, "This is going to take a long time."

Ran responded, "Yes. If we don't fix this problem her crops will fail. She lives off the land. A few sheep, maybe a couple of goats, some chickens. She butchers a sheep now and then, kills a chicken when they stop laying eggs. She survives."

Corderus asked, "Why is she all alone? Where are her kids? Husband? Grandkids?"

Ran replied, "Good questions shinali. Her husband probably passed. Kids and grandkids leave the reservation

Lake   Doomsday Clock 11:59:59

and don't come back. Modern conveniences and slick promises lure them away from home, supposedly to a better life. Some make it, some don't."

Corderus spoke, "My Mom is half Hispanic and half Navajo. I know my Dad passed in an automobile accident and somehow alcohol was involved. My Mom won't talk about it. I know she feels guilty, responsible. She's never been back to the reservation since Dad died. What happened? I think I have the right to know."

Ran said, "Grab the hoe sonny boy...I'm too old. My back hurts every night. We will talk," He smiled at Corderus.

Corderus had never enjoyed this type of a relationship with a male. It felt good, made him feel like a man.

Ran said, "By the time the Navajo started the long walk home, estimates make the number of child bearing aged Dine' at around 2,000. This led to a gene pool that allowed a recessive gene to be dominant. It's one of the genes tied to alcoholism and alcohol metabolism. It's not the only way the gene effects these areas, just a hypothesis. But it makes sense.

Many Navajo's have the gene tied to slow alcohol metabolism. A normal person drinks a beer and an hour later the liver metabolizes the alcohol, breaks it down. A Navajo drinks a beer, and an hour later half the alcohol from the drink is still in their system.

As a race of people alcohol has been devastating. The Navajo reservation doesn't allow alcohol to be bought or sold on the reservation. It doesn't stop young people from thinking they are the exception to the rule. It doesn't stop lost men and women from drinking 40's and tossing the empty cans and bottles on the ground.

Your Dad, my son, drank a few beers at a friend's house watching football. He was sure he was okay, your mom refused to go home with him. Youth, stubborn and invincible, indestructible. He cut in front of an 18-wheeler just as an accident happened ahead of him. The big rig, unable to stop in time, crushed him.

Lake   Doomsday Clock 11:59:59

Your mom never forgave herself. She thinks she should have done more to stop him. I've talked to his friends who were there and they tell me nothing could stop him after he made up his mind to drive."

Corderus had never heard the complete story of his father's death.

Corderus, changed the subject and said, "Why didn't the old woman ask us to help?"

Ran smiled, "We are proud. You never embarrass a Dine' by telling them they need help. You let them have an out, give them an excuse to stop failing."

Corderus asked, "It feels good to help an elder."

Ran replied, "It should. You might make a good Dine' shinali."

They worked on the dirt slide, shoveling and hoeing to clear a path. Finally, the water was flowing again and the crops were drinking their fill.

They walked along each separate branch and cleaned out weeds and small clogs. They made their way to the house and discovered Char cooking a big pot of vegetables and mutton.

Char said, "Grandmother hasn't been cooking because of the problem with her fields. I thought I'd start a pot of food while you and shinali cut some wood." It wasn't a question, but an order.

Ran said, "We'd be delighted. I'll instruct the grandson on how to properly cut wood, stack it, and then I'll supervise." He grinned at his wife. She shook her head pretending she was upset with him.

The men went outside and Ran showed Corderus how to split wood with an axe. The used a short-handled axe and a long handled one. It was hard work as Corderus' hands were already covered with blisters and his back and shoulder ached from swinging first a hoe and now an axe.

Finally, they had built up a good supply of wood. Because it was July it wasn't needed for heating the Hogan, just a little cooking and maybe some warm bath water or washing clothes.

Chores complete, they told Grandmother goodbye and restarted their journey towards Keet Seel and Betatakin.

Chapter 25

They entered a narrow canyon a few miles ahead. Finally, they came to a blockage of large stones and dead trees. The canyon appeared to be a dead end.

Corderus asked, "What's the plan? Turn back?"

Ran said, "No shinali. The Dine' planned for this day. We have many places to hide. We have not forgotten the old ways. Beauty in front, beauty behind, beauty next to us, stay in balance with mother earth."

Ran continued, "We need to move three boulders and two trees to clear the path. I have a tow rope. Let's get the rope around the biggest boulder first and pull."

Ran was remarkable efficient at knowing where and how to connect to each obstacle. The angle to pull, how many ATV's to use. They worked as a team, within 30 minutes the path was clear enough for the ATV's and trailers to pull thru.

Char took a piece of limestone rock and marked a straight line on one of the rocks.

Corderus asked, "Why did you do that?"

Char said, "We have 5 more families coming back here to live in this valley, including Adrianna's family.

Corderus turned flush again. Char smiled and laughed just a little.

Ran affectionately ruffled his hair and said, "Women will mess up a man's mind every time shinali."

Which made the boy blush just a little deeper and shake his head.

They left the route open so others would have little trouble passing thru. The last group would reverse the process, pull the logs and boulders back in place, in part to keep the large animals from easily escaping the canyon.

Lake   Doomsday Clock 11:59:59

The area was full of game. Corderus could see that right away. Deer, antelope, rabbits, just to name a few. The animals seemed unconcerned if the loud ATV's kept their distance.

Wild horses, a herd of 50 or more ran across in front of them, turned perpendicular to the path they were taking. Animals of every color, shade and pattern flashed in the late evening light. Corderus saw a beautiful young red male and knew that was the one for him.

He told Ran, pointing to the herd, "I want to ride that red one near the front. I like his spirit."

Ran said, "We will see. A horse should want to be tamed. We will see if we can catch him, let you talk to him."

Char said, "Wow, just breathtaking. I've not seen this many wild horses since I was a girl and spending time with my Grandfather on Black Mesa."

Ran said, "Good times. Things were simpler before all the electronics arrived to take away our kid's interest in daily life. It has only been in the last 30 years we've really started losing them to outside influences."

The cattle came next, dotting the landscape in small herds of 20-30, maybe 300 head. Not skinny, not fat, healthy, wild, strong. Nobody had been running these cows for some time. On occasion, an elder would cull a few head for a big ceremony.

Sheep were next. A caretaker sheared them and watched over them, 3 sheep dogs barked furiously at Roscoe and Sam, decided they were okay and laid back down.

The caretaker, an old man stepped out of the Hogan. Corderus thought to himself, man he must be 100 years old if he's a day.

Char spoke first, "Yaateeh Father."

The old man responded, "Yaateeh my little one."

They exchanged hugs and a peck on the cheek.

Lake   Doomsday Clock 11:59:59

Char turned to Corderus, "This is my shinali."

The old man said, "Treavore's boy?"

Corderus said, "Yes Grandfather."

The old man said, "I am Ran's father, Zebedee, your blood Grandfather. Let me look at you?"

He checked Corderus over, failing eyesight, but still possessed a strong sense of Navajo humor.

He ran his hand over Corderus' head, face and shoulders, upper arms.

He said, "Well…he's my grandson…small brain, big nose, puny arms."

He laughed and wrapped Corderus up in a big bear hug, ruffled his hair. "I didn't think I would ever see you my shinali. Thank you for coming to see me, making my life complete." Rare emotion shown by Zebedee.

Zebedee looked up, still hugging Corderus with one arm and said, "Why are you here?"

Ran smiled, "Operation Kit Carson revenge!"

Zebedee smiled, "Okay. I have work to do. You guys need to make base camp by nightfall."

He walked over and petted Roscoe and Sam, gave each of them a big piece of venison jerky.

Zebedee motioned them away with his hands and said, "Go, I have work to do. You have much to do before bed tonight. We've had a couple of Mountain Lions prowling about. Be careful."

A round of "Hagooshii" Bye…for a little while.

They cranked up the ATV's and took off. Roscoe and Sam wanted to stay with Zebedee, but finally took off chasing the group. The 3 other dogs followed a short way and finally gave up, trotted back to their master, stopping to turn around twice and bark, went to the porch, slurped

Lake   Doomsday Clock 11:59:59

some water and laid back down. Their job was over for the day.

The group covered the remaining two miles in 15 minutes. Everybody was tired, but work needed to be done before they could lay their heads down for the night.

The base camp consisted of three buildings. A Hogan, as always, the doorway faced East. A barn like metal structure with hand tools from long ago. No electric, no gas-powered equipment. The last building was for food prep and food storage.

They cleaned out the Hogan and unpacked the trailers. Ran insisted everything be put in its place as a man never knows what tomorrow will bring, have a plan, be prepared.

Finally, thirty minutes after dark, a few candles burning for light, they were finished. Supper was cold mutton, fruit, and fry bread from yesterday. Water to wash it down.

Corderus looked at his Grandmother and said, almost pleading, "Tell me about my clans, please?"

Char spoke, "You have 4 clans. You are "born to" your Mother's clan and "born for" your fathers clan. Then you identify your Mom and Dad's Grandfather's clan.

This helps each Navajo know who they are and helps keep the gene pool strong, have healthy kids, like you."

Corderus asked, "What happens if a Navajo doesn't know their clans or lies about them?"

Char said, "Good question. It happens. First, don't date a Navajo girl who doesn't know her clans. She hasn't been raised in the Navajo ways.

Second, sometimes a person makes a mistake on clans and because our history is so much oral and not written, it happens.

I know a girl who went to NAU in the late 90's and met a handsome Navajo boy. They exchanged clan information, dated, fell in love, married, had two beautiful kids and then discovered an Aunt made a mistake and they were in fact brother and sister according to the Navajo way."

Corderus asked, "Isn't that incest?"

Char replied, "Yes, but what's done is done. You can't put babies back and the heart once given should stay in place."

Corderus said, "Wow! I don't know my clans. What if I met a girl and didn't know she was my sister and I kissed her? Gross!"

Char asked, "Shinali, do you mind telling me what happened between you and Adrianna?"

Corderus took a deep breath in and let it out slowly, "No, I don't mind Grandmother. I was at the skatepark, just talking with the guys. Adrianna showed up and started talking to Keshawn.

Finally, she asked me my name. I told her and I told her I was just visiting my grandparents for a month. She wanted to know who my grandparents were and I told her. Then she asked me for my clans and I didn't know. She said I needed to find out if I wanted to continue talking to her. It embarrassed me and I said she thought she was too good to talk to a boy not from the Rez.

We didn't part as best friends."

Char rubbed Corderus on the head and smiled, "My poor shinali. Native life has been tough on your heart. Next time you see Adrianna you'll amaze her with your clan knowledge. Okay?"

Corderus said, "I still don't know my clans?"

Ran laughed, Char glared at him. Ran wiped the smile from his face and winked at Corderus.

Char continued, "Still background information is needed so you understand our ways. Navajo's refer to their cousins as brother or sister. Fathers and mother's cousins are thought of as aunts and uncles in the Navajo sense.

Lake   Doomsday Clock 11:59:59

Grandparent's brothers and sisters aren't your aunts and uncles, but Grandmas and Grandpas in the Navajo sense. A Navajo has many brothers and sisters, aunts and uncles, and grandparents.

It makes for a big extended family and you'll find loyalty and friendship comes with those relationships. You can move almost anyplace and know a family clan member will lodge you, feed you, and be responsible for your wellbeing.

There were 4 original Navajo clans. Hashtl'ishnii (Mud Clan), Hon'agh'aahnii (One Walks Around Clan), Kinyaa'aanii (Towering House People), Todich'iinii (Bitter Water Clan); the oral history tells about a migration from southern Canada and eastern Alaska, either by the Pacific coast or the plains.

Some settled near the Pueblo Indians and mixed, some went to where present day Albuquerque is located, some went south to where the Apaches live and few went west to the Grand Canyon. We have geographical boundaries. The four sacred mountains.

The clans were created to let Navajo's know how they were related and where their ancestors had lived. There are probably 90 clans or more now, a few extinct as well.

From the original 4 clans we've added 5 major clans. Tabaaha (Waters Edge Clan), Tachii'nii (Red-Running-Into-The-Water Clan), Tse'Njikini (Cliff Dwelling Clan), To'aheedlinnii (Water-Flows-Together Clan), Tsi'naajinii (Black-Streaked-Wood Clan) and all 9 have both related clans and adopted clans. You need a scorecard to tell how you're related to each other. Again, genetics, recessive genes are the reason for many health problems."

Corderus opened his mouth to ask a question.

Grandmother held up a finger for silence.

She said, "I'm almost finished shinali.

Your mother's clan is Naakaii Dine'e' or Mexican clan because her mother's clan is Mexican. So, you were "born to" the Mexican clan.

Lake   Doomsday Clock 11:59:59

Your father's clan, my clan is Bit'ahnii or Folded Arms People. You were "born for" Folded Arms People.

Your Cheii, grandpa on your mom's side is Dziltl'ahnii (Mountain Cove Clan).

Your Nali, grandpa on your dad's side is Tse'Deeshgizhnii (Rock Gap Clan)

You would introduce yourself in this way, using English because Navajo isn't your native tongue.

Hello, my people, relatives, and the rest of you!   My name is Corderus James.   I am of The Mexican Clan, born for The Folded Arms People Clan.   The Mountain Cove Clan are my maternal grandfather's clan and The Rock Gap Clan are my paternal grandfather's clan."

Corderus said, "Wow, that's a mouth full. But I think I understand now. Maybe tomorrow you can help me until I get it down without stumbling thru it?"

Grandmother said, "Yes shinali. Tomorrow we will talk some more."

Corderus said, "I want to hear about the boarding schools. You two are my Nali, right?"

Ran said, "I'm your worst nightmare if you don't stop talking. Both of you. It's been a long day. Many unanswered questions. My body aches. Come over here Grandmother and rub my neck and shoulders."

Char replied, "All you did today was supervise. Your words, not mine husband. I cooked, cleaned and did a man's job today helping you. I want my back and legs rubbed."

Corderus said, "TMI. I'll shut up. Thank you for the day Grandma and Grandpa. I'm still a bit scared for my mom, but I know in a strange way, we're okay, because we're Dine'."

Ran said, "We will survive. Not all of us, some have gone soft and forgotten the old ways. They'll turn to the government in Washington for help. Those people aren't really Dine'. They occupy a physical body, but live in the White world."

Corderus said, "I have to use the restroom, where?"

Ran said, "Behind the barn is an outhouse. Watch out for Mountain Lions."

Corderus was a bit scared. How would he handle a big cat like that without a gun?

Grandmother said, "Don't worry shinali. Roscoe and Sam will protect us. If there was a cat within 200 yards of the camp they'd be barking up a storm. Take a flashlight and go, hurry back."

Corderus went outside, total blackness, the sky above clustered with millions of stars, peaceful, except for the big cat threat, flipped on the Maglite. He was back in 5 minutes, crawled into bed and fell asleep within thirty seconds.

Chapter 26

Morning broke early in July, the sun just starting to peak over the distant cliff and now bouncing off the cliff walls to the west.

Corderus woke up to the sound of barking dogs. Sam and Roscoe were leading Char and Ran as they returned from a morning run. Always running towards the east, before the sun rises, shouting to the gods. In return, they were blessed. It was a Dine' belief.

In the Navajo creation story the Twin Warriors were chosen to slay monsters that plagued the people. They trained for these battles by running, learning everything they needed to win.

They finished their run, both sucking a little air, hands on hips, walking slowly in small circles to recover.

Char said, "Tomorrow you run with us shinali. One more Dine' lesson. Pray for your legs, feet, air you breathe in and out."

Corderus asked, "How far do you run?"

Ran answered, "About 3 miles round trip. We try to finish in 25 minutes."

Breakfast was flour tortillas, with eggs, cheese and sausage. The last of the milk from the Kayenta house was consumed.

Ran said, "I need to check out my barn, inventory some stuff, do basic maintenance."

Char said, "Okay. I'm going to tell Corderus about Boarding Schools and then we'll look for tonight's meal."

Corderus smiled, "I don't like Mountain Lion!"

Grandmother laughed, "You have the Dine' sense of humor shinali."

Char began, "When the treaty was signed in 1868 it was for 10 years. Chief Manuelito and others who signed felt a

Lake   Doomsday Clock 11:59:59

time of peace was needed for the Dine' to regroup and find some stability. Our numbers were so low.

The Federal government agreed to provide 1 teacher for every 30 Navajo kids as part of the compulsory education part of the treaty.

Parents sent their kids off to school, not by choice, but by force.

The school's philosophy was to remove the Indian from the child. Kill the Indian, save the man. The moment they entered school their culture was under attack. The first thing they'd do is cut their hair, a source of pride for many Navajo's. Next was the burning of their clothes and replaced with white peoples clothing. Then it was explained they couldn't speak in their Native tongue. English only was the rule.

The schools were designed to teach European history and Christian values. Many of the schools were located on old Army Fort property. The school masters were old military officers, harsh and rigid standards. The kids spent long hours marching, standing in line.

The schools had a quota system. The police or Indian agent would troll the fields looking for kids. Snatch them up and because education was compulsory there was nothing parents could do about it. Sometimes wealthy Navajo's would pay a family to send a kid in their child's place.

Food was of poor quality. Conditions were unsanitary. Kids housed in dorms, locked in at night so they couldn't run away. Every infraction was severely punished.

When kids returned to their village a sense of mistrust existed. They were not trusted or accepted in either culture. Remember shinali these are oral stories. How true they are, I can't say, but the basic facts are undeniable. Some might have happened to other tribes and at other schools.

The Meriam report published in 1928 stated because of the poor conditions in Indian Boarding Schools the death rate was 6 ½ times greater than other minority groups.

This report suggested 3 reforms. Abolish the European-American course of study. Enroll young kids at boarding schools close to home and older kids could go to boarding schools far away. Last, have the Indian Services provide a course that would allow kids to thrive in both the native and white culture.

Still the popularity of boarding schools grew, by 1970 60,000 Native Americans attended boarding school. Eventually the numbers began to drop as activism got the word out to the public about the horrible conditions. Finally, in 1975 the Indian Self Determination and Education Assistance act was passed.

As a result, many boarding schools closed in the 80's and 90's and by 2007 only about 9500 Natives were in Boarding Schools.

Some Natives think the experience was positive and needs to still be an option, the majority felt it was repressive and needed to be discontinued.

The Phoenix Indian Boarding school, the only boarding school off reservation in Arizona, used to provide summer help for wealthy families by sending their older students to be housekeepers and gardeners."

She stopped speaking, a solitary tear rolled down her cheek. In a span of four days Corderus had come to love his Nali. He wiped away her tear with his fingers.

He said, "That was a terrible time in Dine' history. I'm so sorry Grandmother."

Char said, "Thank you shinali , Did you know the Navajo language contains no word for sorry?"

Corderus said, "Why?"

Char said, "Because if you truly feel bad about something happening, you won't do it again."

Lake   Doomsday Clock 11:59:59

Corderus replied, "I think the Dine' have it right."

Grandmother replied, "I think it's a shame both sides didn't take the best from the other. We believe in a balance. If you take from one side you give back.

Our land is in a trust, we administer it, but the Federal Government still owns the land. We still live under the overriding authority of the Federal Courts. They have the ultimate say so to govern us, override our Dine' choices.

Chief Manuelito knew the first years would be tough so he asked for the creation of the Navajo Tribal Police. The police agency wasn't formed until 1872 and disbanded three years later. In 1959 the Navajo Tribal Council requested it be reformed. This was good, because it meant Navajo law breakers were met with other Navajo's and less violence occurred.

Currently we have 134 officers patrolling 27,000 square miles. That breaks down to 201 square miles per patrol officer. Lots of miles, aching backs and bruised kidneys.

We have a strong local government. There are five agencies on the reservation. Each agency within the Navajo Nation is further broken down into chapters. The Central Agency contains 14 chapters; the Western Agency contains 18 chapters; the Fort Defiance Agency contains 27 chapters; the Northern Agency contains 20 chapters; and 31 chapters in the Eastern Agency for a total of 110 chapters.

This allows for local control of most issues providing the decisions made are consistent with Navajo law, customs and traditions. It also provides a way for local interaction with the Federal government and their agencies."

She paused, no need to load Corderus down with too much information. Still, she was thrilled to share the Dine' history with her grandson.

Ran walked up and spoke, "Grandson, I need your youth and muscles in the workshop. I have a rusty lug nut on a wagon that needs a tire change. I can't make it budge."

Lake   Doomsday Clock 11:59:59

Corderus followed his Grandpa out to the workshop. The wagon was old, an old truck bed from the 50's with a trailer hitch welded to the front. One side jacked up a little.

Corderus knelt beside the tire and turned the lug wrench counter clockwise, remembering an old saying, righty tight, lefty loose.

The trailer rocked forward and the lug nut broke free. Corderus spun it the rest of the way off. He handed the nut and lug nut to his Grandfather.

Corderus asked, "Anything else Grandfather?"

His Grandfather was smiling and it made Corderus feel good to help an elder.

Ran said, "No. Thank you shinali, you are a blessing."

Char and Corderus went exploring, not for pleasure, but for resources. This area had been left unfarmed, uninhabited so no record existed in the Federal records.

The horses and cattle roamed free, the herds were occasionally culled to maintain health and a good gene pool. The sheep had a caretaker.

Roscoe, the sheepdog went with them for protection. They found a large stand of Pinon trees.

Corderus asked, "What do we use these for?"

Char replied, "Pinon nuts are picked by hand. No machine to do the work. Some years we have a great crop, most of the time it's poor. We roast them, drink it like coffee, the toasty, buttery, creamy flavor is highly addictive."

Corderus said, "I've never even had coffee." And on they walked with Char marking a map each time they found something of interest.

They found a large pond, maybe an acre in size. Char showed Corderus how to sit and observe mother nature.

The first rule was silence, which is difficult for a 16-year-old boy. Then observe, birds in the trees, what kind, how many; Char wrote everything down.

Corderus asked, "Why do we care about the birds, how many and what kind?"

Grandmother replied, "Because certain birds live where particular types of plants flourish. We notice the type of bird, follow them and find the plant we need. Maybe it's a plant for healing or eating.

Fauna and flora are important, we must have a balance. Sometimes we remove a natural predator and this allows a type of animal to overgraze, maybe killing too many plants. We then have to reduce the number of the over populated animal to restore balance in nature."

Corderus said, "Nizhoni." Beautiful in every way.

Grandmother replied, "Yes."

They followed the stream that fed the pond. Char took notes. With a little bit of hard work, they could create an irrigation system. Grow crops, corn, squash and beans, the staples of the old ways.

Navajo's adopted so many bad habits from other cultures. Fry bread was one of them. All that grease, led to diabetes and heart disease, kidney failure. How much better they would be to cook the bread like a tortilla, baked.

Sometimes her own people frustrated her. They could be their own worst enemy.

They continued walking and discovered the beginning of the water source. The base of Navajo National Monument mesa. Water was filtering down from on top. If they could combine several sources they'd have all the water they needed and almost be drought proof.

The pond would need to be larger. They'd noticed several Eagles hunting around the pond. It was obviously loaded with fish. One more blessing, but also one more resource to be effectively managed.

Lake   Doomsday Clock 11:59:59

Life is about a balance. The valley offered them a chance to live, thrive, food, shelter. Mismanagement of the wrong resource could spell doom for them. Burn too much wood in the winter and you must start traveling further and further just to heat your Hogan. Waste water and crops or animal die.

Char looked at her watch and realized it had been 24 hours since she'd heard her grandson shuffling around in his bedroom.

They had survived the first day. The first day was easy for them, a return to the old ways. The Dine' were prepared.

Ann's Story

Chapter 27

00:00

Baltimore, Maryland

25th floor, Ann glanced down to the street, nervous. And truth be known, a little frightened.

The crowds were swelling. Violence seemed to follow bad news. The media had played up each crisis around the world to the maximum rating possible.

Food supplies were short in her neighborhood. Beer and hard liquor deliveries were getting thru. Milk, eggs, butter, water, life essentials were not arriving on a regular schedule.

Lake   Doomsday Clock 11:59:59

Electricity was lost all along the eastern seaboard yesterday. It hadn't come back on and nobody was able explain why. The media seemed to be ignoring this problem. Cell phones were down, EMS wasn't responding and even the police were absent from the unruly group of people down below.

There had been other famous power outages in the United States. On November 9, 1965, a relay switch tripped at the Sir Adam Beck Station on the Ontario side of Niagara Falls. The 230 Kilovolt transmission line caused a domino effect. In New York City, it was 5:16 and the power outage stranded 800,000 riders on the subway system.

The power overloads and automatic shutdown systems effected 30 million more in New Jersey, Connecticut, Massachusetts, Rhode Island, New Hampshire, Vermont, Quebec, and Ontario.

In addition, 10,000 National Guardsman and 5,000 off duty policeman were called in to keep the peace. It turned out to be relatively calm, and within 13 hours power was back on for almost all customers.

Northeast United States and Canada, August 13-14, 2003. A minor incident in Northern Ohio caused a high voltage line to shut down. The alarm system that should have alerted First Energy Corporation failed. The incident was ignored. In the next 90 minutes, while operators were trying to trace the problem unsuccessfully, three more major power lines shut down because of the first line shutting down.

The dominos started to fall and by 4:05 PM, Southeast Canada and 8 States in Northeastern United states were without power. 50 million people were inconvenienced for up to two days, 11 deaths and 6 billion dollars in damages.

Canada officials blamed a Nuclear power plant In Pennsylvania, state officials denied that charge. Months later the cause was determined, overgrown trees in Northern Ohio brushed against the first power line causing it to shut down.

Lake   Doomsday Clock 11:59:59

Ann turned away from the 25th story window, a luxury high rise in an area ripe for rejuvenation. She walked towards the home office where her Dad was yelling at the internet.

The computer was on, as were the lights, A/C, hot water, because the building was billed as indestructible, impenetrable and with backup power, generators.

The generator was designed for a hospital. Costing $85,000, 408 KW, 208V, diesel unit. Multiple generators were built into the 35-story structure.

A huge underground tank held 10,000 gallons of diesel fuel to feed the thirsty generators trying to keep up with the July heat in Baltimore. Smaller 1,000-gallon fuel tanks were on various floors.

The internet was down and her Dad was smart with numbers, a CPA, but got hit twice with the stupid stick containing common sense.

Ann yelled from the doorway, "Daddy?" No response.

She yelled again, this time banging on the door frame, "Daddy!"

Nothing. She resorted to an old trick her Mom used, "Brian, Brian Alvin Matheny."

Her dad looked up. Smiled with his goofy grin and red hair and said, "What? This stupid computer won't send my email with my attached returns for Mr. Turner. Why do I spend all this money on foolproof systems and when I need them they don't work?"

Ann was 15. The adult since her Mom died two years ago from cancer.

Brian was a ginger, bright red hair. Pretty much a dork growing up. Chess Club, Band, Thespian, Debate Club, a social misfit. Medium build, 157 pounds on a 6-foot frame.

Ann was an athlete. Five and a half feet tall, short brown hair, blue eyes, maybe weighed 115 pounds soaking wet.

She played club volleyball, gymnastics, club softball, and with a double dose of common sense.

She got along well with people. She never hesitated to roam the neighborhood waiting for gentrification. She had seen drug deals go bad, watched the police sweep down to bust gangs. It almost seemed like an effort was being made to discourage the poor from staying.

She knew drug dealers and old people. She talked to everybody. A drug dealer had befriended her when Ann helped him find a hiding place during a drug sweep. She walked the streets with immunity under his protection.

Her Mom was a throwback to the 60's, a flower child, a hippie. Free thinking, an artist and a writer.

100 times Ann had wondered how her nerd Dad and hippie Mom connected. Then Sherry, her mom got sick, tired all the time. Old story, went to the doctor and discovered she had breast cancer, metastasized to her spine and lungs. Surgeries, drugs, radiation, exorcisms or so it seemed.

After 18 months, her body gave up. She'd tried to prepare Ann for life with her Dad.

She even wrote a series of letters for Ann to open on her birthdays. From 12 to 21 years of age. Ann's birthday was tomorrow, she'd turn 16 and would open the envelope titled, "Sweet 16, my lovely Ann".

Ann realized her Dad was speaking.

He said, "Ann, are you listening to me?"

She blushed, "Sorry Dad, brain fart. What did you say?"

He took a breath, "I said my damn computer won't send this email."

She said, "I know Dad, the Internet is down."

Her dad said, "No it's not. My computer is working just fine. That is why I spent almost 1 million dollars on this condo."

Lake   Doomsday Clock 11:59:59

Ann exhaled slowly, "I know Dad. The two are different. You have electricity, but the Internet building where the servers are located don't have electricity. Even the cell phones are off."

Brian said, "What, the phones don't work, why? I automatically pay the bill. My phone is charged."

Ann said, "Look Dad, it's an electricity problem. Not on your end, on the cell phone company's end."

Brian started to speak, "Oh, I under…"

A huge shock wave enveloped the building. The expansion of volume and rising temperature. Liquid becoming a gas in an instant; in this case it was the fuel tank holding 7,000 gallons of diesel fuel that exploded. Traveling out and up the energy tore thru their body causing minor damage. The building shook and vibrated, the steel beams twisted and rivets tore loose.

The energy traveled on the path of least resistance. Up the elevator shafts, thru the HVAC (heating, ventilation, air conditioning) duct work. Glass is weaker than cement so it blew out most of the windows on the first 5 floors. The next 5 floors lost about 50% of the windows, and floor 25 lost 10%. There were 35 floors in the building and a Penthouse on top.

Pictures and anything on the walls were tossed and shattered. Plumbing lines and electrical conduit ripped open. Drywall cracked and crumbled on walls, and floor tiles shattered from movement.

The explosion fatally wounded the dream building of Architect Kathy Frank, who resided in the Penthouse.

Brian and Ann's brain still hadn't processed what was happening. The boom from the explosion finally found the occupants on the 25th floor. Both fell as senses were overwhelmed. Ceiling tiles rained down on their heads.

The building shook a little more and finally stopped swaying, leaning to the left about 8 feet at the top.

Smoke and fire detectors went off next. Two seconds later the sprinkler system kicked in and water started to flow and then quickly stopped. The water line feeding the sprinkler system had been severed and the city pumps to keep residential water pressure at 55 PSI had stopped pumping yesterday.

The death toll was enormous. Crowds in the 1,000's were in the street at ground level. 476 people died in less than a second. 232 more died because of the shock wave, internal organ damage and blood loss. 112 more were fatally wounded by falling glass, refrigerators falling from the sky and other objects, including occupants.

Nobody came to help or save the wounded and dying. A few stumbled from side streets trying to find the cause of the explosion and they offered what comfort they could to the people bleeding and cut.

Ambulances didn't roll, firetrucks stayed safely in their bays, hospitals didn't ramp up for a mass influx of wounded. EMS was silent.

Hospitals were struggling just to keep current patients alive and provide staffing as nurses were unable to find fuel to drive to work. The city hadn't had fuel deliveries in 30 days. Firetrucks would have rolled if fuel was available or communication systems worked.

Ann picked herself up off the floor, moved all her joints and tried to stop the ringing in her ears. She looked at her Dad. He had a glazed look in his eyes.

She said, "Daddy. Are you okay?"

He said, "I think so. What happened?"

Ann thought about the possibilities. "A bomb? An explosion of some sort. I can feel the building leaning, plus I smell smoke."

Ann said, "I need to find out what's happening. Will you be okay until I get back?"

Brian shook his head yes, "I think so. I need to finish sending this email."

Ann said, "No Daddy. Your computer is shattered, we have no Internet. Don't worry about your clients right now. We need to find a way out of here."

Brian sat on the floor, trying to get the ringing in his ears to stop and clear the cobwebs from his brain. The shock wave from the blast had given him a mild concussion.

He said, "Sweetie, go make sure your Mom is okay?"

Ann looked at him, "Daddy, Momma died two years ago."

Brian looked at her, a bit sad, "Oh yeah. I remember. I think I've hurt my head a little."

Ann responded, "Stay here. Just sit. I'll be back in 15-20 minutes, tops!"

Ann left her Dad sitting on the floor. She quickly walked to the front door, unlocked the deadbolt and discovered the door stuck. She went back into the kitchen, found the biggest screwdriver in the tool drawer and went back to the front door. She managed to leverage the door open in a few minutes.

She stepped out in the hall, four apartments per floor, nobody was there. Two of the neighbors traveled most of the time, single people, no kids and the third Mrs. Adams was in the hospital with double pneumonia.

She looked around, the elevators were out of course, no electricity. Two of the corners held emergency stairwells. One stairwell went from the ground to the 13th floor and one went from floor 13 to the 25th floor.

She went down to the 13th floor and opened the door to the stairwell going down and was immediately engulfed in smoke. She shut it, that wasn't an option.

So up it was. 10 stories to the top of the building. She took the stairs as quickly as possible. All her cardio training was coming in handy today. She made it to the 30th floor,

Lake   Doomsday Clock 11:59:59

passed a guy going down. Kept going, down was a dead end.

Up to what? She hadn't thought about that. How would they get off the building? Maybe helicopters?

She kept going. Finally, she made the top floor and flung it open. The Architect, Kathy Frank stood out in the open, slowly looking around.

She saw Ann and said, "I'm sorry young lady, we're not giving tours today."

Ann thought, she's a bit touched in the head, but kept that thought to herself.

Ann said, "Yes Ma'am. Did you notice the explosion and the building is leaning just a bit?"

Kathy Frank replied, "I did. It will probably need leveling now. I'll call my maintenance guys. Now please go back down."

Ann backed towards the door, thinking this lady is nuts or injured.

She ran back down 10 flights of stairs and passed the same guy coming back up.

He said, panting, "Down is a dead end. No place to go."

Ann replied, "I know that, but how can we get off the building top?"

The man shrugged his shoulders and kept climbing the stairs.

7,000 gallons of diesel fuel exploding caused the dream, indestructible, Condo building to explode.

Wars and terrorism have been fought over and financed by oil.

The October 1973 Arab oil embargo was a passive aggressive move by OPEC Arab nations against countries who supported Israel in the Yom Kippur war. It was an economic war waged with oil, both the supply and the price. This event is sometimes called the first oil shock.

The initial countries targeted were Canada, Japan, The Netherlands, The United Kingdom and the United States. Later, Portugal, Rhodesia and South Africa were added to the embargo.

By the end of the embargo in March 1974 the price of a barrel of oil had risen from $3 to $12, a 400% increase.

The Yom Kippur war occurred when Egypt and Syria launched a surprise attack on Israel October 6, 1973. Initially Egypt and Syria experienced success in pushing Israel forces back. After three days of defeat Israel forces regained the lost ground and ended up encircling Damascus and the Egyptian 3rd Army.

A cease fire was brokered on October 24, 1973. Israel and the United States were the clear short-term winners.

Egypt, Syria, Jordan, Iraq, Saudi Arabia, Libya, Algeria, Morocco, Cuba and the Soviet Union were the losers, short-term. Loss of pride and humiliation in this short, but important conflict.

The United States came to Israel's aid with military supplies and monetary aid.

Long-term, the monies gained by the increase in crude oil by the Arab world would finance terrorist groups for decades and eventually lead to 9/11 and the ongoing war on terror.

In America, the embargo led to long car lines at filling stations. A sharp hike in gas prices and a rationing system in many states. In states where rationing took place, cars with license plates ending in an odd number could get gas on odd days, even number on plates on even days. The 31st was a free day for everybody.

The federal government devised a rationing system for states based on 1972 gasoline consumption gallons. The states losing people didn't suffer as much as states with large population gains.

Lake   Doomsday Clock 11:59:59

In 1979 the world experienced the second oil shock. This was the result of decreased oil production that occurred because of the Iranian Revolution. Despite the fact oil production only decreased by 4% the price of crude oil more than doubled to $39.50 a barrel.

A barrel holds 42 gallons. When refined it produces 20 gallons of gasoline, 12 gallons of diesel, 4 gallons of jet fuel and other products like asphalt and liquefied petroleum gases.

Again, panic ensued and overnight there were shortages in the United States. Rationing appeared in some states. This crisis was more likely caused by panicking consumers and not OPEC or oil companies. People saw long lines and started filling up their cars quicker and adding gas cans to the mix.

President Jimmy Carter went so far as to declare the oil crisis the "moral equivalent of war". In January 1980, he issued the Carter Doctrine, which said, "An attempt by any outside force to gain control of the Persian Gulf will be regarded as an assault on the vital interests of the United States."

Domestic oil production is a battle ground, geographical drilling locations, pipeline routes. Add economics, job loss, jobs gained, pollution versus food production, on and on.

Chapter 28

Ann made it to her floor and went inside the condo. Her dad was trying to put his computer back together.

She said, "Daddy, forget the computer. This crisis is about living or dying."

He said, with a shocked look on his face, "You're serious."

She said, "Yes. What we do or don't do in the next hour will end in us living or dying. I need you to focus."

He said, "Okay, but I don't know what to do. I'm lost. Your Mom would have taken care of things and just told me what to do."

Ann said, "I'm not Mom. I don't know what to do either, but doing nothing will end in our deaths. I'm too young to die. I want to live."

Brian said, "Tell me what we need to do?"

Ann thought about it, "Hydrate yourself, eat a few energy bars, get me a box of energy bars to put in my backpack. Do we have some cash on hand?"

Her Dad replied, "I keep $5,000 in hundreds in the safe. I'll get the rest of the stuff."

Ann went to her room and picked out a sturdy backpack. She loaded it up with some flash drives she'd bought about survival skills. She took the card her Mom gave her for her birthday tomorrow and placed it inside the backpack. She'd open it up tomorrow, if they survived today.

She went back to the living room and found her Dad had done what she'd asked. He handed her the bundle of cash and she stashed it inside the backpack. Bribery money for safe passage and supplies from the local drug dealers.

They stepped outside the Condo door and she stopped.

She said, "I've got to go back and get something important."

Lake   Doomsday Clock 11:59:59

She retraced her steps and found the remaining letters from her Mom. Picked them up and placed them in the backpack. Then rejoined her father outside.

They found the stairwell and her Dad wanted to go down. She explained to him the problem with the fire and smoke. He understood on an intellectual level, but down was a way out, up still left a big problem.

The started climbing up the stairwell. Every two floors her Dad would call for a break. He was breathing heavy.

When they got to the top floor they found the guy she'd passed twice pounding on the door. He noticed them and turned around.

He said, "The stupid psycho lady has blocked the door. I can't force it open. Maybe we could combine body weight here?"

Her Dad said, "Sounds swell. I'm not much help, but my little girl is a trooper."

Ann rolled her eyes.

Why was the touted indestructible building dangerously close to collapse?

Design flaw? Inferior materials? Building codes? Shoddy workmanship?

Everybody did their job. Kathy Frank was narcissistic, and suffered from several forms of mental illness.

The city of Baltimore Building department was thorough and professional. They made sure the proper materials were specified, and a civil engineer had signed off stating the building was safe. The right materials were used in the construction.

The workmen weren't union, but they did their jobs in a professional manner.

The culprit was imported rebar from China used in the foundation and floors. An excessively high amount of boron was used in the rebar by the manufacture to earn a

Lake   Doomsday Clock 11:59:59

tax credit. This made the steel weaker when welded by the technique used in the construction.

Blame free trade? The Chinese produced almost 50% of the World's crude steel. 808 Million Metric Tons in 2016. Not all of that needed in China, 106.6 Million Metric Tons exported to 122 countries.

Much has been written about Free Trade. A common argument is that every country should make what they make the cheapest. Which sounds good unless you live in an underdeveloped third world country. No valuable resources and no way to play the game.

Can you make a cell phone in one country? Does anybody make all the required parts? Have the needed raw materials?

300 plus parts and materials used, no one country has them all, not even close. So, trade is important.

The workers in Pittsburg, Pennsylvania who lost their jobs because of cheap imported steel aren't happy. Somebody wins and somebody loses in every transaction, every deal. Uber smart men and women study economics all their life and still disagree. We call that a floating target, what you hit is what you were aiming for.

Ann and the stranger pushed against the door with everything they had, nothing moved.

Suddenly the clank of a key being inserted and turned could be heard. The door opened.

Kathy Frank, standing prim and proper said, "The elevators won't respond. I'm going to have to walk down 35 flights of stairs. Unbelievable. My entire maintenance department will be fired after today."

Nobody said a word. They let her pass and walked out onto the roof, leaning now. Smoke poured over the lowest side. The steel was heating up and starting to groan and creak. The fire was being fueled by all the wood subflooring, wood studs, and particle board cabinets. It didn't help that people had installed illegal fuel tanks inside their Condo's, just in case. Oxygen was provided by all the busted-out windows. The perfect scenario.

The penthouse sat on the rooftop, three stories high, 6,000 square feet. A small structure for maintenance tools sat in a corner.

A metal latticed media tower stood 200 feet high. Loaded with cell phone, radio, internet and TV relays. It was positioned on the tilting side.

The building covered a city block. It was surrounded by older, but smaller commercial and apartment buildings. Kathy Frank's gift to the world was 508 feet high, add the 200 feet of the tower and it was listed at 708 feet in the City travel guide.

Ann told her Dad to go explore the Penthouse, but be ready if she yelled for him. She found a hammer Ms. Frank had been using to beat on the elevator call button laying on the ground.

She ran over to the maintenance shed and beat the Master lock with the hammer. Again, and again she slammed it with everything she had. Nothing. No progress. She was close to tears. Their lives were at stake and a stupid lock was winning the most important battle. She needed options. Something to help them get off the roof or over to a different building.

Superman? Spiderman? She'd take the Hulk right now.

The guy who helped beat on the door was standing at the edge of the building, looking down. He turned around and walked over to Ann who continued beating futilely on the lock using the hammer.

He asked, calmly, "Do you need that door open?"

She wanted to say, using sarcasm, no, I'm practicing my backhand for a tennis match tomorrow.

She screamed, "Yes!"

Lake   Doomsday Clock 11:59:59

He pulled her back, by one arm, pulled a large looking handgun out of his waist band and shot the lock off. The sound of the gun discharge left her ears ringing.

He smiled, and using a lame Australian accent, said, "You just got to have the right tool for the job mate."

Ann mumbled, "Thanks!" And opened the maintenance room.

A few nylon ropes, safety harnesses, window cleaner, squeegee, an axe, wrenches, screwdrivers, a floor scrubber, walkie talkies with spare batteries, a jump box, pliers, sockets, 14/2 electrical wire, a Monopoly Game, Uno Cards, PVC Pipe, PEX tubing, glue, two 20-ton jacks.

Her Dad came running up and said, "OMG. I heard what sounded like a shot."

Ann pointed to the stranger, "John Wayne shot the lock off the door."

Her Dad looked at the stranger and walked over, stuck at his hand, "Mr. Wayne, nice to meet you. I'm Brian.

The stranger looked very confused.

Ann said, "Dad, that was sarcasm. I don't know his real name."

Her Dad laughed, a little awkward, "I get it. Because he used a gun. Sorry Sir, but Brian is my real name."

The man said, "I'm Tatum, Tatum Thorne."

Her Dad said, "Which floor do you live on?"

Tatum responded, a bit sheepish, "That's a bit embarrassing. I lost my job as a day trader 18 months ago. I know the night watchman. He used to be a day trader as well. He knows which Condos are vacant, who's on vacation, who's in the hospital, and so on. I just move every few weeks to a different floor. It's cheap and nobody seems to notice. I'm frugal, tidy, move out a few days before they get back. I find odd construction jobs as a day laborer. Now this crap has happened. My friend was on

Lake   Doomsday Clock 11:59:59

duty when the explosion happened. I can't imagine anybody made it out alive."

Ann thought, survivors guilt, PTSD?

She said, "We need a plan. Any ideas?"

Her dad, Brian said, "I have no idea. The wind is getting hotter. The building is creaking. I think the bolts and screws holding the steel I-beams are starting to melt or pop."

Tatum said, "Anyway we can knock that tower down and hope it lands on top of a building across the street?"

Ann said, "I was thinking the same thing. I wish we had a cutting torch. We could cut the bolts off the base and it would topple. Maybe catch the roof top across the street. That building looks about 10 stories lower than this one."

They ran over to the edge. Ann estimated the height difference to be 130 feet and the distance between the two buildings to be 60 feet. The street below was two blacktop paved lanes, narrow, small cement sidewalks. Now the street was red and littered with body parts.

Ann did the calculations in her head. The Pythagorean Theorem, side A squared, + side B squared = side C squared. C = 143.1 feet is what they needed for the tower to lean over the building and catch the next roof. It was their only chance.

The tower was 40 feet from the edge of Kathy Frank's Taj Mahal. It worked theoretically. If her estimations on A and B lengths were correct or even close. They had 17 feet to spare.

Then she thought about the variables. What if it didn't fall at a 90-degree angle. Too much to think about. They needed a plan to topple the tower. How much longer would the building stand?

She remembered watching footage of the two World Trade Center buildings disintegrating on 9/11/01. She wasn't born yet. But, just watching the footage made her sick to her stomach. All those people who were still alive when the buildings came down. She shuddered. They needed a good plan.

Tatum said, "Why don't we use the two jacks and try to leverage the tower loose?"

She said, "It's all we have. Let's get started. I'll grab one and you take the other."

The plan had faults. It was soon apparent that they couldn't jack the tower high enough using the roof as a base. They needed more height.

They looked around and a dozen people had joined them on the rooftop. Everybody was in a daze. People were muttering to themselves. Some were crying out to God. Some wanted to be saved right then. Some were silently praying and preparing for death.

A man was yelling about the Devil and Satan and how he wouldn't burn. He walked to the side of the building and without a word jumped to his death.

Tatum watched silently and solemnly said, "Reminds me of a joke."

Ann said, "Keep working. What reminds you of a joke?"

Tatum quietly replied, "That man who just jumped."

Ann sarcastically said, "Really, a joke at a time like this. I might have a minute left to live. I'm only 15."

Tatum said, "Look, you can't change what is or isn't going to happen. You might as well keep working and listen to my joke."

She shook her head, but didn't say no.

He said, "Two guys are drinking at a bar. The first guy says, did you know you can jump out off a tall building window and if there's a building next to it there is an updraft that will carry you back up to the window you jumped from.

Lake   Doomsday Clock 11:59:59

The second guy says, No way.

The first guy says, I'll bet you $100. I'll show you. He walks over to the window, opens it and jumps. A few seconds later he flies back in.

The first guy hands $100 bill to the bartender. He tells the second guy it's his turn and give his $100 bill to the bartender before he jumps.

The second guy jumps, falls to his death.

The first guy collects his money from the bartender and leaves.

The bartender turns to a 3rd guy at the bar and says. That Superman is such a jerk when he's drunk."

Ann smiled and said, "That's so stupid and inappropriate right now."

Tatum said, "But it made you smile for just a second. Sometimes humor is all you got in life. My life has gone from making $500K a year to living in other people's Condos. I lost my wife, I haven't seen my little girl in a year. My parents disowned me, my friends forgot about me. All because I failed at life."

Ann said, "You can start again. You're not even 30, right?"

Tatum said, "I'm 35. What can I do?"

Ann said, "Off hand, how about being a comedian?"

Tatum looked at her with new found respect. She might be a kid, but she was street smart, life wise.

He said, "Touché' Kid!"

Brian, her dad, ran over, "Ann, I just remembered. I saw a cutting torch set in old lady Frank's art studio."

Tatum ran to get the tanks and torch. Within 5 minutes he was back.

They started cutting the bolts. There were four, one on each corner. The tower had a base of 4 feet.

Lake   Doomsday Clock 11:59:59

They had no idea how much it weighted. They cut off the first bolt in 2 minutes. The second bolt came off just as easy. The third bolt was removed. Seconds ticked by, the building rood was hot. The fourth and final bolt came off. The tower stood still.

They tried to rock it. No luck.

Suddenly the building shuddered and shook violently. The tower jumped a little from side to side and started to tip to one side. Away from the street. Ann started to cry out and scream, "No!"

The building hiccupped and the tower suddenly toppled over. Sliding across the rooftop as it fell and then hit hard, bounced once and shuddered to a stop.

Ann and Tatum ran to the edge. The tower was indeed on the top of the building across the street with 10 feet to spare.

A young man ran up and grabbed a metal piece of the frame and swung himself up. He quickly moved across the street. Looking like a monkey as he used the inside of the lattice to cross.

He jumped out and did a "Rocky" dance. The next guy walked across the tower, on the top side, hopping from one metal strip to the next, he made it and did a "Muhamad Ali" dance, "float like a butterfly, sting like a bee". Others started to cross. Several young people helping the old, two husbands helping wives or two wives helping husbands depending on physical condition.

The group on the burning building top was down to four. Ann, Brian, Tatum and Kathy Frank who had rejoined the group.

Brian said, "I'm afraid of heights. I can't do this. This is my day to die."

Ann sternly said, "No, not happening Daddy."

Tatum softly said, "We'll help you Brian."

Lake   Doomsday Clock 11:59:59

Kathy stood silently off to the side.

Ann said, "Staying here isn't an option. I've already lost Mom. I'm not losing you. We're a team Daddy."

Brian said, "I'm scared. I'm paralyzed. My feet won't move. I can't breathe."

Tatum said, "Sir, take a deep breath and let it out, slowly. Do it again. We'll be there every step of the way."

Ann said, "I'm going to get a safety harness and a lanyard. I hope that will make him feel better."

Tatum looked at Kathy Frank and said, "Are you coming."

Kathy looked around and said, "No, this is my ship. I'm going down with it."

Tatum said, "Damn noble thought, but stupid. Live to see the sunset."

She said, in a moment of clarity, "I can't."

Tatum left her to her thoughts and final minutes of life. It was in his opinion, a chicken's way out. Face the future, learn from the past mistakes. Help society, make your neighborhood better.

Ann had managed to get Brian strapped into the safety harness and attach the safety lanyard to the first piece of metal. She was encouraging him to take a step.

The building was quickly dying. Any moment and it would collapse.

Tatum noticed Brian was frozen and Ann couldn't get him to move. He had an idea. He ran to the maintenance shack and found an old beanie. He found a second lanyard and a coil of rope and took that as well.

He took it to Ann and told her to have her Dad put the beanie on and pull it down to cover his eyes. What he couldn't see could be helpful. He added a second lanyard so Brian would be attached to the tower frame every step.

Lake   Doomsday Clock 11:59:59

They started slowly. Brian was indeed frozen with fear. Tatum managed to get him to stand on his feet and moved him forward like a baby walking on top of a parent's shoes. It was torturously slow. Take a small step, move the lanyard, another small step. They had 160 feet to travel, 2 feet at a time.

Finally, they hit the half way part. The tower was beginning to vibrate. The building was going to collapse at any second and they were 80 feet from safety and 400 feet from death if they fell.

Tatum said, "We're not going to make it. Stop. Take the lanyards off the metal. Attach both of us to your Dad's safety harness."

Ann replied, "By what?"

Tatum was uncoiling the rope and motioning to the two guys left on the roof where they were headed. The first two across, "Rocky" and "Muhamad Ali".

He said, "Wrap it around your chest, or your belt loop. Make it secure."

He pulled a large pipe wrench out of his back pocket and attached the rope to one end. He had one chance to throw the wrench and then they could run and jump when the tower collapsed. Because it was going to collapse any second.

He tossed the wrench and the "Ali" caught it. He tied the other end around Brian's safety harness. They moved Brian reluctantly to the top of the tower. Started walking, 60 feet, 4 more steps, 50 feet, still not close enough.

10 more steps, 30 feet, 5 more steps, 20 feet, 2 more steps, 15 feet and the tower collapsed. They jumped and landed just short of the edge. Maybe 5 feet from the top. They hit hard. Both clinging to Brian and his safety harness like a baby and an umbilical cord.

The two guys at the top pulling hard, 450 pounds of dead weight. They were struggling, but refusing to give up.

Lake   Doomsday Clock 11:59:59

Three feet from the top. Tatum hooked his arm over the ledge and helped pull them up a little.

Then it was over. They were on top. Safe for the moment. They looked back at Kathy Franks big moment. She was waving a white hanky in the air, surrender? Goodbye?

It didn't really matter. She'd made her choice. The building shook and collapsed, gone in a few seconds. All of them turned and ran to get away from the edge.

The building they were on shook as well, rumbled, creaked and groaned as the energy from the collapsing building pushed out.

Then it stopped, just smoke and heat coming from the collapsed building.

They all looked at each other. Survivors. Somehow, they defied the odds and made it across from a burning skyscraper. What else could go wrong?

They took a quick inventory. Ann had her backpack with the energy bars, jump drives and cash. Tatum had grabbed the Jump box. Not much, but it was all they had.

Brian was just happy to be alive. The two guys who helped pull them up took off in search of food and supplies.

They all agreed they needed to get off the roof top and head west, out of town or hunker down in the tunnels until the world regained its sanity.

Twenty-Five floors, stairs only, because of course the elevators required electricity to move up and down. Not that elevators worked daily in a slumlord building.

Which is kind of the point. The people living there were elderly, disabled, some young hard-working families. Everybody shared a common trait, no money. Life had kicked them around a bit, or just life's way of being cruel.

If the owner repaired the building the rent would go up and people would be forced to move and find a new old building, with cheap rent.

Lake   Doomsday Clock 11:59:59

Free Market forces this conundrum on the poor. Which of course made the neighborhood ripe for gentrification.

They made it down two flights, in the dark, light only on the landings; where windows used to be and now gaping holes existed.

A rag tag cluster stood on the landing. Four young teens, making a living as runners in the drug trade. An unexpected day off, without pay, because the illegal drug trade isn't unionized or even legal.

So, they were trying to make money the old-fashioned way, protection. Protection from other thugs like them, guys too lazy or unskilled to find a regular 9-5 job.

If the building across the street hadn't exploded and burned they could have stolen a car and run some drugs to a suburb or sold some stolen cell phones to "Gato's Pawn Shop", on their day off.

Ann, Tatum and Brian stopped at the foot of the 23rd floor stairs. The 4 thugs, a leader, two Lieutenants, and a runt, the designated gopher stood 6 feet away on the landing and blocking the next set of stairs. The way to freedom and the only way out of the building.

Brian said, holding up his right hand, in a Vulcan sign, "We come in peace."

The thugs were confused.

Tatum said, "That's live long and prosper."

The thugs were impatient.

The leader said, "There's a toll for using the stairs. You guys look rich, so $200 each."

Ann said, "We have safe passage."

Brian said, "We have $5,000 cash. $200 each is no problem."

The thugs, like most people, were also greedy. They didn't think the group carried $600, maybe $100 between them and after scaring them a bit, frisking them, feeling up the chick, they would have let them go. But $5,000 was real money.

The leader said, "The new toll is $5,000 or we throw your sorry asses out the busted window."

Tatum said, "We have a get out of Jail Card!"

Tatum, the cowboy, showing a practiced, smooth move, pulled his six-shooter out of his waist band and cocked it, pointed it at the thug leaders head.

Tatum said, "Go ahead punk, make my day!"

Brian laughed and said, "Clint Eastwood. "Dirty Harry", awesome!"

Ann said, "Knock it off, both of you."

The leader said, "You guys are making a mistake. We'll take $200 and you guys leave."

Ann said, "That's fine. I'll give you the $200."

Tatum, feeling emboldened said, "No. Don't give them anything."

Brian said, "I agree. These guys are hooligans."

The leader said, "You guys are making a big mistake. What's a hooligan?"

Tatum, Ann and Brian moved past the group of four thugs. Headed back down the stairs.

The four thugs fled to their apartment one floor up. Where they had guns and walkie talkies and alerted the group on the 15th floor. Who went to their apartment and got their guns so they could teach the millennials a lesson they wouldn't ever forget, maybe even take the girl, certainly the $5000 was rightfully theirs. They might even toss that cowboy out the window.

The group of three kept going down the stairs, floor by floor, looking back occasionally to see if the thugs were following.

Lake   Doomsday Clock 11:59:59

They were between the 16th and 15th floor when a hail of bullets, warning shots, pinged off the metal balusters.

Up above, warning shots arrived as well. They stopped. Unable to move forwards or back.

The group down below was the first team. Still thugs, still a leader, two lieutenants and a gopher. They had an extra year of practice as runners, lookouts.

The leader below said, "Cease fire. Let me set your terms of surrender."

Ann said, "I have safe passage." Which everybody ignored.

Tatum said, "I'm a good shot."

The leader above said, "But you only have a six-shooter. There are 8 of us."

Brian said, "He only has 5 bullets. He shot a lock off earlier."

Ann shook her head in disbelief.

Tatum said, "I have three speed loaders in my pocket. 17 bullets to shoot 8 of you and I'm shooting the leaders first."

The leader below said, "My guys will defend me and you have to shoot them first."

The gopher said, "Hell no. I'm not giving my life up for you homie."

Tatum said, "I have a Smith and Wesson Model 29, .44 caliber. I can shoot thru two, maybe three of you with one bullet."

Ann said, "Shut up, all of you. I have safe passage. Call your boss on the radio and tell him Skate Girl needs some help."

The thug above said, "Why should we do that?"

Ann said, "Because if you don't, all of you will die when he finds out you harmed me and my family. You will die and your families will die as well. Don't believe me, go ahead, shoot. All it takes is a 30 second call to your boss."

Silence. Shuffling feet, murmurs and a distant radio static.

A minute later the thug below waved a white pair of underwear, boxers. around the corner.

He says, "Sorry Skate Girl. Safe passage granted. We didn't know it was you. Please tell the boss we treated you right."

Tatum cleared his throat, ready to talk. Ann said, "Shut up Cowboy. Don't say a word Daddy!"

They walked past the thugs, Ann said, "I'll give him a good report."

Down they went, 15 more flights of stairs.

They went out the back door, on the sidewalk stood "Rocky" and "Ali", drinking from a jug of water and eating energy bars, smiling, still happy.

Tatum, in disbelief, said, "How did you guys get past the thugs?"

Rocky said, "What thugs?"

Brian said, "The thugs on floor 25 and 15?"

Ali said, "Didn't you use the fire escape?"

Tatum said, "Hell no. We used the stairs."

Rocky said, "Always use the fire escape in a low-income building. Gangs operate on the stairs. Common knowledge dude."

There are rules in every level of the world, all classes. The poor just want food, enough food, the middle class wants their food to taste good, and the wealthy want their food on fine China with the meat, veggies, in the right place.

You change classes, expectations change. The poor want a roof over their head. The middle class wants large square footage and the wealthy want a zip code, an address.

The poor want clothes for the season, the middle class wants name brands and the wealthy need designer clothing.

The poor depend on public transportation, the middle class wants a working car, the wealthy want a car that few have.

Change worlds and you feel a bit stupid, until you learn the rules. It doesn't make any group better, just different. The wealthy tend to look down on the middle class. The middle class tend to look at the poor and say, there for the grace of God go I. And the poor are too busy struggling with housing, food and clothing to worry about others.

Life can be fickle at times.

They went to see the neighborhood boss. The drug dealer, protection racket, fenced stolen goods, hit man, and Ann's friend. Sometimes people become who they are because of where they are born.

He liked to be called Bugsy, after Benjamin "Bugsy" Siegel, American Jewish mobster. The real Bugsy, he hated the nickname.

Bugsy avoided sponsoring prostitution because he considered it harmful to the family and disrespectful to women. He didn't mind selling you enough coke or meth to kill you. He also would coordinate hits on rival gangs. Fancied himself as a modern day, Murder Inc.

It was his respect for women that allowed him to form a friendship with Ann. He called her skate girl because she loved to ride her board everywhere. She had an original "Navajo Nando" board.

They talked about art, and music, social changes, politics and how to make your neighborhood better. He considered himself to be something of a Robin Hood. We all justify our actions.

Lake   Doomsday Clock 11:59:59

Bugsy was in a jovial mood. He was selling hoisted generators left and right. A good business man hedges both sides. You sell guns and band aids. He pirated electricity from the electric company and sold it to the poor at a discount. Now he was selling generators to the same group. Life was good. He was going to make a killing on water tomorrow.

The meeting was short. Bugsy was busy. He needed to finalize plans to kill two rival gang leaders caught trying to infringe on his territory. Hijack a trailer loaded with water bound for a homeless shelter and meet with a City Councilman about a donation to build a baseball diamond. He thought maybe he'd also gift a skate park in honor of his favorite skate girl, Ann.

He charged Ann $1,000 for saving her life. He lectured her on not knowing to use the fire escape, common sense he told her.

Ann asked about transportation. Something small and able to hold the three of them and a few supplies.

He gave her a great deal on an old Cushman used as a US Postal truck, from the 1960's, white, faded blue postal decals, but ran like a champ. He tossed in a full tank of gas and a 5-gallon spare full. What a guy?

The Cushman was on 3-wheels, two in the back and a single front wheel. The steering was handlebar style, like a motorcycle or a bicycle. The doors on both sides slid back like a closet door and the back doors swung open.

You could see the faded decal from its postal service days. It ran on a small 3-cylinder engine and somebody had upgraded the tires and suspension. Bugsy explained they used it long ago to transport confiscated (stolen) goods in underground tunnels that crisscrossed the city of Baltimore.

Ann paid $500 for the trike, and $100 for a box of easy open prepared food and a 5-gallon jug of water.

They were adapting.

Lake   Doomsday Clock 11:59:59

Bugsy told them about the nuclear explosion in Hamburg, Germany. The country seemed undecided. Was this a real disaster that would throw the world into uncontrollable chaos or just a hiccup. In a year or two it would be old news, markets would adjust, wealth among the 1% would be redistributed.

Bugsy believed it was temporary, Ann felt it was a fatal blow and war would follow. As always, they had a spirited discussion, each one defending his/her position. Time would tell who was right or if something in between happened.

Bugsy gave them a map of the tunnel maze. That cost $10, they were friends, but business was business and he had a large payroll, three ex-wives and 8 kids to support.

Bugsy told Ann to stay in touch.

She asked, "How?"

He said, "Your part of the postal service now, send a letter." Everybody was a comedian.

They left Bugsy's neighborhood. It had been less than 5 hours since the G20 explosion. It seemed like forever. Their bodies were crashing. The adrenaline rush from surviving the burning skyscraper and the subsequent gun battle with the gangs in the stairways was too much.

Brian and Tatum soon fell asleep in the back of the Cushman. Ann drove for almost 10 miles, at a brisk 15 mph pace, because the tunnels were in fairly good shape. She finally found a side tunnel that went back about 100 feet and drove the trike there.

Brian and Tatum kept sleeping and so Ann curled up on the cool ground outside. She used an old, scratchy, green army blanket found in the Cushman, wrapped it around her body, and fell asleep.

Chapter 29

Society was changing at a rapid pace.

The advent of steam had pushed the industrial revolution in the late 1760's to about 1840. Machines took over the tasks previously done by hand. Chemical manufacturing and iron production increased.

Lewis and Clark attempted to find a practical route across the western part of the continent from 1804-1806.

1830 the first steam railroad opens on the east coast, by 1869 the transcontinental railroad is complete.

Imagine living in a time when the country went from 12.9 million people in 24 states in 1830 to 38.6 million and 37 states by 1869.

In 1800 6% of the population lived in cities and 94% lived in a rural setting. By 1840 11% lived in cities and 89% lived in rural setting. In 1880 28% were living in the city and 72% were living in the country. 1920 51% were living in cities and 49% were in the country. 1960 63% were living in cities and 37% were living in the country. 2000 76% living in cities and 24% rural and in 2016 82% were in cities and 18% in rural setting.

The population shifted because of technology and the rise of the middle class. Farms were modernized and 1 person could do the work of many.

Millennials, kids born between the early 1980's until the late 1990's. Each generation is unique in the challenges they face. Each person is unique, there is only one person like you. But, there is a difference between being unique, and feeling special or entitled.

The Greatest Generation label given to people who grew up during the "Great Depression" of the 1930's and then went on to fight World War II, either as a participant or a war material provider.

They were unique. They did without during the great depression. People learned to grow gardens in the city, Lake   Doomsday Clock 11:59:59

repair or reuse what they had. Single men rode the rails looking for work. Government embarked on a Public Works program to put the men to work who were unemployed. Infrastructure in the United States improved, roads and highways were upgraded, parks were built.

World War II created a new set of hardships. The country needed raw materials converted to war supplies. Ships built, tanks, airplanes, ammunition, and they needed workers. Everybody or almost everybody went to work to support the war effort.

Women left small towns and farms to work in factories building airplanes, ammunition, secretary work. They lived in dorms and with families who had spare bedrooms with sons off fighting overseas.

Rights were suspended. Let me rewrite that sentence. Rights were suspended. The government told manufactures what they needed for the war effort. You couldn't buy a new car, tires, refrigerators or stoves from the early 1940's until 1947. If you were in a job deemed essential to the war effort you had to get permission to quit and change employers.

Food was rationed. Sugar, milk, eggs, flour, butter, meat, all had to be bought with coupons. People created their own barter systems. They were unique, but not special nor did they feel entitled.

The men came home, the women were released from factory work and the economy was booming. Babies were born, by the score. What's a score? Google it.

The Baby boomers were the next generation. So many barriers had been knocked down for women and minorities during World War II.

Family vacations for the middle class became the new norm. People took two weeks off during the summer and bought tents, or travel trailers to pull behind their station wagons and suburban's or pickup trucks. They went to see the new National Parks and other places they'd just read about in US history books.

Lake   Doomsday Clock 11:59:59

People had leisure time. Men and women developed hobbies and started supporting causes. The middle class started sending their daughters to college in droves. Women stayed in the workforce and began sending their kids to daycare.

Each generation wants life better and easier than the one before. Two-week vacations started to include trips to resorts and ocean cruises. Camps for kids during the summer. American's middle class had disposal income and time.

The baby boomers protested anything and everything including the Vietnam war. The women burned their bras and many wanted sexual freedom. The sang songs of protest, marched in the streets. The Civil Rights Act passed in 1964 based on Martin Luther King's civil rights movement ushered in a new group; the Black middle class.

The sexual revolution ended in the 1980's with the AIDS epidemic.

Generation X were kids born from the late 1960's to the middle 1980's. More disposal income, and this was the last group who seemed destined to surpass their parent's lifestyle.

These were also the MTV kids and the ones who went from 4 basic channels on TV to 200+. These kids experienced the beginning of Microwaves and pagers. You carried several quarters with you to call your parent's back, or friends when your pager went off.

Enter the Millennials and the skyrocketing technology. These kids didn't have landlines. Technology is changing so fast that careers last years instead of decades. They grew up with cell phones, pay phones became a rarity.

College became such an expensive burden that many of them start adult life feeling like indentured servants.

The housing market crash of the late 1990's and early 2000's ended many of their hopes for home ownership.

Lake   Doomsday Clock 11:59:59

They have become somewhat jaded as a generation and yes feeling a bit entitled.

The world has been at war most of their adult life. Terrorism headlines and fake news are their headlines. The world of technology marches on faster and faster. Keep up or drop out.

They grew up in schools that gave everybody a trophy or a certificate just for showing up. They came to expect to be great because everybody told them how special they were each day. Remember these kids were raised and educated by Baby Boomers and Generation X parents and teachers.

Many are disillusioned with life, yet with a feeling of entitlement. Where is my piece of the American Dream?

Chapter 30

Ann felt a rat move across her lower leg. She was awake. She hated rodents. Music, Rock and Roll, floated down from the Cushman. Bob Seger serenading her with "Against the Wind".

She tossed the scratchy blanket off and the rat scurried away. Ann shivered, not from the cold, but from the whiskered animal crawling on her.

The only light was from the cell phone screen, Brian's.

She asked, "You still have power? I thought your phone would be dead by now."

Her Dad replied, pointing into the Cushman, "I plugged my phone into this cigarette lighter."

Ann asked, "How long have you been charging the phone?"

Brian shrugged his shoulders, "About 8 hours. The same time you went to sleep."

Ann asked, "Where is John Wayne?"

Brian responded, pointing to his right, "He walked down to the end of the tunnel. Wanted to see what was down there."

Ann said, "Daddy, see if the trike starts?"

Brian turned the key and the Cushman just clicked. No power.

Ann looked at him, a bit irritated. "Daddy. You ran the battery down charging your worthless cell phone. You've got to start thinking."

Brian's feelings were hurt. "Geez Ann, I didn't know a cell phone would kill a vehicle battery. Besides, Tatum charged his phone too."

Ann said, exasperated, "I'm traveling with two no common-sense adults."

Lake   Doomsday Clock 11:59:59

Brian said, "What are we going to do? How do you suggest we fix the problem?"

Ann said, "You tell me Dad."

He said, "I don't know. Can we push it and pop the thing, what do they call that thing? I've seen that in the movies."

Ann rolled her eyes, "It only works if we have a standard, a clutch. This trike is an automatic."

Tatum came back from his tunnel exploration.

He said, "Did you know there's a sign outside in the main tunnel that says, 1561 miles to Wall Drug. What's that all about?"

Ann said, "Wall Drug is in Wall, South Dakota. Ted Hustead moved there in 1931, a pharmacist. Wall had a population of 231 people. Business was slow even though traffic was heavy because of the newly opened Mount Rushmore National Monument 60 miles away.

Ted's wife, Dorothy, suggested they give away free ice water. Ted went out to put up signs advertising the giveaway and the rest is history. Two million visitors annually visit the remote town. You want to go there Tex?"

Tatum said, "No thanks, high semi-arid desert. Hot in the summer and cold as a witch's tit in the winter. No!"

Brian said, "Witch's tit?"

Ann said, "Drop it Daddy. Let's focus on this problem. Okay?"

Brian said, "What problem?"

Ann, exasperated now, "The Cushman won't start because you two drained the battery charging your cell phones that won't work."

Tatum said, "Ann, not a problem."

Ann said, "What are you going to do, push it, get it rolling and pop the nonexistent clutch?" She rolled her eyes.

Lake   Doomsday Clock 11:59:59

Tatum looked a bit hurt from the stinging criticism.

He said, "No, we have a jump box from the maintenance shed. And for the record, I charged my phone off the jump box which is fully charged."

Ann said, "Sorry. I'm stressed out."

They attached the jump box and the engine purred to life. They turned around and headed out to the main tunnel.

Ann knew they wanted to go West and look in the direction of I-70 and then South. She was aiming for the George Washington Forrest.

She wanted to be in Moonshine country, field corn and creek water used to make "White Lightening". She knew they might find an old abandoned still which would be isolated and away from people.

First, they had to find a way out of Baltimore. The side tunnel they were in emptied into a larger train tunnel for the mass transit. Only half of Maryland residence drive so the subway-train-bus system is extensive and links up with other major metropolitan area. No electricity meant no trains running.

The tunnel finally ended in a switching yard. Nobody was around in the early morning hour. Daybreak, silence, no trains running, no people waiting to rush to work. It was as if the world had stopped and was waiting for the next huge event before deciding where to go.

They ended up on a train track headed to Washington DC. Ann knew that couldn't be their destination. They'd need to circle around the DC swamp and head to West Virginia.

They made steady time, 15 mph, the large tires helped, but poor suspension still and the tracks made the ride bouncy and hard on the kidneys. Her dad and Tatum were once again sleeping. They were like kids on a cross country trip.

Ann reached under the seat of the trike and discovered a small handgun, fully loaded. She put it back and decided to keep that secret to herself, just in case.

Lake   Doomsday Clock 11:59:59

They bounced along, putting miles between them and Baltimore. Suddenly, the Cushman engine sputtered and died.

The silence woke up the two kids.

Ann explained, "Out of gas. We need to think about finding some more."

Brian suggested, "Can't we just drive up to the interstate and get some?"

Tatum said, "No, we need electricity to pump the gas."

Brian said, "This is really a crappy thing, no electricity."

Ann kept her mouth shut. She carefully poured the 5-gallons of gas bought from Bugsy into the Cushman. Placed the can back in the back with explicit instructions to the boys not to lose it. She pumped the gas pedal to bring gas to the carburetor, old fashioned engine, no electronic fuel injection or mother board on the vehicle. She turned the key and the engine sputtered to life, smoothed out and Ann slipped it into gear, and off they went, at 10 mph.

Four more hours of driving, 40 more miles and she looked at her watch.

24 hours had passed since she walked into her Dad's office, just before the generator fuel tank caught on fire and the skyscraper housing their condo burned.

They had, being lucky, and a now 16-year old's guile survived day one. She knew when they stopped next, she'd read the letter from her Mom. She thought, "Happy Sweet 16 Ann."

Four Square Ranch

Chapter 31

North Central Montana

00:00

Four friends, nothing got between them. They worked hard and played hard.

They lived on and off the land, no neighbor for 15 miles in any direction. Their fathers had owned the land before them; given it to the kids when they finished college and had semi-retired. All of the old men and their wives were alive today, in their 80's. The four sons were in their mid-50's.

The dads had been neighbors, kids growing up during the depression, too young for the great war, WWII, in the 1940's, but all served during the Korean War as Rangers

Lake   Doomsday Clock 11:59:59

in the 3rd company. Special men. Special skills. Special forces, men you didn't want to challenge or piss off, even in their 80's.

The four older men and their wives lived in the original central house; a semi-retirement home. The grandkids cooked their meals, cleaned the house, and drove them to doctor appointments. It was how life should be in every family.

Their Grandfathers had served in the war to end all wars, WWI, and before that their family farmed the frontier with horses and plows. Before that, trapped and hunted. Before that, they crawled out of a tar pit. They were descendants of the families that settled Montana.

Montanans solve their own problems. Back in 1864 when Henry Plummer and his gang decided not to worry about local law enforcement; local vigilantes rounded them up one by one and hung them. Left a note on the body, 3-7-77, cryptic. Many believe the numbers stood for the dimensions of a grave, 3 feet wide by 7 feet long and 77" deep.

The current group, now in their 50's, went to school together as youngsters. A small district with less than 150 students from kindergarten thru 12th grade. They played football, basketball and baseball together.

They lost the 6-man football state finals as freshman and then reeled off 3 titles in a row. Heath and Dan were the blockers and Andrew and Eddie the fast and swift. Leave Dan or Heath alone and a 5-yard shovel pass turned into a long, slow TD. Both ran like arthritic rhinos, even in high school.

In basketball, it took a bit longer. They didn't win a championship until their Junior year. Heath and Dan controlled the boards and swatted anything shot within 5-feet of the basket. Dan was 6'8" and Heath 6'3". Eddie and Andrew ran the offense, shot 3's like Pistol Pete Maravich and Spud Webb. Both were excellent passers and ball handlers.

Their senior year in Basketball they were undefeated.

Baseball was a different story. They made the playoffs each year, but never made it past the semi-finals. As Heath said, "They sucked at baseball, damn little white ball moving too fast."

They graduated together and went to college together. Heath and Dan were on the four-year plan. Andrew was on the 5-year plan and Eddie took 6 years.

They complimented each other, smart enough to make life plans early.

Heath had a dual degree in Business and Agriculture, farming was his specialty. He knew to use organic methods to grow crops. How to replenish seed and plan for lean years when the drought and heat withered crops and animals. He made sure progress was planned and measured by the decade.

Andrew was the medicine man. He specialized in both human medicine and animal health. They were isolated and having an expert to drive a tractor and look out for the health of the humans and animals was a huge benefit. He was also responsible for the breeding, genetics of the numerous animals they raised. Nobody likes a 3-legged cow in the herd. He had a dual degree in Nursing and Genetics.

Dan was the mechanic. He could fix anything, mechanical or fabrication. He could work with wood or metal, a jack of all trades and strong as an ox. He also understood irrigation systems, fluid dynamics. He designed the ponds, irrigation system, windmills, and drinking water. He didn't lose many drops of aqua and made sure they recycled everything possible and waste was at a minimum. Dan had dual degrees in architecture and engineering.

Eddie could fly anything, drones, ultralights, helicopters, single engine or dual engine planes. He could piece them together when they broke and drive a tractor all day. He had degrees in aeronautical engineering and alternative energy. In addition, he designed the electric grid, solar, wind, thermal, and hydro.

They lived in separate houses. All together in a big compound, with the original house in the middle, all the men were married. Heath had a boy and a girl, Dan had three boys, Eddie had two girls and a boy with a set of twins mixed in that threesome. Andrew had one boy and two girls. It was a motley crew at best, but loyal and loving.

The women all worked as well. From cooking, to canning, gathering eggs, making the milking operation run smooth, it depended on the females.

The men worked out away from the houses and the women ran the tiny village. Everybody seems satisfied with the arrangement.

Heath was the unofficial leader. The voice of reason, moderation. Taking life in easy measured steps.

Andrew was calm, resourceful, a deliberate response, never panicking.

Dan, was calm on the outside, cool demeanor, but don't irritate or anger him. If he lost his temper get out of the way.

Eddie was the risk taker, always pushing the envelope.

They had memories, from childhood. They, built, tweaked, and raced old "Muscle Cars" on the dirt roads, tossed eggs at neighbor's houses on Halloween, occasionally knocked down mailboxes in the nearest town with a baseball bat. Played practical jokes on each other, and occasionally went too far, always settled and forgotten over a beer the same day.

This morning was the continuation of a long running joke. Dan loved to dress up in a bear outfit, very realistic. His favorite target was Eddie. The last time he pulled the prank one of the grandkids pulled a video off a security camera and posted it on YouTube. Dan jumping out and chasing Eddie. Eddie running as fast as possible, stumbling, falling, crawling on all fours trying to get away. As of last week, it had 3.4 million views.

Today, Eddie planned to turn the tables on Dan. He had heard Dan was going to chase him with the bear outfit. So, Eddie packed a big Clint Eastwood Dirty Harry gun, complete with blanks.

That morning Heath and Andrew were in the control room, watching the scene unfold.

Eddie walked along the edge of the building and casually rounded the corner.

Dan stood up, like a ferocious "Grizzle Bear". Eddie took off running. Dan followed.

Eddie turned around and pulled out his big revolver. The bear stopped and started waving its arms, trying desperately to remove the head piece.

Eddie took careful aim and fired off 4 shots. The bear fell back believing it was fatally wounded. Eddie started laughing.

It was epic. Dan changed his pants and boxers when everybody stopped laughing, knew he had been had and started plotting his revenge. 4 good friends.

Chapter 32

Their Ranch, "Four Square" was legendary in Montana for combining organic farming and free-range ranching. They grew corn, and winter wheat, as their main crops. They raised cattle, sheep, and goats. The animals had summer and winter pastures.

Roads crisscrossed their property for easy access and they did much of the patrolling by drone. Eddie was the expert and he had drones up every day the weather cooperated. Two of the college graduate grandkids manned the room filled with monitors, it was an important job. The drones had advanced software provided by a company that did defense research for the military. The software was adept at finding problems, predators, animals or human.

The drones were exempt from several FAA rules. They occasionally exceeded the 400-foot ceiling limit because of the need to see over the horizon and they rarely were in line of sight of the operator.

Technology was becoming more important in their business. The 3rd generation were still arriving into this world, and all under 25 years old.

The ranch was almost 100,000 acres. An acre being 43,560 square feet. A square mile is 27,878,400 square feet. 100,000 acres is 156.25 square miles. If the ranch were a big square it would be 12.25 miles on each side. Which it wasn't a square, but a patchwork of land parcels requiring many miles of fences to funnel livestock. Neighbors tend to frown when your cattle herd mingles with theirs.

It was a fine July day, noon, when the warning alarm sounded in the monitoring room. The screen flashing the warning was on the top row and the camera was from an area in the northwest corner of the ranch. The code flashing on the screen, "Unscheduled Cattle Loading Detected".

Lake   Doomsday Clock 11:59:59

On a different screen, bottom row, a different warning flashed. Low level, "Unscheduled Gate Opening". No camera there, just an electronic beam broken when the gate was opened. Three trucks pulled thru the opening, one of the men got out of his truck, relocked the gate, got back in his truck and the convoy resumed its path towards the compound. The warning light stopped, nobody noticed it in the control room.

The two warnings were related. It was part of a coordinated attack by two rustling groups waiting for the world to enter a chaotic stage where the rule of law would face temporary suspension in America and outlaws and thugs could move in and takeover big, sparsely populated ranches.

The first group was rustling 200 head of cattle right now. That might draw some attention. All the men involved with that operation had combat experience with the Mexican drug cartels. They were confident they could handle four hick Ranchers and a few employees.

The second group, also cartel veterans, were headed to the main compound to take over the ranch. They hadn't decided if they would kill everybody or just enslave them. They were the "A" team and supremely confidant.

Joyce, Joycetta to her Mom, checked the screen in the monitoring room. The room was manned three times a day for an hour, and warnings and video footage from the previous 8 hours were checked. It was fortuitous for the "Four Square Ranch" that the initial warnings happened during one of the three manned daily times.

She zoomed in on the four semi-trucks, each with a large sleeper and a cattle trailer. Behind the semis was a Dodge 3500 dually pulling a long toy hauler.

Each trailer probably held 50 head of cattle. They had an unwritten rule, a weight limit, of 50,000 pounds per trailer. How much could 200 cows be worth? $400-$500K, an approximate value based on current prices, supply and demand.

Lake   Doomsday Clock 11:59:59

The big payoff would come in selling the remaining 10,000 head of cattle in the months to come as food shortages would lead to starvation. The rustlers stood to make millions of dollars in the next 12 months.

Joyce followed protocol, contacted Heath who had stopped laughing long enough at Dan to come to the control room.

Heath checked out the video and was immediately concerned. This was a brazen daylight rustling operation. 200 head of cattle were being rounded up and loaded.

He called Eddie.

He said, "Eddie, we have a group of rustlers loading up 4 big haulers, about 200 head, right now on the north-western pasture."

Eddie responded, "I'm on it. I'll take the ultra-light, it's only about 15 nautical miles up there. It will take me 20 minutes to do a pre-flight check, take off, check it out and contact you guys. Those guys aren't going to disappear in 20 minutes."

Heath said, "I think we'll head that way. They've got to be confronted and the sooner the better. Better to stop them before they have our cows in the truck and maybe topple over in a stupid attempt to get away, kill a bunch."

Eddie, "Makes sense. I'm at the hanger now, starting my pre-flight. I'll contact you when I have eyes on the bad guys. Are you contacting the game warden?"

Heath responded, "Can't get thru. We only have service thru our local cell towers covering the ranch. We're using backup power now. The electricity has been cut since yesterday. Don't know what's happening in the outside world."

Heath added, "Eddie, load that revolver with live bullets before you leave, just in case…"

They both laughed and the connection was quickly ended.

Heath contacted Dan and Andrew, told them what was happening. The rest of the family heard the news and hopped into action. They were self-sufficient. Everybody had a job to do.

The men rustling the cowboys didn't care about the animals. They were in it for the money.

They had spent time choosing this ranch. In part because of the isolation, and the bios on the websites didn't list military experience. College graduates, soft men, educated, but not accustomed to hard dirty work.

Late last night they'd parked close and crossed a neighboring ranch, cut the fence and driven on the Four-Square Ranch road. They'd unloaded their ATV's early in the morning.

They'd used google maps to locate holding pens in an isolated area. They figured at some point they'd be spotted, but they felt capable of fighting off a group of greenhorns without law enforcement backup.

They swarmed around the herd in the ATV's, driving them into the pens. There were 12 of them and 8 ATV's. One of the lookouts caught sight of the drone. It was programed to fly in an effective pattern and not to avoid criminals. Eventually the drone was shot down. The bad guys hoped it wasn't a live feed drone.

Eddie was airborne, flying a Challenger II Special from Quad City. 300-foot takeoff roll, 95 MPH cruise speed and a 26-foot wingspan. It was light and maneuverable.

Eddie was a cautious. His job was to spot the Rustlers and let them know they were being tracked. Game up, pack up and go home. He was talking to Heath the entire time.

Eddie said, "I can see the semi-trucks. I'm going to circle around and look from the other side."

Heath, "Be careful. We lost the drone. Don't know what happened. Could have been shot down."

Lake   Doomsday Clock 11:59:59

Eddie said, "I'm at 4,000 feet and I'm staying a mile away from the loading pens. How long before Dan and Andrew arrive?"

Heath said, "20 minutes or so."

Eddie said, "There is a girl running from the toy hauler. She looks like she's running away."

Heath spoke, "Eddie, it's not your mission to rescue this girl. Don't move any closer. Just keep us informed of the rustlers. Okay?"

Eddie responded, "I got you."

The plane circled twice more and Eddie kept watching the girl run desperately down the dirt road. In four minutes, she'd come about a half mile.

He moved in a bit lower, dropping to 2,000 feet and making his loop around the holding pens at ¾ of a mile. The girl was running hard and Eddie watched an ATV break off and head down the road in the direction of the girl. She didn't know the bad guys were after her,

Eddie spoke into his mic, "Going a little lower to try and distract this bad guy and give the girl a chance."

Heath said, "Not worth it Eddie. Back off. We'll help the girl after we stop the rustlers."

Eddie said. "No can-do boss. It's not in my nature to abandon a damsel in distress."

Heath turned to Joyce and said, "I'm out of here. Call one of the old men over to cover for me. Eddie is going to get himself shot down. I'm taking a walkie talkie so I can hear what's happening."

Eddie circled back around and came up behind the flying ATV. He came so low the wheels of the ultra-light almost touched the head of the rustler.

The sudden noise and rush of the plane flying over startled the rustler, Chad. Chad locked up the brakes skidding to a stop and took out his sniper rifle. An old Spanish Mauser sniper rifle, accurate to about 600 yards and using a 7.92 X 57 mm cartridge. The round has a spin rate of 1 rotation every 9.45 inches which gives it excellent penetration. The cartridge was loaded with 12.7 grams of propellant and when fired, traveled at a rate of 800 meters per second or 2600 feet per second.

The speed of sound is 343 meters per second or 1,087 feet per second. Since sound travels much slower than a speeding bullet, you never hear the shot that kills you. If you see a puff of smoke from a rifle barrel that's aimed your way, you'd better be ducking.

Eddie banked the plane and turned back to pass over the rustler again. The man was standing next to his ATV with a large bore rifle and a scope.

Eddie threw the plane into a turn and saw the smoke come out of the barrel of the gun. It missed. Eddie's plane climbing hard now, turning away from the rustler. The engine RPM's maxed out. He'd made a big mistake in not even considering these guys had sniper rifles.

Chad, the rustler, lined up the engine of the climbing airplane thru his scope and squeezed the trigger.

Eddie could hear the engine scream as he passed thru 2,000 feet, and suddenly it went quiet. The engine was dead. He'd been hit. SOB!

Eddie didn't panic. He looked at the altimeter. He knew he had a glide ratio of 9:1. If he was a mile high, he could glide 9 miles. But, he wasn't a mile high. He was at 1800 feet. 1800 X 9 = 16,200 feet, divided by 5,280 feet = 3.1 miles. He was in trouble. He set the controls for a maximum glide path and keyed the radio mic.

Eddie said, "Mayday, Mayday! I've lost power and will land at the furthest point from the conflict. 1800 feet when I started my glide. Heading due north."

The four-old grandpas had arrived and were monitoring the situation. Bob, Chuck, Roy, and Lance, listening to their boys handle some modern-day rustlers.

Lake   Doomsday Clock 11:59:59

Bob spoke first, "You milk that glide for as long as you can Sonny boy, but put down in the flattest possible spot."

Eddie said, "I got it Pops. Make sure somebody heads this way."

Bob said, "We rescue you first. It's called prioritizing. Still got a mission, just changed a bit."

Roy said, "Hot dog, a mission. We've got some excitement, just like old times fellas."

The others agreed it was good to feel a little adrenaline for a change. Old friends, the four of them.

Joyce said, interrupting the feel good and nostalgic moment, "A drone has spotted three trucks flying United Nation and Mexican Flags headed our way."

Chuck said, "How far away?"

Joyce replied, "About 15-20 minutes away. Maybe 10 miles."

Lance said, "I'll go help the kids. You three deal with the morons rolling up on an armed fortress driving pickups and packing a few long guns and handguns."

Chuck added, "Let's roll out the HUMVEE's and put on a small show of force. Let them decide how they want this to end."

Eddie was reading out his altitude, "1200 feet, 1,000 feet, 800 feet, 600 feet, 400 feet, I'm going down."

Bob said, "Stop being so dramatic. You're doing a landing without power."

Eddie said, "200 feet. I'm going to focus on landing now."

Bob said, "Good idea. Heath is on his way and knows where you're putting down. He'll contact Dan and Andrew. They'll pick you up and then you four need to deal with the rustlers. Oh, and Lance is headed your way with a HUMVEE. Land easy son, don't jam the brakes."

Lake   Doomsday Clock 11:59:59

Which is what Eddie did, landed smoothly, but hit the brakes too hard, pitched forward and busted his nose. Blood everywhere.

He unbuckled, opened the door and stepped out. His foot found a fresh pile of cow manure.

Eddie said, "Bullshit."

Wiped his shoe off and headed for a clump of trees 100 yards away. First rule of evasion, hide. Don't let the enemy see you. He couldn't hide the plane, but he could make sure if the rustler who shot him down came looking for him, he'd make it difficult.

He wiped his bloody, and still bleeding nose with a rag. He'd picked up his Clint Eastwood handgun, a Smith and Wesson model 29, .44 caliber, two bottles of water, plus an emergency kit with energy bars and a first aid kit.

Chad wasn't a happy rustler. He'd joined this group at the last minute as a local Americano guide. He'd had a small drug problem several years ago, lost his job, couldn't pay his drug tab and became a facilitator for the cartel just to stay alive.

He'd started life as an adult with dreams of being a rodeo star. Rodeo was his life, the next Cody Jesus. He'd drive from Texas to Wyoming, back to New Mexico, all within a week just to compete. Ride Bulls, 8 seconds, the ultimate adrenaline rush in his opinion.

He'd torn up a shoulder and a knee riding in a Podunk rodeo, small town, lousy rides, and a small purse. He'd gotten careless and hurt. Ended up needing three surgeries, a big hospital bill and hooked on pain killers. Turned to illegal drugs when the prescriptions stopped flowing. Lost his job, a story told 100,000 times in America.

Now he was in bigger trouble. His job was too retrieve the girl, not shoot down a plane with a college educated city boy at the controls. He'd lost the girl in the excitement of the cowboy versus plane battle.

His cartel boss was very clear on the walkie talkie radio. Find the girl, kill the pilot, do both and you'll live. Do only one and the boss would shoot you on sight. Do neither and your living family tree will be uprooted and placed in Boot Hill as fertilizer.

He had followed the path of the plane going down, it took him 10 minutes to locate the aircraft. He carefully approached, hoped to find a dead or unconscious body, found neither.

Thought about where he might go if the roles were reversed. Noticed the grove of trees and headed that way, chambered a round, moved the safety to off and started walking.

Dan and Andrew were behind the careless Chad, the rustler, the drug user. Chad was focused on the grove of trees and his stealthy approach. Tunnel vision. Completely oblivious to the sounds two men made creeping up behind him. The earbuds in his ears banging heavy metal music didn't help.

Eddie was watching from behind two fallen logs. He wasn't sure if Dan and Andrew could see him, but his job was to stay out of the line of fire. He thought about what to do next and decided to distract the rustler by giving up without being seen. This might allow Andrew to get close enough to the rustler to convince him to surrender without a fight. Dan wasn't the stealthy one, so he was following 20 yards behind and watching their backs.

Eddie cleared his throat and said, "Hey, I give up. Don't shoot me."

Chad grinned, he had the little turd, "Okay Senior, show your face."

Eddie said, "Did you shoot my engine?"

Chad said, "Yep. If I shoot down four more airplanes, I'll be an "Ace".

Lake   Doomsday Clock 11:59:59

Andrew, placing the barrel of his M4 Carbine, 5.56 X .45mm NATO cartridge, speed of 2,970 feet per second, gently brushing against the back of Chad's neck.

Andrew sniffed the air, and said, "Did you just poop your pants?"

Chad sighed, "Oh man. Please, I'm in deep trouble."

Eddie stepped out of his hiding place, and said, "You and Dan, brothers, Ace."

Andrew had to smile.

Dan said, "Maybe we'll just let him shoot you Eddie, then negotiate."

Chad said again, "Guys, let's make a deal."

Andrew said, "Place the gun down, slowly. Then maybe we'll talk."

Chad took a big breath. Slowly bent down, laid the gun down, sat down and cried.

Sometimes tears are all that's left when you realize how badly you've screwed up in life.

Dan gave him 5 minutes to cry, called him a snowflake. Picked him up and did a frisk job that basically involved picking him up by the ankles and shaking him like a pecan tree. One handgun, two knives, and a pair of brass knuckles fell out. Dan left a pair of shriveled nuts attached.

Then they talked.

Dan said, standing over Chad, "Short version sonny boy, no extra words."

Chad gulped, started talking, "There are 11 rustlers. Counting me, 12. 8 ATV's, now 7 and 4 lookouts. We want 200 head of cattle, but we have a hard stop time at 1:30. There is a group of three trucks, 9 guys, going after the main house and capturing the command center. That attack is supposed to be beginning at 1:00.

Lake   Doomsday Clock 11:59:59

We've also got 6 chicks in the toy hauler, sex slaves picked up in Canada, imported from China and Mexico, I think. None of them speak a word of English.

The cartel wants your ranch, the land because of the isolation and the livestock for food. They seem to know something is happening right now around the world. Like total chaos is hitting and law enforcement doesn't exist here.

They're going to kill my family if I don't return with the pilot and or the girl who ran away."

Eddie walked over to Chad, placed a hand on his shoulder as if to comfort him and kneed him in the privates.

Chad fell to his knees, rolled over on his side in a fetal position, panting and coughing.

Andrew said, "For crying out loud Eddie. Why did you do that?"

Eddie replied, "He shot down my plane. He could have killed me."

The sound of an approaching ATV diverted their attention from their prisoner. Heath showed up. Two minutes later Lance drove up in a HUMVEE.

Everybody exchanged stories. Chad sat alone. Reflecting, not sure what to do or say next. He was screwed any way this went down. The cartel had firepower and experienced people. The ranchers weren't as green as they'd been led to believe. They didn't seem concerned about anything Chad told him, and they didn't seem careless or stupid. He was missing a piece of the puzzle and he couldn't figure out what piece, but it was important.

Chapter 33

Sun Tzu says, *"The art of war teaches us to rely not on the likelihood of the enemy's not coming, but on our own readiness to receive him; not on the chance of his not attacking, but rather on the fact we have made our position unassailable."*

Back at the control room and at the main house, preparations were under way to repel any attempt the bad guys might make. Everybody who was out working on the ranch was warned, take cover, lie low, do not engage.

The four main houses were evacuated along with the houses for temporary workers. Everybody collected in the big house. They went down to a storm shelter. Food was served, a DVD was playing and the ladies prepared for the wounded, because there would be casualties. Their men were fighting to protect their families. This was a case where you either killed the enemy or be killed. But, they believed in even helping those who tried to hurt them. Love thine enemies. Body bags were available for those who refused to surrender and chose to check out.

The house was almost fire proof. Most of the outside was metal siding, metal studs, walls were ¼ inch steel plate covered by drywall, and a metal roof.

The 200-yard driveway leading to the house was lined with trees, all close enough together that once you entered the driveway you either went forwards or backwards, no turning around.

Traffic barriers had popped up to protect the house from ramming or a crazy suicide bomber. Prepare for the worst, hope for the best.

Roy and Bob, body armor on, weapons fully loaded, went out in the HUMVEE to confront the group of trucks approaching from the south. Chuck took up position in the sniper's nest perched atop the main house. Several other grandsons and granddaughters and long term loyal employees were positioned in a 150-degree arc, a sniper and a spotter on two-person teams. The idea was to create a saturated field of fire without shooting at each other. Pin the enemy down by leaving them exposed on one side. Force them to make a choice, surrender or die.

Roy and Bob hung a white flag on the HUMVEE. They found the small convoy 3 miles from the main house.

They stopped and waited, out in the open, clearly inviting a meeting. The flag flapping lazily in the light breeze.

The trucks stopped, two stayed still, the third one drove up slowly.

The leader opened the passenger door and stepped out. Roy opened his passenger door and stepped out as well.

They met in the middle. The bad guy snapped a salute, he was wearing a UN uniform with a blue UN helmet.

Roy didn't return the salute for various reasons. He said, "How can I help you?"

The man said, "I'm General Garcia with the UN. Your farm has been confiscated for meat production. The world is at war and the UN needs to feed people. I appreciate your cooperation. We will give you and your family one hour to gather some belongings and leave or else?"

Roy said, "I'm going to quote General Mattis, an old friend, "I come in peace. I didn't bring artillery. But I'm pleading with you, with tears in my eyes: If you screw with me, I'll kill you all."

General Garcia calmly said, "One-hour Sir, or you and your family will die."

Roy turned and briskly walked back to the HUMVEE. Bob reached out and tossed the white flag to the ground, popped up an American flag in its place. They headed back to the main house. Sometimes a conflict can't be avoided. Fight to win. Be prepared, yesterday, not today or tomorrow.

Sun Tzu, *"So in war, the way is to avoid what is strong, and strike at what is weak."*

The idea is to avoid a fight. Make the enemy give up. Create so much chaos they go home.

They were fighting on two fronts. North, 11 men against 4 warriors and an old veteran. South, 9 guys versus 3 ornery old veterans and a few savvy grandkids.

They talked via walkie talkie and came up with a plan, one they hoped would discourage the enemy and encourage them to go find a weaker victim.

Chad, the rustler, agreed to help. They got a bit of blood on Eddie, took enough gory pictures on Chad's phone to make it look like he had killed him.

The women being held against their will in the toy hauler complicated matters. Nobody was watching them, so it was possible to create enough chaos, release the cattle, disable the ATV's and Semi trucks and take the hostages away from the bad guys.

Complicated plan with only five good guys to pull it off and one unreliable rustler.

Chad's job was too return to the rustlers with phone pictures and a story about how the pilot was dead, but the girl had gotten away.

Lance took off on the ATV, going after the girl who got away. 45 minutes had passed, and a drone was tracking her from a distance.

Heath and Andrew had the dangerous job. Wait for Chad to open the gate and start a stampede and then they would attach grappling hooks to the opposite rails and open the holding pen to allow the cows to escape.

Eddie's job was to race in with the HUMVEE and somehow convince 5 girls who didn't speak a word of English to jump in with him.

It wasn't a perfect plan. The biggest concern was part one, relying on Chad, he was an unknown, now a reluctant spy.

Chad noticed how, at least after Dan roughed him up a bit and Eddie rang his family jewels, the guys treated him with respect and didn't threaten him. The said if he failed to execute the plan and told the cartel about them, he was on his own. They didn't smile when they told him this part.

Eddie reluctantly gave up his prized .44 Magnum, but now loaded with blanks for Chad.

The rustlers were confident and a bit arrogant as they went about their business of rounding up cattle. The shipping pen held about 150 and the cows were restless. A small herd of 25 or so were approaching. The lookouts were focused on the task at hand, filling up the pens.

Chad had sold the story and now the boss wanted the plane as well. Chad convinced him the plane would be there for a long time and the girl who was running, could, well, run forever and not leave the ranch. They had time to find her, toss her back in with the rest of the toy hauler trash.

Colin Powell, *"No battle plan survives contact with the enemy."*

The plan fell apart within seconds. Chad fired his gun in the air. The cattle stampeded. The rustlers turned their guns on Chad.

Within seconds the cattle had moved between Chad and the other rustlers. Chad pulled off a quick thinking move. He held the gun away from his head, pulled the trigger and committed suicide. Fell on the other side of the fence, away from the stampeding cattle.

The remaining rustlers, now ignoring the dead Chad, managed to turn the cattle back towards the holding pen. However, Heath and Andrew had pulled the back fence down and blended in with the rustlers.

Everybody started shooting their pistols in the air to stop the herd.

Lake   Doomsday Clock 11:59:59

The cattle, all 175 of them by now, went thru the pen and out the other side. The rustlers finally realized what was happening, tried to give chase. Only three of the ATV's headed towards the cattle.

In the chaos and confusion, Chad restarted his ATV, because his gun was loaded with blanks and his acting job of suicide only fooled the rustlers. He quickly joined Heath and Andrew following the three rustlers.

The three rustlers on ATV's stopped to regroup and wait for their friends to catch up, help them form a plan to move the cattle back into the pen.

Heath, Andrew, and Chad arrived, guns drawn, handkerchiefs covering their nose and mouth to block the dust and help disguise their faces, blend in with the rustlers.

Handkerchiefs down now, surprised looks, reality quickly set in.

Heath said, "Gentlemen, and I use that term loosely, drop your weapons."

Andrew said, "You've been waiting all your life to say that."

Heath said, "Correct, I have!"

The rustler leader, now very pissed because their timing and plan was shot to hell looked at Heath, Andrew and Chad.

Rustler leader said, to Chad, "You're dead. With my own eyes, I saw you shoot yourself."

Chad pointed his 44 Magnum at "El Jefe" or the leader. Pulled the trigger and watched him fall off his ATV, laying on the ground, moaning.

Chad laughed, "Get up snowflake, it's loaded with blanks."

Dan broke the silence, "Did you poop your pants?"

El Jefe didn't understand why the four gringos laughed so hard.

Lake   Doomsday Clock 11:59:59

They hogtied the three individually and then lashed them back to back to back. Punctured the gas tank on each ATV and then headed back to the remaining 8 rustlers. Now it was four versus eight.

Heath looped around and away from the group. His job was different. The rustlers sensed the dynamics had changed and were watching the ATV's approach.

They'd watched from a distance as three of their group were tied up. Confusion kept them from reacting.

Andrew raised a white flag, waved it back and forth. A universal sign you want to surrender or call a truce and talk.

The remaining men weren't hard core. They were with the group for different reasons. Most of them either had a past drug problem, a debt to repay, a relative with a debt to repay or just wanting a job.

They found a dirty t-shirt, semi white and raised it in the air.

El Jefe Junior walked out to meet Andrew. They met in the middle, about 150 yards from each group.

Andrew nonchalantly said, "Nice day for a picnic."

El Jefe Junior laughed, "Nice day to load some cattle."

Andrew smiled, "Look, I understand you came here to rustle some cattle. Take what isn't yours. My job, and we're good at it; stop you partner."

El Jefe Junior said, "We were told you guys were college softies."

Andrew laughed, "Maybe. But we were raised by Korean Veterans, Army Rangers. We learned to survive on our own from the time we were 8. We hunted from the time we were 6. Moved cattle to summer pastures for 2-3 months in our teens. Fended for ourselves. Dude, you guys aren't anything to us."

El Jefe Junior asked, "How's my boss?"

Andrew said, "Rubbing asses with his close friends and not going anywhere. Look, be smart, live to fight another day. Regroup, comeback, try to kick our asses again. We have too many weapons."

El Jefe Junior, spreading both arms wide, said, "I appreciate you trying to leave me a way out. But, if I go back without cattle and empty trucks, I'm dead."

Andrew sighed, "I'm going to help you. I have a guy out there in a sniper's nest. He's got a Barrett M82 50 caliber sniper rifle, fires a 50 Browning Machine Gun cartridge, 12.77 X 99 mm NATO round. Damn round is twice the length as a dollar bill is wide, think about that Chief. Travels 853 meters per second, effective range of 1800 meters, over a mile. He's 800 meters out there. Whatever he shoots at will be hit within a second. Care for a demonstration?"

El Jefe Junior said, "If I go back with empty trailers, we all die."

Andrew said, "Let me solve that problem, okay?"

He held up 4 fingers and within a second the boom of the 50-caliber echoed across the pasture. Hit the first semi, engine compartment, a little steam, the engine stopped immediately.

The second, third and fourth shots followed. Four dead semis'. No cattle hauling today.

El Jefe Junior said, "I'd admire you're style cowboy. I don't think you're very smart. My bosses will be pissed."

Andrew said, "Now my guy is going to shoot your ATV's. You're going to rejoin your group, climb in the 1-ton truck we left you, pull the toy hauler and go home. Also, the group attacking our compound, you guys are lucky. You got the "B" team. They got the "A" team, the old retired Rangers. Those guys have been drooling, waiting for one last fight."

Lake   Doomsday Clock 11:59:59

El Jefe Junior said, "We will leave now. My guys won't be happy. Tell Chad he's dead. What about my three guys out there?"

Andrew replied, "They're mine. I'll pass along your message. One last thing, the girls in the toy hauler. They're under my protection now. I have them. Go now, tell your bosses you ran into a group of 100 crazy cowboys, or better yet, run to Canada. If I catch you or your boys on "Four Square Ranch" land again, Sir, we will kill you and that's not a threat, but a promise."

El Jefe Junior walked back to the group. Heath fired a warning shot near their feet to move them along. They were all armed. None of them twitched, the 50-caliber demonstration convinced them they were no match for the college boys.

They didn't kill the ATV's either. They needed them to haul everybody back to the Ranch house.

El Jefe Junior and his band of highway robbers quickly walked back to the pickup, defeated, pissed and the bravado on display earlier was gone. They were sure they'd enjoy an easy victory over soft college boys.

Andrew returned to the group, told them what he'd said and off they went to round up the 3-naked rustlers left in the dirt, and covered with cow pies.

Lance didn't have any problem talking to the girls. English is spoken all over the world. These women were victims, not dumb and two spoke a dialect he'd picked up in Korea.

They were eager to leave the cartel, the violence and sex abuse. They quickly found the girl who ran, thanks to the drone keeping her in sight. She saw her friends and climbed right into the HUMVEE.

They all met up where the three cartel members were left. Everybody had a different idea how to deal with the three.

The women wanted to castrate them, splay them out and cover them with honey or raw meat, leave them for a day or two, see how they did with the wildlife. Nobody could

Lake   Doomsday Clock 11:59:59

come up with a logical reason why not, but humanitarian reasons forced them to decline the plan.

Heath decided they needed to take them back to the house, let the old men question them, alone. They might provide valuable information about future cartel plans. Better to have them and let them go, faraway, then to wished they'd kept them to ask a few questions.

They loaded the prisoners into the HUMVEE, shackled, still naked, a little humiliation can help compliance. Andrew reminded them the "Four Square Ranch" was not a signee of the Geneva Convention. And yes, they were prisoners of war.

The girls were a different problem. They needed to be handled with kid gloves. They were sex slaves, abuse victims. They would need other women to help them, talk to, find a way to help them recover and cope with trauma.

They took off, a 20-minute ride. Lance and Heath, along with the three prisoners in the HUMVEE. The 6 women and 3 guys on ATV's, riding, thinking, reflecting on the events.

They programmed a drone to follow the pickup and toy hauler to make sure the remaining 8 cartel members left the ranch proper.

As the convoy, now 11 ATV's and a HUMVEE approached the main ranch they noticed smoke rising.

Lake   Doomsday Clock 11:59:59

Chapter 34

It was "A" team versus "A" team.

Trouble started as soon as Roy and Bob turned the HUMVEE around and headed home. Small arms fire pinged off the HUMVEE frame and back window.

The tires were military grade run flats and the glass was bullet resistant with a rating of UL 752 level 8, able to withstand 5 hits from a 7.62 mm bullet.

The number of hits on the HUMVEE became non-existent after the three trucks started following them, because shooting from a moving platform is tough, not like in the movies. It didn't help that they were bouncing over dirt roads.

The cartel led by the pseudo UN General Garcia followed at what they considered a safe distance, 800 yards.

Chuck, up in the tower was using the M24 military sniper rifle. It has the "long action" bolt version of the Remington 700 receiver, but is chambered for the short action 7.62 X 51 mm NATO cartridge. It can be reconfigured for substantially larger cartridges.

Cartridges are described by, case type, diameters of different parts of the bullet, case length, and case capacity. How much powder will it hold. A grain is 1/7000 of a pound, takes 7000 grains to make a pound. A cartridge with 250 grains will have an effective firing range longer than the same cartridge at 200 grains.

Chuck had reconfigured the M24 to use .338 Lapua Magnum ammunition, with 250 grains. The same cartridge used by the British military to establish the new record for longest confirmed sniper kill at 2,707 yards, or 1.5+ miles.

Chuck waited until they were 1200 yards away to shoot the engine in the lead truck.

The HUMVEE was ready to turn into the tree lined driveway.

Lake   Doomsday Clock 11:59:59

The convoy stopped and Chuck took out the other two trucks. This was a dangerous strategy, but one they'd discussed. Now the enemy had no way to leave except on foot. Surrender, slink away in the night, or die moving forward.

They chose a different strategy.

RPG launchers came out.

By this time Bob and Roy were back safely and taken up positions to defend the family.

The walkie talkies were alive with chatter.

Bob said, "What the hell are they doing?"

Roy responded, "I don't think they read the manuals on RPG's."

Chuck laughed, "What's the maximum effective range?"

Bob answered, "About 200-400 meters. They have a maximum fuse of 4.5 seconds. They could get here."

Roy asked, "What rules are we operating under?"

Bob answered, "Full engage. Shoot to kill, no wounded. They forced this fight."

Chuck said, "I'm feeling a bit naked up here. I think I'll come down and find a new position."

Roy said, "Good idea Charlie. I'd hate for them to get in a lucky shot."

The first salvo of 3 RPG's shot out of the tubes, running solid for a few seconds, most just blew up when they ran out of fuel, looking for a target that didn't exist. One found a storage barn, exploded and the hay inside started to burn. Russian designed, RPG-7, 9 million plus made had a maximum range of 1.000 yards.

The horses were frightened by the noise. The chickens, after a quick outburst shut up, the goats and sheep moved as far away as possible.

Lake   Doomsday Clock 11:59:59

The group left in the storm shelter heard the booms and explosions.

One of the kids asked what was happening.

One of the older kids replied. "Our granddads are kicking butt."

Which was true.

The cartel members were disorganized and a bit confused.

El General said, "How did they shoot our engines so far away?"

First Lieutenant said, "They obviously have different weapons than what we were told and obviously the old men aren't quite so feeble as we were led to believe."

El General responded, "I need volunteers."

Nobody spoke.

El General spoke again, "I'm offering a battlefield promotion?"

Nobody spoke.

El General said, "I want one volunteer from each truck. If you don't give me a volunteer, I'll shoot the leader of the truck."

Three volunteers soon materialized. What choice did they have?

El General told them the plan, fan out, stay low, cover fire will be provided. Shoot and scoot.

Reluctantly they left the protection of the truck body, which was a misconception because the ammunition used by the "Four Square Ranch" would have torn right thru it.

The three Korean veterans were patient. They didn't fire immediately. They had 400 yards of ground the bad guys needed to cover before they were within range to effectively fire their weapons.

They waited. Let them move in 200-yards. The next time they popped up and cut loose with a 3-round burst, each received an overdose of 250 grains to the head. Shame to waste life in such a manner.

El General didn't want to die. He'd just lost 3 men. The remaining were eyeing him warily. Thinking, maybe it makes more sense to just shoot the crazy guy wearing a stupid blue helmet pretending to be a General than it is to die needlessly.

El General asked, "What do you all think?"

The Second Lieutenant stood up, waved a white flag, a handkerchief, a gift from his mother.

El General said, "What are you doing fool. I'm in charge here."

The Second Lieutenant turned and swiftly raised his pistol and shot El General in the head.

Second Lieutenant said, "Not anymore."

The new El General said, "Anybody disagree? Time to call it a day. We've been out planned, out gunned and out fought at every turn. Three old guys stuck it to us."

They laid their weapons down, stepped out in the open and laid down, face first, arms and legs spread.

Chuck said, a bit disappointed, "Damn, their giving up."

Chapter 35

The surrender went smoothly. They needed 4 body bags and now they had 5 prisoners. When the other group returned they ended up with 8 prisoners and 6 freed sex slaves.

The United States has a long history of sexual exploitation tolerance. From colonial times and indentured employees being forced into sexual relationships involuntarily.

Slavery and black men and women being forced into sexual relationships with slave owners and men of power.

Chinese women were imported to provide sex to the Chinese railroad workers, often hooked on opium and spent their entire life as a prostitute.

Modern times, children and women are lured to the United States with false promises of employment and then forced into a life of prostitution to pay off their debt. The best guesstimate is 14,500 to 17,500 women and children annually are forced into the sex trade.

The "Four Square Ranch" had 6 of them.

They heard the news about the suspected atomic blast at the G20 summit in Hamburg, Germany. This helped explain the 2-prong attack from the cartel.

The four dead cartel members were bagged and tagged. No place to send them. Heath dug a trench and buried them. Dan said a few words about their life. Even a bad guy deserves a simple funeral.

What to do with the prisoners? The "Old Men" made them watch the burial.

They blind folded them, lined them up, used Eddie's 44 Magnum and blanks again.

Bob said, "First one of you who tells me a true story about your orders from your bosses gets to live."

Nobody spoke.

Lake   Doomsday Clock 11:59:59

Bob went behind the first prisoner and pulled the trigger. They all jumped.

Bob said, "Holy mackerel, did you see those brains splatter. Next!"

They all started talking at the same time.

Dan said, "Who pooped their pants?"

The good guys all laughed.

They sat them down, they talked. Found out a onetime cattle buyer the month before wore a miniature camera and cased the ranch. The information seemed to indicate an easy mark, college educated ranchers, blended generation of families.

This was a well-financed and planned attack.

Life was still happening at the ranch. Eddie and his daughter went to pick up his ultralight. The one Chad shot forcing Eddie to make an unplanned landing. They had to remove the wings from the fuselage and winch the plane on a flatbed trailer. Three hours to retrieve the plane.

Chad was extended an olive branch. He'd started the day as an enemy, switched sides, and earned a small degree of respect and trust. His fake suicide was brilliant, quick thinking, and an Academy award performance.

He was given the choice, stay with them, take his chances; or they had an old 1996 Chevy farm truck, full tank of gas. His ex-wife and small child lived 200 miles away.

He drove away, headed back home, wearing a clean pair of boxers and an old pair of Wranglers. Eddie didn't wave goodbye.

The eight prisoners were a problem. They felt they had few choices. Shoot them, keep them locked up, or turn them free.

A person who can't play by a loosely constructed set of social rules is a burden to the hard-working person. If you want to take from others, what's not yours, we lock you up.

Lake   Doomsday Clock 11:59:59

Feed you three meals a day, give you basic medical care, a bed at night, exercise, a TV, a place to shop, books to read. That doesn't seem like a bad life, and it's expensive to the taxpayers. But you lose your freedom.

Shooting them seemed like an easy option. Dig a trench with a backhoe, find a volunteer to pull the trigger. Push them in, cover them up. The price? A little gas for the tractor, the cost of eight bullets.

Letting them go is fraught with risk. What if they come back with more guys? Bigger weapons? Now they know the enemy. Make a new plan, adapt, overcome?

The locked them up in an old underground cistern. A few didn't go willingly, nobody like to be in a cave. That was solved by wrapping them in plastic and lowering them thru the opening. No humans were hurt during this operation.

They "Four Square Ranch" gave them two tasks. They were to pick a leader. Somebody to negotiate their future, and the vote had to be unanimous. Their lives depended on compliance and a plan. Their choices were three, death, incarceration for life, or leave and assure us you won't return. Come back with a plan; one hour.

The ranch held a general council. Four generations, because everybody had a stake in the future.

The news filtering in from the outside via short wave radio was grim. Riots in the city, food shortages, no gas, no electricity, buildings burning, no emergency services, no plan.

What about the ranch? Could they run 10,000 head of cattle, take care of crops, chickens, sheep, goats, with about 50 people?

What was the new goal? Feed people? Feed themselves? Their neighbors? A brave new world?

After a spirited discussion, they decided to take it day by day. Nobody knew for certain what was happening across the globe. Give it a month, things might return to normal. Trains and trucking would resume. Cattle and crops would

Lake   Doomsday Clock 11:59:59

go to processing plants and feed the masses. Ranchers and cattle men feed the people. Risk takers, gamblers, the heart that pumps life thru America.

What farmers and ranchers need is a steady price. They don't need more loans. More loans just mean a higher payment to be made to the bank. The bank doesn't care because agriculture loans are guaranteed by the USDA. A defaulted loan means a forced sale to a big conglomerate. One more farmer kicked off their land.

The big conglomerate leases the land to a first-generation immigrant who wants a piece of the American dream willing to toil for pennies an hour. The farmer whose land has been in the family for numerous generations moves away. The rural town slowly dies. Self-sufficiency is lost. Happens everywhere.

Water wasn't a big problem. They had access to several large streams, holding ponds to collect rain water. They had graded the slope of the land to collect run off. Grazing rights and longevity of land ownership helped put their ranch near the top of the list for water rights.

They collected roof rainwater draining off barns and all homes. They had a water purification system to make drinking and cooking water.

Electricity was a different matter. They couldn't meet the needs of a large ranch on the solar, wind, and hydro they currently owned. They could meet their private houses requirements and it would be better if they consolidated houses. A/C was out, heat would need to be supplemented with firewood.

The cartel dudes were having trouble forming a census on leadership.

Bob decided to motivate them a bit.

He opened the hatch and said, "Incoming!" Tossing a smoke grenade into the cistern.

Lots of scream from below, lots of laughing from above. Lots of profanity below as they realized it wasn't a real grenade.

Bob opened the hatch again and shouted, "You'll have 5 minutes. Send me a leader."

Three minutes later a head popped out of the cistern. A leader.

They sat down at a long table located in the dining room of the main house.

Eight men and a woman on one side and the lone cartel member on the other.

Neither side spoke. The eight men sat with their arms folded. The woman, Jan, Chuck's wife sat up straight with her hands folded in her lap.

Finally, the cartel leader, Henry, cleared his throat and said, "What are your terms?"

Lance snorted, said, "Terms? There are no terms. You're not surrendering you moron, you're captured, a prisoner of war."

Jan spoke, using a soft, but firm voice, "Young man, we are trying to decide what to do with your group. I'm here because the men want to execute you. Do you understand?"

He sighed, "Yes Ma'am."

Jan spoke again, "Your group attacked our family unprovoked. You tried to steal our cattle. You fired weapons and RPG's at our house. You tried to kill all of us. Convince me you deserve to live?"

Henry took a few seconds to respond, "We are men, proud. We followed orders. We made bad choices. We believe the world is ready to fall apart. That's the only reason our bosses would send us on this mission. We want to live. We'd like to leave. We'll never come back."

Heath said, "I don't know what to do with them. Killing them doesn't seem right, but it's what they deserve for trying to kill us. I'm sure as hell not going to house you and feed you as prisoners."

Dan said, "You guys can't be trusted. We can't let you live here. We'd never sleep easy at night. Always wondering when you might return."

Jan said, "Here's what we're going to do Henry. We have semi's and we'll place all of you in a cattle hauler and drive you to the Canadian border. I suggest you keep going and find a new life and different bosses. If you ever return, the women will pull the trigger to shoot you Sir! Do I make myself clear?"

Henry said, "Yes Ma'am, thank you for sparing our lives."

They departed. Two of the grandkids had picked up one of the cattle haulers and returned to the main yard. The eight men were shackled and locked in the trailer. Two more grandkids liberally spread cow manure on the floor, for comfort and a soft ride.

Dan driving and Heath riding shotgun departed with the prison wagon. They had a 5-hour round trip ahead of them. It was almost 9 PM by the time they departed.

The dinner table was filled with a spirited discussion. The day's events were discussed, sliced and diced. The heroes were bigger, the villains were slain and the old men lived in glory one more time. They fell asleep with full bellies and only slightly concerned about tomorrow. They were self-sufficient yesterday, and today; tomorrow wasn't here yet.

The night passed, the control room with the drone cameras monitored all night. It just seemed like a prudent move.

The sun came up in the east. Bright, sunshine, the world's problems still existed. The "Four Square Ranch", slowly came to life.

There were cows waiting to be milked, eggs needed collected, animals to feed. Chores, everybody had a job.

Lake   Doomsday Clock 11:59:59

From the oldest of 85 years old to the 3-month-old great grandbaby, life was being lived. Two granddaughters were pregnant and there was much at stake for the families living on the ranch.

Animals were giving birth. Blood lines were extended, or ended. You took care of your animals because they provided you with food on the table.

Animals on the farm work. Cats catch mice, dogs warn of intruders, and nobody raises gold fish. It is in many ways an uncomplicated life, but harsh as well. Animals live and die, it is part of the life cycle.

Bob took a walk late in the morning. Went out to the family cemetery to talk to his dad and mom, visit the little girl they lost in the 70's to drugs.

Told his dad about the intruders yesterday, how they came close to losing the farm. Told his mom he loved her and cried a tear over the loss of their daughter. Life was complicated at times. You have wins and losses, good times and bad. He wasn't sure how many more days like yesterday his body would survive.

He walked back to the main house. Took a nap before lunch.

Heath was in the control room monitoring the drones. They'd rechecked the tapes from yesterday and realized they'd missed a warning. The second group approaching from the south that tripped the gate lock. They'd need to work on that part.

If the world went crazy others would want what they had.

His daughter Lacy said, "Daddy, it's been 24 hours since our warning yesterday. Do you want me to tape over the footage or keep it?"

He said, "Keep it rolling. Yesterday is history."

Johnny and Rachel's Story

Chapter 36

00:00

Denver, Colorado

Mercy Hospital

Love.

True Love.

Best love story in history or literature?

Romeo and Juliet? Two teenagers from feuding families, fall in love, marry. Juliet falls into a deep sleep, Romeo believes her to be dead and takes poison. He dies, Juliet wakes up and discovers Romeo dead. Tries to poison herself by kissing his lips, ultimately falls on a dagger. The

Lake   Doomsday Clock 11:59:59

two deaths unite the feuding families. A tragedy based on loss of life. Not true love.

Cleopatra and Mark Anthony? The tale of two people who fell in love at first sight, marry, become a powerful Egyptian couple. Their power outrage the Romans. During a battle Mark Anthony gets word of Cleopatra's death, fake news. Fake news isn't so new. He falls on his sword. Cleopatra takes her own life upon hearing the news. Again, a tragedy based on loss of life.

Lancelot and Guinevere? The knight and the Queen were unable to keep their hands off each other. This is part of the Arthurian legend. They resist, but finally succumb to temptation. King Arthur discovers the affair and Sir Lancelot makes a daring escape from her boudoir. Guinevere is condemned to burn to death and several days later Sir Lancelot, with his pants on this time, rescues her. Sir Lancelot lives out his days as a lowly hermit. King Arthur's power base is eroded. Queen Guinevere lives as a nun in Anbury where she dies. Love based on betrayal to a kingdom and infidelity. Not true love.

Tristan and Isolde? Isolde was the daughter of the King of Ireland. She was betrothed (think sex slave) to King Mark of Cornwall. Mark sent his nephew Tristan to escort her back. They fell in love. The affair lasted until King Mark found out, he forgave his wife, but banned Tristan from the country of Cornwall. Tristan moved to Brittany. He was attracted to Iseult of Brittany because of the name similarities. They married, but Tristan wouldn't consummate the marriage because of his true love for Isolde. Tristan fell ill and sent a ship for Isolde in hopes she could cure him. If the returning ship had white sails Isolde was coming to see him, if black sails she had not come. Upon seeing the white sails, Iseult lied to Tristan, telling him they were black, he died of grief. Isolde soon died of a broken heart. A twisted tale of love.

Paris and Helena? Helen of Troy and the Trojan War. Helen was married to Menelaus, king of Sparta. Paris, son of king Priam of Troy falls in love with Helen, kidnaps her and off they go to Troy. The Greeks launch a great flotilla

Lake   Doomsday Clock 11:59:59

of ships. Helen, the face that launched, 1,000 ships. Troy is destroyed. Helen returns to Sparta and lives happily ever after. Forced love and kidnapping is never true love.

Napoleon and Josephine? A marriage of convenience. He was 26, she was older and politically powerful. They both cheated, but still loved each other. Eventually they split when Josephine couldn't give Napoleon an heir. Love doesn't promote infidelity.

Odysseus and Penelope? Married, war separated them for 20 years. She resisted the 108 suitors trying to replace her husband. He resisted a beautiful sorceress's offer of everlasting life and eternal youth. This story comes close to true love.

Paolo and Francesca? Made famous by Dante's masterpiece, "Divine Comedy". Francesca is married to Paolo's brother, a brute. She falls in love with Paolo and takes him as a lover. They read the story of Lancelot and Guinevere and fall deeper in love. The brother discovers them together and kills both. Love shouldn't tear a family apart.

Scarlett O'Hara and Rhett Butler? Civil War era story. Love versus hate. Passion versus fickle. They find lots of passion, unfortunately at different times. Mental health issues in this story.

Jane Eyre and Rochester? Two lonely people find love in friendship. Edward appears to be gruff, but is tender. Unfortunately, he hides the fact he is already married and Jane discovers this fact on their wedding day. She runs away. Later Edward's house catches on fire and his first wife dies and he is blinded. Eventually Jane returns and they find bliss. Love can't be found based on a lie.

Marie and Pierre Currie? Marie, unable to study in Poland because she was female traveled to Paris in 1891 to attend the Sorbonne. She met Pierre who wooed her and made several marriage proposals. They finally married in 1895. In 1898, they discovered the elements polonium and radium. In 1903, they were co-winners of the Nobel Prize in physics for discovering radioactivity. Pierre died in 1904 and Marie carried on his work, carrying on his memory. In 1911, she won a second Nobel Prize in chemistry. All for love. Not a bad story.

Queen Victoria and Prince Albert? Became the Queen of England in 1837. Married her first cousin Prince Albert in 1840. They had nine kids. Albert died in 1861 and Queen Victoria mourned for three years in seclusion. She continued wearing black until her death in 1901. This is a good love story as well.

Jesus Christ? God sent His only Son to die for our sins. He was crucified, suffered, died, and three days later rose to fulfill the scriptures. The best love story of all time.

Love is complicated. True love is rare.

Corinthians I, chapter 13 verses 4-8:

[4] Love is always patient and kind; love is never jealous; love is not boastful or conceited,

[5] it is never rude and never seeks its own advantage, it does not take offence or store up grievances.

[6] Love does not rejoice at wrongdoing, but finds its joy in the truth.

[7] It is always ready to make allowances, to trust, to hope and to endure whatever comes.

[8] Love never comes to an end.

Chapter 37

The alarm on Saundra's phone went off, Bob Seger, *"Hollywood Nights"*. She opened her eyes, it took a few seconds to orient herself. She was sleeping in an empty hospital room, fourth night in a row.

The world had gone ballistic in the last week. Electricity no longer flowed. No communications, no internet, gossip only. Like fake news was the only source. Filling stations were closed. Grocery stores had quickly sold out and now private security guards with itchy trigger fingers patrolled the parking lots.

She lived 25 miles away, her car was almost out of gas. She was stuck at the hospital, but taking care of newborn babies was her life. Her husband, Ronnie, was self-sufficient so she didn't worry about him. The world could come to an end and he'd still get up in the morning and take care of the animals and the crops on the small 10-acre farm they owned.

They were down to five babies in the maternity unit. Newborns who were available for adoption.

A judicial system whose wheels had stopped turning because of the electronic age. No electricity in Denver for a week. No servers, no records, so the courts closed for all but serious criminal matters. Looters weren't arrested anymore. Shoot at a policeman though and you got your butt thrown in jail.

Adoption agencies stopped picking up kids for placement because of legal questions created by lack of court documents. Thirty kids were in the newborn unit ten days ago; moms and dads took 25 to their homes. Now they were down to five, all healthy, almost two weeks old.

She wedged the door shut to her room. She was a mess, all of them were a bit tired and worn out from maintaining 12-hour shifts for almost 10 days without a break.

She looked in the mirror, still fit, average looks and height, dirty blonde hair, blue eyes, almost 50 years old.

Lake   Doomsday Clock 11:59:59

She washed her body with wipes. Water was for medical and drinking. The hospital electricity was supplied by diesel generators and the fuel supply was almost exhausted. They'd been holding meetings with administrators twice a day for 5 days.

Nobody had any answers. They'd discharged all the patients possible. The ones in ICU were being transferred to a long-term facility better equipped to handle a long period with no electricity.

All elective surgery was cancelled. Recovering surgery patients had been sent home as quickly as possible. They gave the patients a generous supply of pain medicine and antibiotics. Nobody had practiced a scenario like this one.

Saundra walked down to the nurse's station and heard laughter well before she arrived.

Everybody was in a room, 20 feet by 20 feet. It was the only place with A/C, courtesy of the diesel generator. The rest of the newborn ward was stifling hot in the July heat.

The remaining nurses were all there. Nick and Taylor were arguing about football. Who was the most important offensive player on the field? Quarterbacks? Wide Receivers? Kickers?

Nick swore he could kick a 54-yard field goal in college. Taylor swore his Dad was in Pro Football's HOF.

Andy, the old man, like Saundra, enjoyed tutoring the kids. A veteran nurse has been spit on, puked on, peed on, pooped on, bled on…and everything in between.

The guys were BS'ing and Kim and Kelly were holding two babies, now awake and needing a bottle. Kelly was a young nurse as well.

Kim was the true hero, not just a nurse. She volunteered at the hospital. A double heart transplant survivor. The first transplant lasted 19 years and now she was on her second heart. What a life to wear out two hearts and a need a third heart.

Lake   Doomsday Clock 11:59:59

Saundra asked Andy, "Why is everybody in such a good mood?"

Andy said, "Because in 15 minutes we get to go home."

Saundra laughed, just a little, "What? How am I getting home?"

Andy said, "While you slept, I performed a few miracles. An adoption foster care home in western Colorado has room. They've sent a plane and a nurse to pick up the fab five. And I got a message to Ronnie, he's out front, a stretch ATV, waiting for you."

She laughed, a big laugh, "A stretch ATV? The only thing stretched on that will be my butt riding behind my husband for an hour or so, 25 miles. Really? He couldn't drive the truck?"

Andy said, "You're going home. Look, the roads are not safe. That's 25 miles he rode, back roads, trails, to pick you up. It will probably take you 3 hours to get home, but you'll be home."

Over the next 5 minutes the young nurses and transplant volunteer said goodbye and headed home to new struggles and an uncertain future. Now it was just the two veteran nurses.

Andy said, "You want to stay and close up shop or you want me to do it?"

Saundra replied, "No, you go. How many miles do you have to ride?"

Andy had a mountain bike he often rode to work.

He said, "Eight, but most of it is thru a green belt. It might take me 90 minutes of easy riding. Okay, good luck, be safe."

They hugged and then Saundra was alone with five babies, three were hungry and the other two needed diaper changes.

The A/C cut off.

Lake   Doomsday Clock 11:59:59

Three minutes later two maintenance members showed up. Jack and Evelyn, each grabbed a crying baby and popped a bottle in their mouth. The room was quiet.

Jack quietly said, "Message from the bosses, abandon ship."

Saundra said, "What?"

Evelyn said, "Quarantine. If these babies aren't out of here in 10 minutes you can't leave. One of the last patients we admitted from an International China flight has a highly infectious disease."

Chapter 38

Same time, outside the hospital. The bright yellow Piper J-3 Cub turned on final approach to land at Mercy Hospitals small airplane strip and Helicopter pad.

Almost 20,000 J-3 planes were built between 1938-1947. Cheap, costing between $995 and $2,461. Empty weight of 765 pounds. Maximum takeoff weight of 1,220 pounds. 455 pounds of passenger, cargo, and fuel. Cruising speed of 65 knots, 75 mph, max cruise range of 191 nautical miles, 221 miles. Service ceiling of 11,500 feet. Powered by a Continental 4 cylinder, 65 horsepower power plant.

The Piper Cub holds 12 gallons of fuel and burns between 4-5 gallons per hour. 6 pounds per gallon, 72 pounds for fuel. 455 pounds minus 72 pounds equals 383 pounds available for passengers, supplies and five babies.

The flight from Gunnison to Denver had taken two hours. The distance by car is 191 miles,133 air miles.

Two passengers on board, male and female. 300 pounds between them, a nurse and an ex- Air Force pilot.

Rachel, the RN was alone, 35 years old, biological clock ticking, no suitors in sight. She really didn't have any potential friends. She hadn't dated in 10 years, since Johnny, her husband, walked out because she wasn't able to have kids. She never thought about intimacy anymore. Maybe a little the first year or so, but after that it just became easier to be alone and not complicate her life with a relationship.

Khalid, the pilot, was divorced with 2 boys, Jibril and Korey. His call sign was "Mustang", because he'd played football for Southern Methodist University in Highland Park, Texas.

The Cub was a forgiving plane and during WWII almost 80% of the military pilots received their initial training on this aircraft. The landing was smooth and Khalid taxied over to the fuel station.

Lake   Doomsday Clock 11:59:59

Rachel stepped off the plane and headed to the main hospital building 300 feet away. The lone Medivac maintenance guy rolled a 55-gallon barrel of avgas out to the tiny aircraft to refuel using a hand pump. None of the Mercy planes or helicopters had flown in three days because of fuel shortages. He'd siphoned the fuel in the barrel from a Bell 206 Air Ambulance this morning after hearing of the effort to rescue the five orphans. The lone pilot left on duty was in the basement, the dungeon.

Evelyn waved to get Rachel's attention and the two met by a side door. Evelyn led Rachel to the nursery.

Saundra was gathering supplies, formula, diapers, warming blankets, medicine, anything she could think of that five babies might need. It was a bit like throwing darts blind folded. Too much? Not enough?

They introduced themselves to each other as they multi tasked getting the babies ready for the trip.

Saundra asked, "Can you think of anything else? We must be out of the building in 3 minutes. Security will lock us down tight. The CDC designated our patient case from China as a Bio-Level 4."

Rachel whistled softy, "A level 4? Holy bananas!"

Saundra grimaced and responded, "The patient flew in on one of the last Air China flights from Wuhan. Sick as a dog. The CDC says they've never seen this flu variant and it's deadly. She isn't going to make it and nobody is supposed to know but three other patients on her floor are showing symptoms along with a respiratory tech. A nurse who worked with the patient during admitting left town on a flight to LA and nobody can locate her. We are in a load of trouble Sister."

Nobody spoke for 30 seconds. Finally, Jack said, "Let's roll these five little stinkers out to the ambulance. Fixed wing or rotary?" Jack served in the military as well.

Rachel said, "A Piper Cub."

Saundra laughed, "You are kidding, right?"
Lake   Doomsday Clock 11:59:59

Rachel said, "I'm not. None of our aircraft are flying. This is Khalid's personal plane. His toy, boys with toys."

Saundra, "How are you going to secure these babies?"

Rachel said, "The best we can. I'm going to sit in the back and surround myself with the kids for the two plus hour flight to Gunnison. The plane isn't perfect. Do you see a different option?" She was frustrated.

Rachel continued, "I had to jump thru hoops to even come here. Khalid was generous enough to leave his two boys and fly me here."

Saundra said, "We don't have a choice. We need to save these kids. Remember we have a level 4 quarantine situation here."

The four-started walking towards the bright yellow fixed wing Cub. They passed Khalid half way there.

Rachel said, "Where you going Khalid? We need to be airborne ASAP."

Khalid said, "A man has to take care of business." And continued walking.

Rachel said, "Find a bush. This hospital is under a level 4 quarantine."

Khalid laughed and said, "Okay. Let me go around the corner and water a bush."

The four continued towards the plane. Khalid rounded the corner to urinate and 30 seconds later the group heard a gunshot and Khalid yell.

Saundra pointed to Jack and Evelyn, they set their babies down, and headed back to the building to find out what happened. Rachel and Saundra hurried the last 50 feet to the plane. Then returned to pick up the two remaining babies.

They started loading the plane with supplies. Saundra suggested they wait until Khalid got back to load the babies.

Lake   Doomsday Clock 11:59:59

Jack and Evelyn rounded the corner and saw Khalid laying on the ground, moaning, clutching his right hand, blood pulsating, and bone showing. A frazzled security guard standing nearby.

Jack asked, "What happened?"

The security guard said, "This dude didn't stop when I ordered him. He just kept walking and gave me the finger. So, I shot his damn finger off."

Khalid moaned and said, "I told you I needed to pee. What an ass."

Evelyn said, looking at Khalid's hand, "He can't pilot the plane."

She looked at the rent a cop, and snarled "You just might have condemned five infants to death. This guy was going to fly them to safety."

Rent a cop whined, "How was I supposed to know?"

Jack had stepped inside the lobby to find a first aid kit.

He returned and said to Evelyn, "Go down in the dungeon and fetch Johnnie."

She rolled her eyes, "I get to wake up Mr. Happy, thanks."

The lobby first aid kit was woefully inadequate for a gunshot wound severing the middle finger.

Jack wrapped the stub and applied pressure. Tried to get Khalid to relax just a bit.

Jack said, "You know, there's an interesting story about the middle finger gesture."

Khalid spat, and said, "Don't tell me that bullshit story about the "Battle of Agincourt", and the French severing the middle fingers of English longbow men and it led to the saying, "pluck yew" from the defiant archers."

Jack laughed, "No, but that's a good story. I'll have to remember that one. What branch were you in young man?"

Khalid said, "Navy."

Jack said, "Good, this story is about the Navy."

Saundra came up and checked the dressing. She had rummaged thru a kit from the Bell helicopter ambulance and found a 400-mcg fentanyl lollipop for Khalid to suck on for pain relief. The fentanyl is absorbed quicker thru the mouth then a morphine needle into a muscle.

Jack said, "USS Pueblo January 23, 1968. Also called the Pueblo Incident or alternately the Pueblo Crisis.

The crew, 82 of them, 1 was killed during the capture, was held by the North Koreans for 11 months. These kids were abused and tortured during their captivity.

The North Koreans held staged photo ops for publicity and a few of the soldiers gave the finger each time. When the soldiers asked what it meant they told their captors it was a "Hawaiian good luck sign" like the shaka or hang loose sign.

Eventually the North Koreans caught on and the beatings intensified."

Khalid had slipped into a drug induced sleep.

Saundra said, "It was a great story Jack!"

Jack shrugged, "Thanks."

Chapter 39

Evelyn ran to the dungeon; the lockdown was imminent.

Johnny was dreaming. In his dream, he was married to his college sweetheart. They'd had two kids, traveled the world from posting to posting. The kids were air force brats. His wife was the Queen of the house. Everlasting love, true love.

Evelyn shook him. "Wake up Johnny. Wake up, emergency!"

Johnny quickly sat up, "What?"

Evelyn said, "We need you to fly 5 newborns to Gunnison."

Johnny shook his head, "Why do they need to go to Gunnison? Never mind. We don't have any fuel."

Evelyn said, "They have a plane here. The security guard shot the pilot's middle finger off. He can't fly the plane."

Johnny laughed, "Barny Fife shot somebody. I hope they take his gun away. What an ass. Okay, Saundra going with me? And you said plane. I don't fly planes. I'm a helicopter pilot."

Evelyn said, "Saundra isn't going with you. They bought their own nurse. You'll like this plane, bright yellow, cute."

Johnny said, "Oh man. A Piper Cub. I flew one of those on weekends going to the Air Force Academy."

Evelyn told him, "We're on a level 4 quarantine. They're locking the hospital down any minute. Nobody in or out."

Evelyn looked at the manila packet on the bed.

She asked, "Did you open it?"

He said, "Yes. Let me give you some advice. Don't marry a psycho German broad when you're stationed overseas, and have a couple of kids with her."

Evelyn responded, "Where is she now and how are the kids?"

Lake   Doomsday Clock 11:59:59

Johnny spoke in a low voice, "They moved to Hamburg, I haven't seen my kids in five years. Now, leave me alone, so I can get dressed."

Evelyn said, "I'm old enough to be your grandmother, get dressed, you don't have anything I want to see. Let's move sonny boy!"

The climbed the stairs and went thru the abandoned lobby. A guard was starting to lock the door with a heavy chain and a huge lock.

Johnny said, "Wait a minute Chuck. You got one more."

He stepped outside and walked over to Henry, AKA, Barny Fife. Grabbed him by the collar and drug him to the lobby door. Knocked on the glass, Chuck opened the door.

Johnny tossed him in, and said, "Put scumbag in the same room as the quarantined patient."

Evelyn couldn't help but admire his style.

Khalid stirred a bit. Johnny walked over to him.

He said, "Hey. Khalid, I remember you from Guard weekends."

Khalid said, "Are you flying the babies?"

Johnny said, "Appears. Anything I need to know?"

Khalid, "Yeah, the nurse is hot."

Johnny laughed, "Right. Do you have a flight plan?"

Khalid said, "Yes, it's in the Garmin. The fuel tanks are full, 12 gallons. You have enough to make Gunnison with a gallon or so to spare, but no screwing around, no scenic tours. I'm serious."

Johnny said, "I got it. Look, what are they going to do with you?"

Saundra replied, "Ronnie is rigging up a stretcher on a maintenance wagon. We're taking him to our ranch. I've got pain medicine, antibiotics, minor surgery stuff. He won't like the next few weeks, but he'll survive."

Johnny grabbed Khalid's good hand and squeezed. "Take care brother", He said.

Johnny and Jack walked towards the plane. Johnny started doing his walk around, checking everything on the plane.

Rachel stepped off the plane and their eyes met. Even ten years hadn't diminished the feelings of hurt and betrayal. Those feelings came rushing back in a heartbeat.

Rachel said, gruffly, "I'd like a different pilot."

Jack, who was maintenance, but an old Marine Sergeant said, "Ma'am, we'd all like something different. I'd like twenty years off my birth certificate, thirty pounds off the scales. He's the only pilot we have."

Johnny said, "Look Rachel, I know you're still mad. I know it's been ten years."

Rachel said, "Ten years, one month, three days and four hours."

Jack looked at Johnny, looked at Rachel, and said, "Do you two know each other?"

Johnny started to speak, "Please don't ask…"

Rachel cut him off, "Shut up Johnny. This man left me because I couldn't bear children for him, give him an heir. I was his wife!"

Jack said, "What do you want me to do? I can't kill him. He's the only pilot we have young lady."

Rachel said, "Can you castrate him with a dull, rusty knife?"

Jack looked at Johnny and said, "Man, you really screwed up. Look, you two need to stand each other for two hours to save five babies. Can you put aside the past bitterness, for 120 minutes, for five kids?"

Lake   Doomsday Clock 11:59:59

Evelyn walked up and placed the last bag in the plane. She'd stuffed Johnny's shoebox full of letters in among the cloth diapers.

They had no choice. A crisis can make strange bed fellows. Two people, former lovers, best friends, needed to put aside harsh feelings and bitter memories to help transport five innocent lives. Denver, Colorado, the mile-high city, elevation, 5.280 feet to Gunnison, Colorado, elevation 7,703 feet.

The Rocky Mountains, 53 peaks above 14,000 feet, the Piper Cub with a service ceiling of 11,500 feet. Johnny knew he couldn't fly over them so they would need to fly thru the valleys and over the smaller peaks.

The highest peak east of the Mississippi River is Mount Mitchell at 6,684 feet. The west is wild and high!

He familiarized himself with the route. Khalid had done a nice job of minimizing the turbulences on the flight back. The babies of course. Five little kids. Infants made him nervous. His heart was racing as the Piper Cub started its roll and needed almost 850 feet to take off, normal was 730 feet. Johnny knew they were over the maximum load weight by 50-75 pounds.

Seeing Rachel again had tossed his thought process out the window. Did he still love her?

Rachel was in the back of the plane with five sleeping babies. A miracle they were all asleep at the same time. The plane climbed gently and headed southwest. Home, Gunnison, a simple life. Seeing Johnny made her gut twist up. Did she still love him?

She moved bags around and a shoebox fell out and spilled its contents, letters. She recognized the handwriting on the envelope as belonging to Johnny. Each one addressed with her name, no address, each one with a date of June 4 and a different year. The latest one dated a little over a month ago. She counted, ten in all, one for each year.

Lake   Doomsday Clock 11:59:59

She had three choices, put them back and pretend they never existed, dump them out the plane window and watch them disappear forever, or read them and accept the contents and damage to her already scarred heart.

The babies were sleeping; Johnny seemed focused on flying. She opened the first envelope and began reading.

June 4, 2008

Rachel,

It's been a year since I left you. I wanted you to know I feel bad about hurting you so much.

I really want my own kids. I don't want to adopt. It's a man thing I guess.

I graduated from the Academy last month. (applause)

It looks like I'm going to Germany. I wish you were here with me to see the world. We talked about different postings and how much fun it would be to see Germany in the fall and go on excursions to other European countries.

I hope you are okay. I don't know if I can mail this letter or not. I still care about you.

Sincerely,

Johnny

Rachel slid the letter back in the envelope. What a piece of work this guy was, hoping she was okay. She opened the second letter.

June 4, 2009

Dear Rachel,

Wow, what a year. I'm married. Can you believe it?

Her name is Gretchen and she's a local girl, German I mean.

She cooks me dinner, we go to pubs and drink stout beer. It just seems surreal that a year ago I was living in the states and wondering where I was going. Feeling lost without you.

Here I am, living a good life with a wonderful woman.

How are you? I do think of you quite often. Did you finish nursing school? Are you seeing somebody?

I hope you are happy. I hope you found Prince Charming.

Sincerely,

Johnny

Rachel silently folded the letter and placed it back in the envelope. What a jerk. Maybe she could keep the letters. As kindling, to start a fire and throw the pilot out the window.

June 4, 2010

Dear Rachel,

OMG, I'm a Dad. Let me repeat that sentence. I'm a Father. A beautiful baby girl. Maria is perfect, 7 pounds, 4 ounces, blonde hair, blue eyes, I think. They keep changing colors.

You would be proud of me. I'm changing diapers, wet only of course. LOL

What a difference a year makes. I think I'm going to be posted to Japan in a few months. Gretchen isn't happy and has talked about staying here. I don't know how we can do that and live on my salary.

I hope your happy. I just know you finished nursing school and maybe found a dashing doctor to marry.

Sincerely,

Johnny

Rachel folded the letter and slid it back in the envelope. She didn't know what to think.

June 4, 2011,

Dear Rachel,

Hello from Japan. I'm working hard. The Japanese don't love us. Of course, we haven't behaved very well near the base. Sex attacks, rapes, drunk sailors, just a few ruined it for everybody.

My wife stayed in Germany along with our daughter Maria. I haven't seen them in three months and then it was only for 24 hours. I want to be a Dad, but the family must be together for that to happen.

Life goes on I guess. How are you doing? Still in Colorado?

It seems like a long year. Nothing else to report. I really miss us. That's crazy I know. But, you were my best friend.

Very Sincerely,

Johnny

Rachel folded the letter up and placed it back in the envelope. She didn't like that Johnny hurt, even though it was seven years ago. They were, at one time, best friends. She opened the next envelope.

June 4, 2012,

Dear Rachel,

I have a son. Francis, 8 pounds, 13 ounces. My heir, my namesake, a kid to carry on the family name.

I'm elated and deflated at the same time. Gretchen filed for divorce and is trying to garnish most of my wages.

Japan is a great country. History everywhere and I made a trip to China with a group of guys in the Spring. We spent a week touring the great wall of China and temples and dynasties. Wow…wow…wow. You would have loved it and snapped 1,000 pictures every day.

How are you? I miss our talks and how you call me out when I spouted out bullshit. You kept me honest.

Missing You,

Lake   Doomsday Clock 11:59:59

Johnny

Rachel didn't know what to think. She folded the letter back up and slid it back into its envelope.

June 4, 2013,

Dearest Rachel,

My wife won't let me see my kids. I have a family and no access. I don't know where to turn or who to talk to anymore.

I find myself thinking about God and remembering how strong your faith was in Him. I'm feeling dark right now. I saw your profile on Facebook. I'm a lurker. Maybe I'll start going back to Church. I need inner strength right now.

I really need a friend like you. I don't deserve you. I've come to realize a family is made from the pieces around you. Biological, adopted, step-kids, they are all the same. Too late for me.

I hope God has treated you kindly. I hope your life is fulfilled. I hope you found a family.

Love,

Johnny

A tear rolled down Rachel's cheek. She folded the letter up and slid it back in the envelope. The babies were still sleeping.

June 4, 2014,

Dear Rachel,

Are you sitting down? I'm sterile. I bet your laughing reading this admission. The man who left you because you couldn't have children can't father children.

God has a sense of humor. I deserve this affliction.

Gretchen has served me papers to have my parental rights terminated. It seems she wants to marry the biological father of the kids. I am stunned.

Lake   Doomsday Clock 11:59:59

The military made me take a complete physical and that's when I discovered my almost non-existent sperm count.

I have one more year of military service and have decided to not make it a career. The Air Force has been good to me. I've asked to be placed in the Colorado Air National Guard.

How are you?

I'm going to church and learning to give my troubles and concerns over to Him.

I was a fool to abandon you. Can you somehow forgive me?

Much Love,

Johnny

Rachel didn't know what to think or even feel. It hurt her to read how badly he was hurting. She folded and slid the letter back in the envelope and reached for the next year.

June 4, 2015

Dear Rachel,

I'm free from active military service and living in Denver. I know from Facebook you live in Gunnison.

My shame prevents me from contacting you.

I'm active in a small church near Mercy Hospital. I found a job as a helicopter pilot flying for the company that services this area.

My church has a community service to work with kids on the street. Denver is loaded with them, terrible home lives, abuse of every kind. Drugs, sexual exploitation. I'm coming to terms with my most grievous sin of abandoning you.

Can you ever forgive me? I have no right to even ask the question.

I hope you are enjoying your life. I know God is a big part.

Much Love,

Your Johnny

Rachel smiled, folded the letter and slid it back in the envelope. Reached for the next year. Johnny was a Christian and that made her heart sing with joy.

June 4, 2016,

God is good. I hope you are well?

I have decided not to date anybody. Not that I have since Gretchen, but a woman at the church asked me to dinner and I realized, hold on, I'm yours.

How can I ask God to forgive me for leaving you and then not be prepared to be reunited with you if the opportunity arises?

I know it's crazy. I know you don't think about me. I know you probably hate me. You have every right and reason to feel revolted at the sight of me. I'm rambling.

I miss you. I would give anything to redo my decision to divorce you.

Love,

Johnny

Rachel saw Johnny in a different light now. She carefully folded the letter and slid it back in the envelope. She needed to think about how she felt. One more year.

June 4, 2017

Dear Rachel,

I love you, I love you, I love you. Even if you don't love me. Even if you hate me; I still love you.

God gifted you to me. I screwed that part up.

I'm wearing our wedding ring. It has caused a few people to be confused, but it makes me happy and reminds me each day of my commitment to be ready if the opportunity

Lake　　　Doomsday Clock 11:59:59

presents itself to tell you how sorry I am for abandoning you and throwing away our friendship.

How can you ever forgive a total ass? I don't know. I've forgiven myself and that has helped.

I'm still involved in the youth ministry with homeless kids. I want a family and others toss their kids out in the street. It doesn't make sense to me. God has a plan. I'm part of that plan for those kids.

Until we meet.

Love in Christ,

Johnny

Rachel folded the last letter and slid it back in the envelope. The wall, impregnable for ten years from love, cracked, fell apart, a Humpty Dumpty reenactment, love rushed inside.

The Piper Cub swung violently to the left. Boxes and bags crashed against the wall, the babies were restrained in a makeshift five-point harness.

The plane dipped to the right, packages and boxes went the other way.

Rachel wasn't seat belted in and was flung left and right. She saw the wall approaching and tried to raise her arms to cushion the blow. She hit the side of the plane with her head, a metal strut, and everything went black.

Chapter 40

Johnny managed to level out the Cub. A military helicopter appeared flying next to him. The crew signaled for him to talk on the radio.

He said, contacting to the helicopter, "This is an approved medical flight. What is wrong with you guys?"

A voice came back, "Put her down Sir. Orders."

The nation was under martial law. The military controlled the skies and the roads and the shipping lanes.

He searched for an open spot and found a small dirt road with a long straightaway. The Cub handled like a champ. He set her down, stopped, cut the engine, and looked back, saw Rachel laying in the back, bleeding. The babies were all crying. His life suddenly seemed out of control. Five minutes before he was flying at 2,500 feet above the terrain wondering if Rachel would garrote him from behind. But, it was the right day to be the only pilot in the plane.

The Blackhawk kicked up a huge dirt cloud landing in front of him, effectively cutting off his rolling runway.

Rachel regained consciousness just as the Cub landed. She felt something drip from her nose and realized she had hit her face on the plane wall and was bleeding.

Johnny opened the pilot side door and jumped out. He looked back again at Rachel.

He said, "You're injured. Give me your hand and let me help you out."

Rachel's head was spinning, not from the blow to the head, but from the letter contents. She gave her hand to Johnny and stepped out of the plane. She felt dizzy and stumbled.

Johnny yelled, "Do you guys have a medic? Your crazy shenanigans up there caused my flight nurse to hit her head."

Lake   Doomsday Clock 11:59:59

The Blackhawk crew all knew Johnny from National Guard duty. They were trying to stop Khalid, it was his plane. One went back to retrieve a medical kit.

The Guard pilot spoke, "Sorry Sir. We thought you were Khalid. He's a damn Texan. I admit we did come in kind of fast."

Johnny said in response, "She's the only flight nurse I have. I hope she didn't suffer a concussion."

Guard pilot said, "Doc will check her out. You got crying babies in there?"

Johnny rolled his eyes, "Yes. I need to check on them."

The next few minutes were spent with Doc checking out Rachel to make sure she was okay. She didn't have any signs of a concussion and her nose had stopped bleeding.

Johnny and the Blackhawk crew fed the babies, changed diapers, burped them and rocked them back to sleep. They finished settling them into their restraints. Five happy campers, good babies.

The Blackhawk pilot said, "You and that flight nurse have a nice family. Five kids, wow!"

Johnny laughed, "That flight nurse is my ex-wife and she hates my guts."

Rachel was sitting up now and said, "Doc, I want to talk to Johnny."

Doc yelled, "Johnny, the patient is asking for you."

Johnny shrugged his shoulders and said, "Dead man walking."

He walked over to where Rachel was sitting. She was smiling and he thought maybe she had a head injury. Thirty minutes ago, she'd wanted his manhood cut off.

Doc stood up, Rachel motioned for Johnny to sit next to her. He nervously sat down.

Lake   Doomsday Clock 11:59:59

She said, "I'm going to do something and you'll think I'm crazy and then I'm going to say something and you'll know I'm crazy."

He muttered, "Okay."

She threw her arms around his neck and kissed him. Softly at first and then a hard kiss.

He didn't know what to do at initially and finally returned the embrace and the lip lock.

The embrace ended and the catcalls started.

Johnny was grinning from ear to ear. He said, "Doc, I think she's got a serious head injury."

Rachel said, "I read your letters you wrote every year on the divorce anniversary. Do you still love me?"

Johnny said, "Yes, I love you Rachel. I don't think…"

She hushed him, placing two fingers on his lips, "Stop, I love you. Your letters written with raw emotion say more about your heart and feelings than 1,000 words right now."

The Blackhawk pilot walked over and said, "Sir, I do have a serious message for you. No flights allowed over 400 feet until further notice."

Johnny said, "Why? I don't know if I have enough fuel to make Gunnison with those restrictions."

The pilot said, "A credible rumor is being floated about an old DC-3 plane, painted in DPRK colors, loaded with North Korean special forces planning on making a parachute launched raid on a major American city."

Johnny said, "You're serious."

Blackhawk said, "Yes Sir! If a F15 or F22 sees you above 400 feet they have been instructed to put a missile up your tail and make radio contact after."

Johnny said, "Message received Sir. I'll hug the ground between here and Gunnison and hope for the best."

Lake   Doomsday Clock 11:59:59

The Blackhawk pilot responded, "How about we share a few gallons of fuel with you and help out a fellow Guard?"

They spent 15 minutes BS'ing and topping off the Cub's fuel tank.

The Blackhawk spooled up and took off in a cloud of dust leaving Rachel and Johnny standing alone. Holding hands, new or rediscovered love? True love?

Johnny broke the silence. "I feel better with full tanks."

Rachel said, unhooking her necklace, "Look, I've worn our wedding ring around my neck for ten years. Will you do me the honor of placing it back on my finger?"

Johnny was in tears, so much, in so little time.

The wedding ring is worn on the left hand, fourth finger. Before modern day anatomy, it was thought that a vein ran from the fourth finger straight to the heart.

He gently slid the ring on her finger and said, "I love you Rachel. Please forgi…"

She stopped him, "No need to ask for forgiveness my love. Your letters convinced me of your sorrow. If indeed, you are sorry about something happening, you make sure it never happens again."

He asked, "Why did you continue to wear your wedding ring on a necklace? Why not just toss it in a jewelry box?"

She responded, "You don't know women very well. I was jilted. I needed a cross to bear, to keep you out of my heart. It worked, you and every man that expressed one iota of interest in me were repelled by the ring hanging on a chain.

I believe that God was saving me for this moment, to be reunited with my husband. Maybe that's a bit of a stretch, a fairy tale. I believe in true love. You broke my heart and now you've healed it. End of story."

One of the babies started to fuss which really ended the discussion.

Lake   Doomsday Clock 11:59:59

Rachel asked, "Who changed their diapers?"

Johnny proudly said, "I did, two of them."

Rachel said, "You put them on backwards."

He asked, "How many are boys and girls?"

Rachel replied, "Three girls and two boys. Why?"

Johnny asked, "Names?"

Rachel sighed, "No. These kids will be adopted and their new family will choose a name. It helps to not get attached. Each one tugs at your heart, especially the kids being adopted. Nurses always spend extra time with these kids because the mother isn't at the hospital to hold and feed them."

Five minutes later they were airborne. Johnny kept the Cub under 400 feet, which gave him zero tolerance for mistakes. He was constantly on the lookout for electric lines, cables strung between two old mines on opposite hills. The list of hazards was staggering.

It took an hour of nerve racking flying to reach Gunnison. Numerous columns of smoke drifted up, reaching for the mountain tops and beyond. Black smoke, oil based, shingles, cars, anything made from petroleum products.

Johnny circled the airport once, just to check out the runway, see if there were any obstacles in the way.

A man in a white biohazard suit stood next to a 55-gallon barrel, three boxes stacked on top of each other, and a United States flag hung upside down on a pole. An upside-down flag is a distress sign.

Indeed, the nation, the republic, was in trouble.

Johnny landed in a mere 440 feet. He taxied over to the man and cut the engine and opened the door.

The man said, in a metallic voice, "Where's Khalid?"

Johnny said, "He took a bullet from a trigger-happy security guard, lost a finger. I'm his replacement."

Lake   Doomsday Clock 11:59:59

Bio man said, "Where's Rachel?"

Rachel popped up, "I'm here Freddy."

Freddy said, "You can't stay here."

Johnny said, "We have to. We have no place else to go."

Rachel said, "Why can't we stop here? We have five babies to drop off and then we're headed back to Denver."

Freddy said, "Nope. We are under a level 4 quarantine. Denver is quarantined. We have an avian flu variant that's never been seen before and Colorado is ground zero and it's spreading fast.

We have reports of all the cities on the west coast, LA, San Francisco, Seattle, all reporting outbreaks."

He held up a finger. "Just a minute. I'm getting an updated report right now."

Freddy listened intently and walked over to the stack of boxes and sat down, slumped over.

Rachel said, "What's wrong Freddy?"

He answered, "A nuclear explosion has been confirmed in Hamburg, Germany at the G20 conference. Everybody attending the conference appears to have died. You know every country in the world had either the number one or two person there, not just the 20 bigwigs."

Johnny appeared a bit stunned and Rachel noticed the look on his face.

She said, placing her hand on his arm, "What's wrong Johnny?"

He said, "I just got a package from my ex-wife. She taunts me a bit once a year or so by sending me photos of the kids. They just moved to Hamburg last month."

She hugged him, which caused a confused look from Freddy.

Johnny said, "Rachel is my wife."

Lake   Doomsday Clock 11:59:59

Which caused more confusion.

Rachel said, "True. But, we took a 10-year sabbatical for somebody's bad behavior."

Johnny felt sadness from the news overseas. His heart was happy standing next to Rachel and the future she represented. He couldn't live in the past or change what was happening 6,000 miles away.

Rachel's playfulness was part of what he missed. The friendship, companion, confidante, and wife.

Freddy said, "Look, you guys need to be airborne in 10 minutes. Nonnegotiable, you can't stay here. This area is closed to new arrivals. I'm sorry."

Johnny said, "Where do we go?"

Freddy said, "If it were me, I'd head west. Maybe the base of the Rockies. There are a few old mines and maybe one can be used as a shelter. You need, food, water, shelter."

Johnny looked back at the plane, "I have five babies to feed."

Freddy said, "And we are going to help with that part. These three boxes contain powdered formula. Enough to feed five kids for three months. Certainly, this crap will be straightened out before then?"

Johnny shrugged. He didn't know. So much had changed, so little time.

He said, "Rachel, what do you think?"

She said, "I don't know how we can do this. We have five babies. I've never been a mom. Johnny?"

He smiled, "I've never been a mom either."

She rolled her eyes, "Look…"

He stopped her, "I know what you asked. You've taken care of babies in the hospital. Love them, change their diapers, feed and burp them, talk to them. It really isn't complicated."

Lake   Doomsday Clock 11:59:59

Freddy asked, "Anything else I can get you?"

Johnny thought for a second, "Yes. Two hunting rifles, a handgun, and all the ammo you can spare."

Freddy spoke into his microphone hidden behind the bio mask.

He said, "It will be here in five minutes."

They waited. Fed the babies, changed diapers, burped them and strapped them back into their seats.

Johnny looked at the map. Where to go?

Rachel sensed his discomfort.

She said, "Why don't we pray?"

He nodded. They clasped hands. She spoke quietly, *"Dear Heavenly Father,*

We don't know what you want us to do or where you want us to go. We need Your guiding light, Your wisdom to help us make the best choice for these five babies.

Dear Lord, we thank You for your gift of life. Johnny and I plead to do Your will.

We ask these things in Jesus's name. Amen"

Johnny checked the map and a reflection from the Cub window danced across the town of Silverton. Rachel saw the sign as well. Both smiled and nodded their heads in agreement.

Silverton, Colorado 9,318 feet, 124 miles from Gunnison, population 670, the new destination.

The ATV bounced across the land between the hospital and the Piper Cub. The rifles and handguns were delivered, only three boxes of ammo.

The finished filling up the tanks with fuel, hand pump of course. The readjusted the load, added more weight with the three cases of powdered formula and prepared to depart.

Lake   Doomsday Clock 11:59:59

The Cubs engine turned over with ease and in 500 feet Johnny pulled the yoke back and they were airborne. Maximum height of 400 feet. The trip was in a southwest direction.

Johnny glanced at his watch and realized five hours had passed since Evelyn woke him up in the Denver basement. So many emotions, so high, so low, so happy, so in love.

They talked.

Rachel, "What are we going to do?"

Johnny said, "I'm going to make love to you!"

Rachel laughed, "Stop it. You know I'm talking about the babies. We can't just keep them forever. There are families waiting for their son and daughter."

Johnny felt something important slipping away and said, "Why can't we keep them? Maybe God meant for us to have a family. Maybe this is how we end up with our kids!"

Rachel sighed, "I wish it were that easy. What if electricity comes back on next week? What if the CDC produces a vaccine for this flu strain in two months?"

Johnny said, "What if Silverton doesn't let us stay?"

Rachel said, "I've been to Silverton. I rode a steam engine from Durango to Silverton and back. Silverton is breathtaking this time of year."

Johnny said, "Let's hope they let us stay."

Rachel said, "We need to give them names. Even if it's temporary. They deserve to be called a special name."

Johnny laughed, "The boy with red hair. He's Pisser. He peed on me when I changed his diaper."

Rachel laughed, "Stop it! We need serious Biblical names. Strong names for difficult times."

Johnny said, "Luke. I knew a kid who changed his name from Alfalfa to Luke in grade school. Smart kid in math. I met him at the Air Force Academy, I think he was from the Navajo tribe."

They went back and forth in a respectful dialogue. Eventually it was decided, Luke and Matthew for the boys, Mary, Rebecca and Esther for the girls. They had a family, an instant group of seven.

The Garmin showed Silverton in the distance, maybe 10 miles. The screen map showed the airport and the runway slowly approaching. Johnny figured GPS was still working because it's satellite based.

The Piper slowly made a wide circle around the small airport to make sure nobody was landing or taking off.

Johnny landed the Cub, bounced once and rolled about 700 feet.

Rachel said, "What kind of landing was that pilot?"

Johnny laughed, "Look Lady, I started the day not knowing I would ever see you again, then I was worried you'd cut my throat, then we were in love. Now we have 5 kids, all under two weeks. My nerves are shot."

Rachel leaned forward and kissed him," I love you. Thanks for being here when I needed you most Johnny."

A woman's kind word and warm heart was all Johnny needed to hear.

They taxied to an open spot. Johnny shut down the engine, jumped out, pulled chock blocks out for the wheels. Grabbed tie downs to balance the wings in a strong wind.

He patted the Cubs engine cowling and said, "I christen you, "Lady Brooke" for running so strong all day and helping us arrive safely."

Rachel looked at him, funny, "What is that all about?"

Johnny said, "A good plane is always named after a Lady. A plane that gives you trouble, becomes undependable or strands you is named after a man. It's a pilot thing!"

Lake   Doomsday Clock 11:59:59

Lake   Doomsday Clock 11:59:59

Chapter 41

An ATV came bouncing towards them with a thin woman behind the wheel. She was elderly, with wind weathered features. She looked like she talked the talk and walked the walk.

The ATV coasted to a stop and the driver said, "Can I help you folks?"

Rachel said, "It's a long story."

The woman cut her off, "I don't have time for long stories. Give me the facts. There's too much crap going on right now. I need to decide in a hurry if you're a friend or a foe!"

Rachel broke into tears. It was too much. A super stressful long day. Starting with a flight from Gunnison. Finding Johnny. Flying back with the babies, being turned away in Gunnison and flying here.

Johnny spoke up, "Ma'am, we have five babies, orphans. We inherited them, my wife and I. Gunnison turned us away because of a quarantine. We are out of fuel. You're all we've got Ma'am."

The woman said, "Holy crap! Sorry about the language. You sound like Mary and Joseph. We won't turn you away. Five babies. Sakes alive."

She picked up a walkie talkie and said, "Joann, stop playing solitaire. Go tell Melissa at the Baptist church to air out the parsonage and borrow five of those baby cribs from First Congregational, set them up in the main bedroom. We got us a real live Mary and Joseph come to visit our little town!"

Johnny noticed the woman was wearing a gun on her hip and a law enforcement badge on her shirt.

She extended her hand and said, "I'm Joy, don't laugh, but I'm the town Sheriff. Ma'am are you okay? Do you need a Kleenex?"

Rachel said, "I'm good now. I just had a little meltdown. It's been a long day. Lots of firsts."

Joy said, "You appear to have a peach of a man to back you up."

Rachel said, "It took me a while to train him, but he's a keeper."

The military had trained Johnny to know when to shut up.

They unbuckled the fab five, Luke, Matthew, Mary, Rebecca and Esther.

Joy looked sternly at the two parents, and barked, "We have a strict ordinance about car seats in this town."

Johnny said, "Ma'am we didn't..."

Joy slapped her leg, and said, "I'm pulling your leg. I'm the Sheriff and I've suspended that law for you two."

Somehow, they managed to fit the five infants and three adults in the ATV and set off for town a short distance away.

They drove across the main street, highway 550, linking Montrose to Durango. Over the Animas river and Cement creek to the church.

The parsonage was a small house, maybe 1100 square feet, wood framed, silver metal roof, the sides of the structure painted dark fern green with a lighter avocado green for the trim. Not what Rachel would have picked.

The front yard was surrounded by a small three-foot high white picket fence. The backyard was open forever.

Somebody had started a fire in the wood pellet stove and the house was a little warm.

It was a well-orchestrated group of Ladies. Food for the two newlyweds appeared, sandwiches, neither had eaten since early morning. The meal tasted delicious, deviled eggs, potato salad and apple pie appeared soon after the sandwiches were consumed.

Lake   Doomsday Clock 11:59:59

Four ladies and one man entertained the kids, changed diapers, fed, burped them and walked around holding them and talking.

Johnny said, "Watch out for the red headed boy, Luke. He'll get you with his fire hose."

So, Luke, Matthew, Mary, Rebecca and Ester were happy and soon fast asleep.

Joy solemnly said, "Look, these kids are yours. I'm going to speak bluntly. We are a Christian bunch here, we'll help you. The world seems to be falling apart. We have resources, a little advanced planning. We're willing to share.

But it's a two-way street. We expect you guys to help us. We can always use a strong guy to move stuff, fix things, hunt, whatever needs done. Rachel as a nurse you are very valuable. I know Johnny can fly a plane, but Air Silverton is temporarily out of business.

Those crazy guys in the military want me to watch for an old DC-3 painted up as a North Korea military plane. Excuse my French, but what the hell is happening?"

Rachel said, "We really appreciate the town allowing us to stay and the help. We didn't start the day expecting to be parents to five rug rats. It seems God has a plan for all of us."

Joy said, "One more thing. We know it's been a long day for you two. Two of us are going to take the babies into the bedroom on the other side of the house and let you guys catch up on your sleep, maybe talk a little. You seem to have a problem keeping your hands off each other. You newlyweds?"

Johnny said, "We were married almost eleven years ago Ma'am."

Joy said, "I'm glad you've kept the fire lit. Raising five little babies isn't going to leave you much time for romance. Enjoy a night of peace and quiet. It might be the last one you get for 6 months or so."

Lake   Doomsday Clock 11:59:59

The evening ended, the babies and their surrogate nannies were in a spare bedroom. Rachel and Johnny made up for ten years of lost conversation and intimacy.

When sleep finally arrived, they slept for almost 8 hours. Their lives had changed in a blink of an eye. In their wildest fantasy world neither would have imagined waking up next to the other with five kids between them. 24 hours had changed their lives forever.

The sound of a plane engine woke them up. The sun was up, midmorning. 22 hours since Evelyn had woken him up. A lifetime ago.

Johnny looked out the bedroom window facing the backyard.

A DC-3, complete with the North Korean red star was being chased by a Blackhawk military helicopter. Two F-15's circling at 5,000 feet completed the surreal scene.

Smoke poured from one engine of the antique plane. The Blackhawk was trying to force the plane to land.

The plane was futilely trying to escape. It was a dogfight mismatch, 60 years difference between airframes and technology.

The DC-3 did a wide turn at 1,000 feet, 180 degrees and was now headed back towards Silverton, maybe 6 miles away.

The Blackhawk backed off and an F-15 unleashed a missile. All of this took about 45 seconds.

The missile exploded as it hit the remaining non-smoking engine and sheared off the wing. The plane tilted up on its side and cartwheeled into the ground, exploding in a ball of fire on impact.

Johnny estimated the distance to be 2 miles from town. The Sheriff drove up and offered Johnny a ride to the crash site. She wanted his input and knew the military would be there.

Lake   Doomsday Clock 11:59:59

The Blackhawk crew was the same one from yesterday. They were arguing over who got credit for the kill. The F-15 pilot claimed full credit and the Blackhawk crew wanted a split because they had shot up the one engine and harassed the DC-3 crew into low terrain flying and an easy target for the flyboy, who turned out to be a fly girl piloting the F-15.

The fire, because of previous rainfall in the area, quickly burned itself out.

The F-15 pilot said the North Korean painted plane had dropped almost 25 North Korean special forces three hours before and a couple of hundred miles away. A fight had taken place between some troubled teens, some US Special Forces and the North Koreans.

Johnny couldn't imagine what had happened to create that scenario.

The sheriff took him back to town, he walked inside their new home. He looked at his watch, 24 hours had passed since Evelyn shook him awake.

Esther woke up and started to cry.

Military Story

Chapter 42

00:00

Near Area 51, Nevada

Todd straddled the SilentHawk, DARPA had a hybrid version of an electric/gas dirt bike. They'd been given two to test out and he felt like a kid with a banana seat stingray on Christmas morning in the 1960's.

It could run on electricity, diesel, gas, jet fuel, whatever you can find and pour in the tank. The engine reportedly would even burn vegetable oil.

He could just imagine finding a McDonalds in an Arab country and stealing from their recycled grease tank to keep moving.

Lake   Doomsday Clock 11:59:59

He was hot. The kid he was trailing was 100 yards ahead and down in a gulley. A trickle of sweat ran down his back.

There were eight of them in the squad. Different branches, highly specialized and now worthless for active deployment.

Todd, aka "Redford", was the planner and leader. He could plug details into a free-flowing plan and make it work on the fly. Nobody better.

Chris, aka "Ironside", the legal wizard, and document expert. He built the teams legends before each mission. They were so top secret only 5 people knew who they were before the unplanned photo-op.

Robert, aka "MacGyver", he could make anything work. The story of Apollo 13 is well known and documented. Following an explosion of an oxygen tank the mission was scrubbed and the Astronauts circled the moon and headed back home.

They moved from the Service module to the Lunar module to save needed power for reentry into the earth's atmosphere. The problem was the Lunar Module was equipped with enough oxygen for two astronauts to survive 36 hours, not three astronauts and 96 hours.

They needed to change the circular CO_2 scrubber filter in the Lunar module because carbon dioxide was reaching dangerous levels. There were no spares. The Service module had several square CO_2 scrubber filters.

The Crews Systems Division of NASA devised a hack using available parts in the modules. They called it a "Mailbox Rig" and it included random parts like, a flight manual cover, suit parts and socks.

Robert could have been that guy all by himself.

Justin, aka "Hathcock" for his prowess with a sniper rifle and any weapon. He seemed to have a knack for picking up the finer points of shooting any gun and all of them have quirks.

Carl, aka, "The Intimidator" could drive and fly anything, boats, submarines, cars, trucks, helicopters and planes.

Jon, aka "Einstein" because he understood the nuclear field. He could assess a threat and recommend the best course of action. He was the only one who wasn't an expert marksman and in fact considered himself a pacifist and often refused to carry a weapon unless ordered by his commanding officer. He was much respected for his principals by the squad.

Pat, aka "John Wayne", for his take no prisoners attitude. He had an attitude that stragglers were shot in life.

Adam, aka "Rudy", because he had overcome so many learning disabilities and physical problems to be a gifted computer specialist. He could fix any hardware device and figure out any system. A graduate of West Point.

The eight were on the sidelines because of social media.

They were in a tiny South American country, waiting to leave, mission complete. The bad guy taken down.

Eating at a Taco Bell, because they were hungry and it was convenient. A group of ten local banditos barged in and started demanding money from the clerk. Without warning, she was executed, an example for everybody.

The restaurant was full of customers. A local soccer team, 6-year old girls celebrating a big win over a rival. More demands, a child executed; over the line for acceptable human behavior.

A decision to make. Star Trek calls in the Kobayashi Maru, a no-win situation. Save the innocent people and risk blowing their cover. Stand down, allow children to die, but the unit lives to fight again.

Jon, the pacifist, pulled his pistol first and shot the terrorist who shot the child. A very brief fire fight ensued. Ten dead and twenty bullets expended, all by the Americans. Double taps or so the story goes.

Lake   Doomsday Clock 11:59:59

The men were heroes. Customers filmed the carnage, blasted it across social media.

The police arrived within seconds, passports collected, a brief public investigation followed. A long private investigation continued; they were confined to their hotel. Body guards followed them everywhere.

The state department intervened and admitted some culpability. The foreign government didn't know what to do. Money changed hands, foreign aid offered. They were finally declared persona non-gratis and deported.

They were flown back to America. They were run thru every foreign power facial data base across the globe and many of their secret missions previously unknown came to light. Not a good day for our heroes.

What to do with them? Highly trained warriors with no place to fight.

Then this gig came open. A group that was on RR and working with troubled juveniles was placed back in the field because of the North Korean crisis.

Some brilliant pencil pusher in the pentagon decided they were a good fit. Talented, on the payroll, can't be deployed. Send the team to Edwards Air Base and let them takeover.

Fifteen troubled kids who didn't know how to get along with others. Didn't like taking orders because they had rights. Failing school because they couldn't do simple tasks like getting up and going to class.

They made "Welcome Back Kotter" kids seem like snowflakes.

Back at Base Camp. The seven soldiers prepared to do battle with the fourteen troubled teens.

Society didn't know what to do with young people who think differently. Who act against the rules. Who don't seem interested in learning or motivated to even try.

Lake   Doomsday Clock 11:59:59

What do you do with a kid who just sits?

There are no easy answers. There is an old saying about the futility of trying to fit a square peg in a round hole. Apollo 13 showed you can make a square filter work for a round box. Especially if your life depended on finding a solution.

So, the squad of 8 decided to make food and shelter a choice, a motivating factor. Water was always available.

Each evening there was a map exercise designed to find shelter for the night. The 15 kids were broken up into teams of three. Three seemed ideal because two allowed one to dominate and do the thinking and four encouraged two against two. Three, like a triangle, strong, each side making the other hold up.

The kids had to use a crudely drawn map to hike three miles. They were dropped off at various points in a three-mile radius and told to hike to camp. They had GPS trackers on their bodies and a drone kept a close eye on the wildlife. Plus, a soldier kept a few hundred yards away.

It was interesting. The first night two of the five teams hiked right to base camp. No argument, no desire to spend the night in the desert. No desire to interact with nature. One team just got lost. Not enough skill to read a topography map and understand a northern orientation. Two teams wandered for hours and finally gave up, scared and tired. Their soldier guided them home.

The next day it was explained to them that they only got one rescue. A class was taught in map reading. Most paid attention. One group chose to ignore the chance to learn a valuable skill.

The next evening, four teams made it back to base camp. The fifth team was hopelessly lost and the soldiers allowed them to stay out all night. The finally found a gully and settled into a restless rest for the last two hours of darkness. The soldiers had access to plenty of animal sounds and made sure they never quite rested.

Lake   Doomsday Clock 11:59:59

The next day a class was again taught on map reading. Proper motivation is amazing. The next night all the groups slept safely and comfortably at base camp.

Each evening the squad of eight soldiers did less and the boys and girls a little more. This morning they were told to make their beds before climbing the hill to get food for the day and fourteen complied.

Retired Naval Admiral William H McRaven said in a famous speech to college graduates, "If you want to change the world, start off each day by making your bed. One task completed leads to another and another. If you can't do the little things right, you'll never be able to do the big things."

The fifteenth, Jeff, was being followed by Todd.

Jeff, upon hearing he had to make his bed, said, "Screw it, I'm going back."

Leaving was always allowed. 40 miles back to Edwards. Here's a map, a gallon of water, a bag of food. See you later, good luck.

Three weeks before they had started this mission. The first week or so every kid left at least once. Everybody came back because they didn't have the willpower or the base knowledge to trek 40 miles across the desert to home. They weren't as smart or independent as they thought. A school based on reality and hardships.

This morning the kids needed to climb a 1500-foot hill to find provisions for the day. They all complied. The first week was a challenge. After you go hungry for a day the motivation to eat and your desire to be obtuse have a brief fight and hunger wins.

The kids were losing weight, detoxed from soda and sugar, and were in fact willing to learn material presented in a natural environment.

Todd continued to watch Jeff from a distance. The dirt bike was relatively quiet at 55 decibels and when it used electricity only, the noise level reduced to 33 decibels or about the level of a normal conversation.

The scene was different at Nellis Air Force base. The military already knew there had been a nuclear explosion in Hamburg, Germany.

They knew chaos was coming to this great land and politicians would try to use the might of the military for political and economic gain.

They followed legal orders. That was their job. They all took the same oath.

I, (NAME), do solemnly swear (or affirm) that I will support and defend the Constitution of the United States against all enemies, foreign and domestic; that I will bear true faith and allegiance to the same; and that I will obey the orders of the President of the United States and the orders of the officers appointed over me, according to regulations and the Uniform Code of Military Justice. So help me God.

The base commander decided to send the kids left on base to the camp where the squad was working with the troubled youth. The problem existed in communications being off line between the base and the squad.

The base commander was responsible for fifty kids and so she assigned twelve soldiers, ten females and two males, to drive two transport buses the forty miles and stay with the existing kids and keep the squad there for the duration.

She sent enough food and water to feed everybody for thirty days. Tents to house them, guns and ammo to defend against all threats, including hunting of game.

Nothing in her twenty-five-year career had prepared her for this situation. Parents placed their kids on the bus with a hug and a kiss and returned to duty. Duty to Country before family. The kept watch 24/7 so the sheeple could rest.

The ability to take home life problems, and place them in a box on a separate shelf is essential to a successful life in the military. These kids leaving were part of families where both parents served.

She looked at it this way; it was her job to move the kids to safety so their parents could focus on their duties. The base was a high-risk target for a suicide, nuclear or a missile attack.

The two buses were loaded and the final goodbyes exchanged. The keys were turned and the buses rumbled to life, both Bluebirds, 250 horsepower, rear diesel Cummins engines, 100-gallon fuel tanks, topped off.

She also sent two DPV's or Desert Patrol Vehicles. These vehicles were designed by Chenowth Racing Products.

They had a range of 200 miles, a 2.0-liter air cooled Volkswagen engine capable of producing 200 horsepower. Top speed of 60 miles per hour and 0-30 mph in only four seconds.

The small convoy headed out the gate. Base Commander, Major General Leslie Gomez's youngest child Albert was aboard the second bus.

The four vehicles were running smooth until they climbed a small hill. The second bus overheated near the top and the driver chose to keep going the final ½ mile.

Both vehicles stopped and the kids were asked to get off and stretch their legs.

Sergeant Monroe was driving the first bus and he called for Corporal Shaffer to look at the second bus.

They told the kids to take a short walk so the engine could cool down. An exhaustive search was conducted to find the cause. Computer software, engine diagnostics all agreed the engine was dead.

It's what happens when somebody doesn't check the oil. Even in the military, routine maintenance can be overlooked.

They couldn't cancel the field trip. This was a run for their lives. The veterans understood that part. Chaos was coming to every large city in the United States. The military would be pushed and prodded to violate citizens' rights. Martial law would be used as a disguise to act.

The bus had to be fixed, pushed or towed the last 28 miles. Leaving it behind wasn't an option. Fixing it wasn't feasible. They didn't have time or a spare engine.

Pushing it was considered and dismissed.

Shaffer said to Monroe, "We have some heavy chains. I believe the first bus will be able to tow the second bus. The problem will come when we head down hill and need breaks."

Monroe asked, "What do you suggest Corporal?"

Shaffer replied, "We have options. We could switch positions with the buses, let the lame bus roll down first and stop it with the good bus. If we do that we need to keep the kids off the bus, the move is risky. We could attach chains to the DPV's and use them behind the lame bus as anchors. The only problem with that plan is if the bad bus goes out of control we'll lose three vehicles."

Monroe said, "Let's pull with the good bus right now and when we get to the big downhill we'll decide which plan to use."

The kids came back to the running bus and loaded up. All the supplies were transferred to the broken-down bus.

It seemed prudent to have the kids transported on the working bus. The heavy-duty chains were attached and tested. Everything seemed to work.

They took off across the plateau, seven miles of easy driving, except the functional bus was towing the second bus now being used as a cargo container. Plan, adapt, overcome, military life.

Chapter 42

How do you explain North Korea without demonizing the leadership?

From 1910-1945 the country of Korea was controlled by the Japanese. Why? Because Japan kicked Russia's butt in a naval war between 1904-1905. It was a huge surprise around the world.

Eight-two years ago there was one Korea. At the end of World War II the peninsula was split into two sections. One controlled by the Soviets and the other by the Americans. Think about East and West Germany. Japan and Germany were the big losers in World War II.

Spoils of war being divided up between the victors, Russia and America. Then the cold war erupted between two super powers, each with a huge nuclear arsenal.

Russia withdrew from North Korea in 1948 and America pulled out of South Korea in 1949. The two Korean halves spoke of separate but equal parts of Korea.

Russia's, Joseph Stalin, encouraged North Korea to attack South Korea. North Korea invaded on June 25, 1950 and they almost pulled it off. All South Korea had was a small contingent of United Nations troops led by American forces. Eventually the Americans regrouped and pushed the North Koreans back to the China border. North Korea was led by Kim Il-sung.

Chinese forces intervened on North Korea's behalf and a stalemate resulted. On July 27, 1953, an armistice was signed. The DMZ separating the North from the South is probably the most heavily fortified strip of land in the world.

A proxy war between America and Russia. Over a million civilians and soldier's dead. Every major building in North Korea reduced to rubble.

Initially the North aligns with Russia and China, aid flows into the country to rebuild the infrastructure and the military.

Lake   Doomsday Clock 11:59:59

The North Korean leadership espouses a word, Juche, or self-reliance economically.

In 1976 China opens trading with the West and North Korea withdraws further into its cocoon, severing most ties with China. This leads to economic stagnation by 1987 and a total economic collapse when the Soviet Union collapsed in 1991.

North Korea returns to trading with China, but the help is minimal because the Chinese have their own set of struggles.

Flooding in the mid-1990's caused mass famine and between 240,000 and 440,000 deaths.

Kim Il-sung dies in 1994 and his son Kim Jong-il eventually takes over.

In all this depressing news, the North Koreans begin a nuclear program. Dating back to 1962 and their all-fortressization stance, building a super military. Even today in a country of 25 million, 1.1 million active military and 8.4 million reserves serve.

The Soviet Union and China provide technical assistance early on as North Korea explores a nuclear policy aimed at cheap electrical energy, they claim.

In 1994 as part of the nuclear disarmament talks Bill Clinton's administration gives North Korea two light water reactors as an incentive to disarm and stop military research. The world thought we could appease North Korea. Place a carrot on a stick to lead the horse to disarmament.

Abdul Qaudeer Khan, remember that name. A Pakistan scientist.

Urenco, is a nuclear fuel company operating uranium enrichment plants around the world.

Urenco, back in the 1970's employed Dr. Khan. Urenco eventually giving him the blueprints to a highly successful

Zippe centrifuge in hopes of solving physics problems associated with the gas centrifuge.

Natural occurring Uranium is 99.2% isotope-238 and 0.7% isotope-235. Fuel from an electricity producing nuclear reactor is 96% isotope-238 and 4% isotope-235.

However, highly enriched uranium, produced using a specific type of centrifuge is 90% isotope-235 and less than 10% isotope-238.

Uranium isotope-235 is the hideous monster that makes Atomic bombs so scary.

Dr. Khan has admitted to helping Iraq and Libya develop their nuclear programs, to build atomic bombs. He has also admitted to helping North Korea develop their nuclear capabilities. He claims it was at Pakistan civilian leader's behest.

The nuclear genie can't be put back into the bottle. Countries are sharing and exporting missile technology.

MAD, mutually assured destruction theory, it is getting closer to being tested.

North Korea has carried out six nuclear tests, the latest one in 2017 was a hydrogen bomb.

North Korea has between 16 and 60 nuclear warheads. ICBM's to carry them. Enough said, their capabilities are scary.

Kim Jong-il died in 2011 and his son, Kim Jong-un took over leadership.

There is no dissent allowed in North Korea. There are numerous human rights violation and evidence to show it is ongoing.

Christian's are persecuted in this country. There is no religion in North Korea. Back to our story.

Chapter 43

30 spies, 30 double agents, North Koreans special forces posing as student's defected to Canada in early 2010. Now, after a circuitous route they were all in Las Vegas. They were prepared to die for their "Supreme Leader".

The DC-3 sat on the tarmac. Powered by two Pratt and Whiney engines capable of producing 1200 horsepower each. The plane carried a pilot and a co-pilot, 21-35 passengers, a maximum of 822 gallons of fuel at 6 pounds a gallon, 4,932 pounds.

Painted a light blue, with a red North Korean five-pointed star on the tail.

16,865 pounds empty weight, maximum weight of 25,199 pounds. Maximum speed of 230 mph and a cruising speed of 207 mph, ceiling height, 23,200 feet. There were 16,079 DC-3's built by the Douglas Aircraft Company, most between the years of 1936-1942 and a few built in 1950. In 2013 an estimated 2,000 DC-3 airplanes were still flying. A testament to the durability of the airframe.

The plane had spent the last two years crisscrossing the United States and Canada. Establishing a legend, credibility for their big mission.

Money is tight in North Korea, especially Yankee dollars. This mission was allotted 10 million precious American dollars.

The cost to purchase a mechanically sound 80-year-old plane, do some refurbishing, then 2 years of routine maintenance. Housing for 30 people, food, clothes, it wasn't nearly enough.

Then somebody in the North Korean group started a go-fund-me for the refugees from the brutal North Korean regime and sympathetic liberals, both American and Canadian public, donated 5 million dollars.

One last night in Las Vegas, in the morning they were headed to Yucca Mountain.

Lake   Doomsday Clock 11:59:59

Lake   Doomsday Clock 11:59:59

Chapter 44

Todd…yeah, remember Todd. He was following the kid walking in the gully. Jeff, was nearing the end of his rebellion.

Jeff had side stepped a rattle snake, been scared to death by a horned toad and drank the last of his water an hour ago.

Jeff slowly sank to the ground, brought his knees up, wrapped his arms around them, lowered his head and started to sob.

Todd had switched the dirt bike to electric ten minutes before and silently glided down the gulley side and slowly rolled up on Jeff.

Todd said, "Howdy partner!"

Jeff let go with a string of profanities. They made no sense, but he was mad, angry and probably a little scared.

Todd said, "You know what my dad told me at 15 years old? Leave home, conquer the world while you still know everything."

Jeff said, a little hate in his voice, "I don't know everything. I just want to be left alone."

Todd responded, "Can't do that because you're screwing up. You won't try in school. You've shut down. You don't seem to want to learn. You don't even go to school half the time."

Jeff said, "Why can't everybody just leave me alone?"

Todd said, "Because life doesn't work that way. We need productive citizens. People who contribute. If you don't learn something, a trade, a skill, a career, then I have to support you with my tax dollars."

Jeff said, "I won't need any help."

Todd said, "Really? How do you plan to make money?"

Lake   Doomsday Clock 11:59:59

Jeff said, "I can win skateboard competitions."

Todd said, "Anybody sponsor you yet?"

Jeff replied, "No, but they will. When I can do this full time. No school to drag me down."

Todd said, "You know, it's a pipe dream. Kids that are gifted in certain areas are discovered early. They have talent scouts for that part. You're good at skateboarding, but you're not the one in twenty million. You're one in a million kid. It makes you good, but not a Tony Hawk."

Jeff said, "Go away!"

Todd laughed, "See what I mean?"

Jeff said, "What?"

Todd spoke softly, "I'm the only person who can save you. I have water and a bike. In 45 minutes, we can be back at base camp. Instead of thinking, you're responding. Sending me away."

Jeff said, "So, if I can't skateboard, what do I do?"

Todd said, "I can't tell you. Everybody needs to figure that one out on their own. Pick something you like. A hobby, an interest, love what you do and you'll never work a day in your life."

Jeff said, "Is that what you did?"

Todd laughed, "No, I joined the military, but found out I was good with the structure it provided. I got into all kinds of trouble at your age. Did time in juvenile detention for theft."

Jeff said, "Do you like what you do?"

Todd replied, "I enjoy serving my country and the friends I've made. You ready to head back? Try again tomorrow?"

Jeff stood up, grabbed Todd's extended hand and hopped on the back. Todd flipped the dirt bike to fossil fuel, rolled the throttle back and demonstrated the bikes speed from 0-30, a rooster tail of sand flying 20 feet high out the back. "Roll Me Away". Boys with toys!

Lake   Doomsday Clock 11:59:59

Lake   Doomsday Clock 11:59:59

Chapter 45

The Bluebird convoy rolled past the dead cow, bulging from heat. The temperature didn't disappoint topping out at 104 degrees. It was hot. The lone running bus avoided turning on the AC to keep the engine from overheating.

The delay in rigging the tow system meant they couldn't get off the plateau today. The White River was the next obstacle and if they were lucky the rain would hold off one more day. With an average rainfall of .5 an inch, July seemed like a good month to travel and not get washed away.

Sergeant Monroe wasn't in charge. He was just the elder statesman in the group and blessed with a double dose of common sense.

The land within ten miles Nellis Air Base was 78% shrub, mostly creosote bush and white bursage, the rest bare desert and artificial surfaces.

Finding a grove of pine trees wasn't likely.

Major Ronda Howard was the officer in charge.

She gave a short speech, "I know you're hot. I know you're tired. I know most of you are hungry. I know some of you are scared.

I can't change the weather, it'll probably be close to 80 tonight for a low. You'll sleep. We will serve a meal shortly. I can't promise you everything will be okay. I don't make promises I'm not able to keep.

These are confusing times. Your folks have a job to do for this country. The best thing you can do for them is do what your told and let's hide out until this crisis blows over. You guys are military brats. I was one as well. You are the strongest. You are mentally strong, use it to your advantage. We need to work together.

We are headed to hook up with the Hogwarts School of Wizardry. Several of you are graduates. The staff at the school is a group of Special Forces. They will help keep us safe.

Any questions?"

One kid raised his hand, "What's for supper?" Food, the whole military seems to live for their next meal.

Major Howard said, "You may have peanut butter sandwiches, PBJ sandwiches or JPB sandwiches, your choice. After we eat let's put up tents, no trash left on the ground. We have no electricity so save your music until later. If you haven't already, put your phones on airplane mode, or shut them down to save power."

Next kid asked, "Lights out?"

Major Howard, "20:00 hours, no noise after 22:00 hours, wake up at 06:00 hours. Let's do this people."

They ate PBJ sandwiches, drank water, cleaned up after themselves. Seems somebody packed two five-gallon containers of vanilla ice cream in dry ice and that needed to be consumed. There were 50 kids, 4 to a tent. The older kids helped the younger ones. The kids were paired up with a buddy, two groups in a tent. Ages, 5 thru 17, it was quite a sight, military brats.

One special tent had two occupants, a pregnant female and her husband, both 17, both entering their senior year of high school.

A few tears of being scared from the younger ones, lights out at 20:00 hours, a few sniffles still at 22:00 hours and finally silence from the humans at 23:30 hours, except the two soldiers on guard duty. The military keeps watch 24/7, a protective shield from foreign invaders, but not in Hamburg, Germany.

They were near the Desert National Wildlife Refuge, 1.6 million acres. Home to approximately 320 bird species, 53 mammal species, 35 reptile species, and four amphibian species have been identified in the different communities on the refuge. Flora includes well over 500 plant species.

Lake   Doomsday Clock 11:59:59

Most mammals and reptiles cannot withstand the high desert temperatures for long periods of time. To adapt to the harsh daytime temperatures, many mammals and reptiles on the refuge are active at night, or nocturnal. This makes it difficult to observe much of the wildlife during the day.

The refuge was originally established for Bighorn Sheep. Bighorn are active during the day, or diurnal as opposed to nocturnal, and can be seen in the hottest part of the summer around waterholes.

Chapter 46

Todd, with Jeff on the back finally made it back to the Hogwarts School of Wizardry. The first school several years before was called, Last Chance. Last chance for some of these kids before juvenile detention. The group of graduates returned so transformed by the harsh realities of working for necessities, food, water, shelter that the kids and parents back at base said it was a magical transformation. Thus, the name, Hogwarts School of Wizardry was hung on the school.

The school had a first-class base camp. Refrigerators running off generators, stoves heated by propane, hot water for showers and cleaning.

Tonight, dinner was hamburger, carrots, and potatoes prepared by Carl. Eight soldiers, eight boys and four girls as students.

It was time for a serious talk.

Adam drew the short straw. He spoke, "When I was a kid, I struggled with school. I was having trouble with reading and writing. Understanding the words and comprehending the meanings. My writing in second grade looked like a 3-year-old."

Several kids nodded in understanding.

Adam continued, "I had a Mom who wouldn't let me give up. I had a Principal who kept looking for resources to help me.

Finally, a program called SOI helped me learn in a way that I could understand. I finally could read and write, do math. I ended up going to West Point, graduating, which is amazing considering where I was at 8 years of age.

My point is, you don't know where you'll end up. You might hit your stride with the next brick falling in place.

We are living in uncertain times. We got word today that a nuclear bomb was exploded in Hamburg, Germany. Many if not most of the top or second leaders from every country in the world except for North Korea were killed.

We have no electric grid in the United States. No internet, no running water, no grocery stores. We are on our own. Your parents are okay. They want you to stay here so they can do their duty. I didn't say job, I said duty. There is a difference. They took an oath to defend the United States against all invaders, foreign or domestic.

I'm encouraging you to use this crisis to get strong, be strong, stay strong. We will protect you the best we can. Right now, we don't know who is a friend and who is our enemy. If we ask you to do something please do it without question. Literally, your life might depend on your response.

One last thing, we expect a group of 50 students tomorrow from Nellis. You know them. Let's all get along and we expect you guys and gals to be the leaders. You've been living the life they now must live.

Any questions?"

Zack raised his hand, "Can we have popcorn tonight?"

Everybody laughed and the tense situation was defused.

Jeff said, "I have something to say. I get it. I won't be a pain in the ass anymore. I'd like to grow up and maybe do something with my life."

They watched two movies, "Grease" and "Agent Cody Banks, ate popcorn and the last of the ice cream. It was a good care free night for the students.

Their teachers were keeping watch 24/7, it is how the military rolls. One team, two guys, and two German Shepherds patrolled the perimeter area. Vigilance, two hours on, six hours off.

The cougar/mountain lion stalking their food supply was out there as well, waiting, being vigilant. A female with three newborn cubs occupied the same area as the school. She weighed 97 pounds, 7 feet long from head to tail, 27 inches high.

She preferred to hunt in the early evening and morning, stalk and ambush her prey with a burst of speed. Mule deer, squirrels, skunks, and porcupines were staple in her diet. She could make a good kill, cache it and eat for ten days.

The squad was trying to move her further away for everybody's safety. A healthy mountain lion population was needed to keep a balance in nature. The mountain lion was both a predator and prey for humans, bears, and wolves.

The night was cloudy, soon turned to thunder and lightning, heavy rains in the mountains, unusual for July in southeastern Nevada.

Chapter 47

The kids from Nellis Air Force Base woke up early. The most dangerous part was below them. The White River was rising from the rains last night, not flooded yet. Rain in the mountain 10-20 miles away profoundly effects the rivers and streams in the valleys. They had to cross it, no choice. They needed both vehicles.

Corporal Shaffer suggested a possible solution.

Shaffer, "Why don't we load up the kids with 30 pounds of stuff. That's ¾ of a ton right there."

Major Howard chipped in, "I've tasked the two DPV's to ferry supplies to the river bank as well. They can run back and forth in the next few hours and help lessen the weight in the hulk bus."

Sergeant Monroe said, "Why don't we just drop the engine out of the damaged bus. It's not like where we're going has a machine shop. The engine is dead, useless weight.

Shaffer said, "Okay. That's actually a good idea. It will take me 90 minutes or so with Private Sanchez helping me to drop the engine."

Major Howard said, "I'll send her over."

The next two hours was spent dropping the engine to save weight. Part of that time was spent retrieving that one tool that was already down at the river.

The kids seemed to think this was still an adventure. A hurried breakfast of instant oatmeal, powdered eggs and untoasted toast. Plain bread.

They loaded their backpacks with whatever they could carry from the bus. Some made two round trips, smaller kids struggled with making the two-mile twisting turn down the 1500 foot drop to the valley floor at 2500 feet.

Finally, the bus was ready to be lowered down the steep twisting incline. Sanchez steered and Shaffer was her ears and eyes. Walkie talkies helped the communication process.

It was a stressful two miles. The bus would take a corner to sharp and need to be pulled back thirty feet. The bus wouldn't turn sharp enough and need to be pulled back thirty feet.

Finally, at 10:15 hours everybody, supplies included, were at the White River bank, ready to cross.

The sound of a piston driven airplane shattered the sound of the rushing river. An old DC-3 flew over at about 1,000 feet with an F-15 right beside it. The DC-3 suddenly climbed and the F-15 had to go around to catch up.

The DC-3 headed to the highest peak at 11,000 plus feet. At about 12,500 feet, high above the valley floor, something tumbled out the side door of the DC-3, then another and another. Major Howard counted 25 packages.

Monroe said, "What the heck, those are people jumping. Did you see the markings on that plane?"

Howard replied, "Hard to miss. I did two years in South Korea. I'd better warn Nellis. Have we just been invaded by North Korea?"

Howard continued, "Get me May."

Monroe asked, "Which one is May Sir?"

Howard answered, "Joel May, looks like he was born a Marine, a little like Sergeant Carter from Gomer Pyle."

The call went down the line for May to see the commanding officer. He hustled over and started to pull himself to attention, snap a salute.

Howard said, "Easy soldier, no need to be formal. I want you to find a pair of binoculars and follow those parachutes." She pointed high in the sky.

She continued, "See where they go and report to me anything you think I need to know to guarantee the safety of these kids."

Lake   Doomsday Clock 11:59:59

May hustled off to find binoculars.

The Desert Patrol Vehicles carried the fifty kids across the swollen, but still navigable White River. It took time and Major Howard had ordered six soldiers to carry their sidearm and the other six to include a M4A1 carbine.

The M4A1 weighs 7.49 pounds, full loaded, holding 30 rounds of 5.56 X 45 mm NATO. The carbine is 33 inches long with the stock extended. Muzzle velocity of 2,970 feet per second and an effective firing range of 550 yards.

Private May hustled over to his commanding officer.

He said, "Crazy Sir. All but two of those paratroopers headed east. Two of them are headed our way. They are armed Sir. One seems to be chasing the other."

Major Howard issued a slew of orders.

She said, "Those of you with Carbines get behind the junk bus. The other six take the kids behind the good bus, now."

Monroe said, "Sir, the buses are on the opposite side of the river."

Major Howard said to Monroe, "Okay. Give me two carbines and I'll cross the river and take the kids downstream. If one of those son of a guns raises a muzzle, you waste them Sergeant. That's an order. They will not hurt one kid in my charge."

Monroe said, "Yes Sir!"

Howard spoke to the remaining soldiers, mostly women, "Which one of you is the intelligence specialist?"

Private Gattu stepped forward, "I am Sir!"

Major Howard said, "Lead the kids down river, look for the best possible cover. Watch those two parachutes."

Monroe and Shaffer watched as Private Gattu pulled a flute out of her backpack and started playing. In fifty yards, she had the kids at a forced marching pace, skipping along, moving away from danger.

Private May was watching the parachutes descending, binoculars firmly in place.

He said, to nobody, "Those are ram-jet chutes."

Several of the soldiers with carbines were watching thru their scopes. Safeties off. Serious now!

Private Grandson, Great-Granddaughter of a Navajo Code Talker said, "I hear the Army is going to change from Round to Cruciform parachutes."

Corporal Schuman said, "It's a pretty big difference. The Round parachutes descend at about 21 mph and the Cruciform at about 16 mph, almost 14% slower, 25% fewer injuries. You jump once a week or even once a month, a 14% decrease in landing speed is easier on your back and knees over time."

Private Dobbs said, "My Uncle has a Rogallo wing, paraglider. He loves jumping off the high peaks near San Diego and seeing how long and how far he flies."

The seconds ticked by and the ram-jet chutes with unknown parties came closer.

Private May yelled, "The highest guy is shooting at the chute below."

Private Grandson said, "Orders Sir?"

Sergeant Monroe said, "Delay firing, unless one of them aims at us. Right now, it's not our fight."

Private May said, "Sir, I estimate the chutes are less than 1,000 feet up. The lower guy is waving an American flag and holding a Bible."

Sergeant Monroe said, "Christians can kill you just as well. A bullet is a bullet. He aims his muzzle at us, waste him."

Private Dobbs said, "How about we shoot the guy doing the shooting, maybe a leg shot."

Lake   Doomsday Clock 11:59:59

Sergeant Monroe laughed, "You think you can hit the top guy at 200 yards? In the leg?"

Private Dobbs said, "Yes Sir."

Sergeant Monroe said, "Go for it."

A single shot echoed back and forth off the canyon walls.

Private May said, "Affirmative on the shot. Left thigh. No more firing."

Sergeant Monroe said, "Good job Dobbs. Everybody stay alert. We still have a high-risk environment. Where did you learn to shoot like that Dobbs?"

Dobbs laughed, "Jack rabbits in west Texas sir!"

The first chute landed and the woman shed her chute. She fell to her knees, hands laced behind his head, blood running from a chest wound.

Monroe shouted, "Medic, Corporal Donnelly."

The second chute landed about 75 yards away. The man struggled to remove his chute. Finally, he released it and slowly reached for his carbine.

Dobbs yelled, "Do not raise your weapon."

The man continued bringing the gun to bear on the person who landed first.

Four shots echoed across the valley. The man laid still, never to move again.

Donnelly raced out to the first paratrooper. Schuman right behind her.

Donnelly poked and probed, took pulse and blood pressure readings, tried to stem the flow of blood.

The woman struggled to speak, gasping for breath, obviously in pain, "I'm a Christian. I didn't want to do this mission, no choice, family is hostage in North Korea."

Donnelly said, "Don't try to talk."

Lake   Doomsday Clock 11:59:59

The woman said, "Hold my hand."

Donnelly clasped her hand. The other soldiers involved in the fire fight gathered around.

Private Elrod started the prayer, Psalms 23;

"The LORD is my shepherd, I shall not want.

He makes me lie down in green pastures;

he leads me beside still waters;

he restores my soul.

He leads me in right paths
for his name's sake.

Even though I walk through the darkest valley,
I fear no evil;
for you are with me;
your rod and your staff—
they comfort me.

You prepare a table before me
in the presence of my enemies;
you anoint my head with oil;
my cup overflows.
Surely goodness and mercy shall follow me
all the days of my life,
and I shall dwell in the house of the LORD
my whole life long."

She quietly passed from this earth. The group was silent for a few seconds.

Chapter 48

Las Vegas Airport 2 hours before

The tanks on the antique DC-3 were full. The plane was empty, except for the pilot and copilot.

The plane was built in Long Beach, California. DC-3's that were modified with a cargo door, hoist attachment, a strengthened floor, a shortened tail cone with towing shackles and an astrodome in the cabin roof were used by the military and called C-47's.

The C-47 and the DC-3 enjoyed numerous aliases. Americans called it the "Gooney Bird," "Doug," " Dumbo ," "Old Fatso". "Charlie 47," "Skytrain," " Skytrooper ," and "Tabby."

Civilian pilots called it the "Three," "Old Methuselah," "The Placid Plodder, "The Dowager Dutchess ," "The Flying Vagrant," and the "Dizzy Three." In Vietnam , it earned the nicknames "Puff the Magic Dragon," "Puff," "Spooky," and "The Dragon Ship."

This plane was old, "Rosie the Riveter" might have worked a shift during WWII, adding some of the 500,000 rivets used to hold her together.

Over the previous 18 months the pilot and co-pilot had put lots of hours behind the controls. A military pilot needs a minimum of 150 hours of live flight time each year to maintain proficiency. In North Korea, it is estimated, the average pilot receives 25 hours of flight time. Simulators help, but nothing takes the place of flying the real thing.

North Korea's Air Force has 940 modern airplanes, mostly obsolete Chinese and Russian aircraft.

The 25 special forces, 20 males and 5 females had blended in with other refugees. They lived in separate towns, went to different colleges and communicated thru a single email address. Messages were saved in draft mode, read by each person, initialed, saved, the control erased the draft and crafted a new message again in draft form.

Lake   Doomsday Clock 11:59:59

No messages sent means no messages intercepted by the NSA. Simple spy craft is the best.

Comment [d]:

The copilot remembered an early training flight near Kansas City. A training pilot from a company was checking them out and a mechanic was on board. The guy was a cowboy from Texas, boots, a blue work shirt with the name "Mifflin" stenciled across the pocket.

His coworker asked what would happen if they lost an engine. Mifflin calmly replied, "Don't worry the other engine will take you to the scene of the crash!"

The trainer and Mifflin thought it was funny. The copilot finally figured it out and thought they had a warped sense of humor.

The DC-3 left Las Vegas at 6:30 AM and made a short flight to a private field. The plane was wheeled into a hanger and the 25 special forces along with weapons were loaded.

Weapons were bought over two years, mostly black market. Because of dietary restrictions in their home country most of the soldiers arrived two years ago weighing less than 130 pounds. Diet, exercise, In-N-Out double doubles, most had gained 30 pounds, except the five females who gained 10 pounds on average.

The company that owned the plane possessed all the necessary documents to film near Nellis Air Force base. The real target was Yucca Mountain.

Yucca Mountain is a proposed nuclear waste site. The history is long and convoluted. The Nuclear Waste Act of 1987 designated the mountain as a deep geological repository storage facility. Congress approved the project in 2002 and ended funding in 2011 under the Obama administration via an amendment to the Department of Defense and full year appropriations act.

The project was highly contested by non-local people, mostly politicians. As a result, nuclear waste is stored across the country instead of at one central, geological

Lake   Doomsday Clock 11:59:59

safe site. The General Accounting Office went so far as to say the project was ended for political reasons and not safety or technical. Congress failed the American people yet again, giving in to lobbyist and PAC money. Blame Harry Reid, or don't. His priorities were to protect Nevada's interest over America's. It is how politics operate.

Nuclear power plants store nuclear waste mostly on site in dry cask storage, cement and steel casks. The military stores their waste in New Mexico at WIPP, Waste Isolation Pilot Plant, in rooms 2,150 feet underground.

The North Koreans were convinced Yucca Mountain contained nuclear waste that they could somehow release and contaminate most of America. It was a one-way mission for their great exalted leader, Kim Jong-un.

The DC-3 left the private airstrip with 25 passengers. It didn't take long for the military to contact them and explain the 400-foot flight rule. No flights higher than 400 feet.

The pilot agreed to the flight restrictions, but he kept breaking the rule so the Air Force sent an F-15 to escort the plane on its approved path. When the plane approached within 50 miles of Area 51 and Yucca mountain the crew was informed they had to turn back, now, or else.

This created some anxiety, but they did have a backup plan. Cheyenne Mountain located in Colorado Springs, Colorado was the secondary target. The plane had a flight range of almost 2,000 miles, so distance wasn't an issue.

The decision was made to drop the special forces near the western portion of the Rockies and let them hike to Colorado Springs on the eastern side.

The crew informed the F-15 pilot of their intentions to climb and cross the 11,000-foot peaks. They were crossing a plateau with an elevation of 4,000 feet. They plane had a climb rate of 1,130 feet per minute at 120 mph. It took the crew just 10 minutes to get to 14,500 feet. The F-15 kept going around because it has a stall speed of 130 knots or 150 mph.

Lake   Doomsday Clock 11:59:59

Communication with the F-15 was delayed because of garbled radio signals and the military getting bogged down in the news about Hamburg.

Down below, Todd and the squad had been notified to watch for the DC-3. They watched the dance between the F15 and DC-3 as the old plane climbed higher.

The F15 buzzing around like an angry bee, unable to fly slow enough to effectively cut off the old bird.

The 15 students were placed in an underground room that held a generator. Justin gave them a harsh speech about consequences.

Justin pointed at them with his finger, "This is my finger."

Then he held up his gun, "This is my gun. One is for shooting, the other for fun! Stay inside, don't screw around. There will be live ammunition bouncing all over. Who's in charge here?"

Jeff said, "I'm in charge Sir!"

Wil said, "I am as well. We'll keep everybody inside and heads down."

Justin said, "That's what I want to hear. We'll come get you when it's all over. You have food, water, bedding, a toilet. Stay relatively quiet, talk, play games, no poker." He knew they would play poker.

He closed the door and rejoined the squad.

Adam, the officer in charge, had finally spoken with Nellis. The instructions were clear, the soldiers in the DC-3 were considered invaders, eliminate. Deadly force authorized.

How do you kill a human being?

Not that many years ago men and women had defined roles. The men did the physical labor, plowed the fields, worked in the factories, came home tired.

The woman kept the house, raised the children, cooked, laundry, sewed.

Lake   Doomsday Clock 11:59:59

Then World War II arrived and the military needed able-bodied men to fight in Europe and Japan. Supplies were required, massive amounts of guns, ammo, tanks and planes; and the young women were the labor force in factories.

In war, you have a choice. Kill to help your country continue the way of life, or be killed.

Todd, Justin, Pat and Adam were the best shots in the squad. Justin was the true expert. He could hit out to 1200 yards consistently. The rest were reasonable accurate within 900 yards.

Carl, Robert, Chris and Jon acted as spotters.

They watched the 23 parachutes come down, floating to within two miles of where they were stationed. They topography gave the advancing force very little choice.

The squad moved into position and waited. Within 45 minutes the North Koreans came into sight. Marching up a long flat field.

They waited some more, until the 23 North Koreans were half way up the hill and about 800 yards away. The shooters were using a SOCOM M-13, bolt action and a .300 Win Mag cartridge.

It wasn't a fair fight. If you want a fair fight, watch an old western fiction movie. In real life the side with the best equipment, best training, best intelligence, usually wins.

The North Koreans expended lots of ammunition. Their weapons were designed for 500-600 yards. Plus, everybody was shooting mostly unfamiliar models, and without target practice their skills were rusty. Outgunned, out of shape, bad combination for the North Koreans.

It took three minutes to dispatch the 23 special forces. Nobody gave high fives, no smiles, just an efficient job. The squad was alive and the bad guys were neutralized.

Robert and Adam went to fetch a backhoe to bury the bodies. Nellis wanted all evidence erased.

Lake   Doomsday Clock 11:59:59

Lake   Doomsday Clock 11:59:59

Chapter 49

Major Howard and the kids were climbing the side of the valley, headed to meet the squad.

The kids had questions.

What happened?

Major Howard, "There was a fight between two parachute jumpers."

We heard gunshots?

Major Howard, "True."

Who got shot?

Major Howard, "The two parachute jumpers."

Did they die?

Major Howard, "Yes!"

No lies, nothing volunteered.

The good bus towed the hulk of a bus. Slow going, sharp turns, nothing was easy.

She decided to send the Desert Patrol Vehicles ahead to scout and find the squad and the exact school location.

The group stopped for a late breakfast.

Corporal Gonzalez was the main cook.

She asked Elrod, "Why do they call you Preacher?"

Elrod answered, "My Daddy was a Preacher and I spent many days imitating him."

Gonzalez asked, "Do you preach now?"

Elrod replied, "I serve. I try to be an example to others. Live my life by deeds and not words."

Gonzalez asked, "Could you say a prayer before the kids eat breakfast?"

Lake   Doomsday Clock 11:59:59

He said, "Sure, I'd be honored."

The breakfast was prepared, simple, and easy. Oatmeal packs, applesauce, orange drink and bread.

Gattu called the kids to breakfast by playing her flute.

Gonzalez said, "Preacher Elrod will bless the food."

Elrod said, "Bow your heads. Dear Almighty Father. We come to you asking for your blessing and safe guidance on this adventure. Please keep the young people safe and give wisdom to the adults guiding them and protecting them. Bless this food for the nourishment of our bodies. Amen"

The kids chowed down.

The sound of a helicopter interrupted the breakfast scene. It was a small military chopper. An old McDonnell Douglas MD-500 defender.

It flew over the small group of students and soldiers, circled around and slowly dropped from 500 feet to 100 feet. It hovered, as if to say, I'm not sure if I'm landing or this is as low as I can go. Finally, a small package floated out of the helicopter and when the package bounced on the ground the helicopter left.

Silence, nobody moved for a few seconds. Shaffer walked over to the package and picked it up.

He said, "Major Howard, addressed to you Sir!"

Major Howard took the package, opened it up and held up a small envelope. She opened it, read to herself. Looked at everybody.

She said, "I'm going to share this letter. It is disturbing. When we find the squad and school kids we'll talk some more.

Major Howard,

We are under a general quarantine. Do not return to Nellis Air Force base under any circumstances. A type of

Lake   Doomsday Clock 11:59:59

unknown flu has appeared all over the world in the last 12 hours. The CDC is working on a vaccine.

Do not attempt to communicate with us. It appears our systems have been hacked and we no longer trust our security.

Good luck, God bless. All of you are in our prayers. Hide, stay low, the squad should stay separate from your group.

Give the squad a free hand in protecting and feeding your family.

They are good, but hard headed.

Sincerely,

Major General Leslie Gomez

United States Air Force

The group loaded up after a hurried breakfast. Nobody seemed sure what to say. The kids, 50 of them, wondered about their parents. Kids are still worriers. A common fear is losing a parent. Each of these kids had both parents or their only parent in the military.

They walked, 5 miles separated them from the squad and the 15 kids in the Hogwarts School. The discussion was awkward.

What are we going to do?

How do we eat with no commissary selling food?

What about clothes?

I'm going to grow out of these pants? Shoes?

I miss my Mom and or Dad?

Major Howard had not been trained for this command. Nobody was prepared for what the world was experiencing right now.

Chapter 50

Hogwarts was experiencing a different type of reunion. The boys and girls were uber happy when the squad returned.

Questions.

Did you kill them?

Do you feel bad about killing them?

How many died?

Would they have killed us?

Did anybody get hurt?

The students walked around outside. After being inside a metal box, breathing fresh air felt good.

They ate a late breakfast of eggs, orange juice and buttered bread. The table was cleared off and the kids sensed life had changed.

The sound of an approaching engine grew louder. After a few minutes, the two Desert Patrol Vehicles came into view.

Schuman was driving one and Grandson the other one. They pulled up, stopped, turned them off. Climbed out.

Schuman smiled, said, "Hogwarts?"

Robert replied, "So we've been told."

Grandson spoke next, "We've got 50 kids and 10 other soldiers coming up the hill, maybe 35 minutes behind us."

Robert asked, "Okay. Orders?"

Schuman said, "Way above my paygrade Sir!"

Carl laughed, "65 kids, 20 soldiers. Do we have a mission?"

Grandson said, "No idea. Our job was to contact you guys and report back to Major Howard."

Lake   Doomsday Clock 11:59:59

Adam spoke next, "We're here. We did encounter 23 North Korean forces this morning."

Schuman said, "We had two near us."

Adam said, "You take care of them?"

Grandson said, "Yes. How about you?"

Adam said, "Everybody neutralized."

Grandson asked, "Was that an invasion? One of the North Korean jumpers told us the original target was Yucca Mountain Nuclear Waste Depository."

Adam said, "I don't know. It wasn't a very good plan. Piss poor planning ensures piss poor performance."

Schuman said, "We'd better head back. Prepare for 62 more guests."

Adam said, "We'll open up the guest quarters, put mints on your pillows." He smiled.

The two DPV's started back up and headed back down the hill to report to Major Howard.

The squad looked at each other. 62 more people in a school designed for 23-25 wasn't going to work.

Pat said, "We need to move. Feeding and housing 65 kids and 20 adults is going to be a major task."

Jon said, "If this conflict goes nuclear we need some distance between us and Las Vegas."

Chris said, "We need good hunting grounds. Some flat land to cultivate crops."

Todd asked, "Do we still have that hydro generator?

Carl said, "It's packed away, still unopened."

They each took two kids with them and started to inventory what they had in camp. There were outbuildings they'd never opened. They needed to know their options, resources available.

Lake   Doomsday Clock 11:59:59

They discovered 10 ATV's in one 53-foot-long storage container. Enough guns and ammo to supply a small army. Also discovered was a container filled with MRE's, Meals Ready to Eat.

Somebody had stocked this camp as a bug out hidey hole. It just wasn't in the right location for 85 people. The sound of a diesel engine straining up the hill brought everybody to the main house.

It was quite a site. The good bus pulling the broken bus. The two DPV's darting in and out of kids and soldiers strung out walking.

Finally, everybody arrived. The bus stopped, turned off, silence.

Major Howard spoke first, "We have a new mission. Nellis has been quarantined. It appears to be either a natural or manmade biological weapon. The CDC in Atlanta is working on a solution. In the meantime, the fatality rate is around 70%. It is worldwide as of 13 hours ago. Nobody has any answers.

Now the bad news. You've all heard about Hamburg, a nuclear explosion. Every country lost either it's number one or number two leader, except North Korea and they stayed away.

Russia has sent a warning and a heads up to the United States. It seems that during the Cold War they smuggled in 100 suitcase small nuclear weapons and planted them in major cities. In case Russia was attacked and the top government officials taken out these bombs are on a 48-hour timer.

Russia claims there is no map showing where the bombs are hidden and no way to stop the count down.

It appears that within 36 hours or so the United States as we know it will cease to exist. Our new President has admitted we also planted bombs in Russia and China and so we have activated those timers as well.

Lake   Doomsday Clock 11:59:59

We have 36 hours to move away from Las Vegas. Get far enough away to escape major radiation. The world as we knew it has come to an end. We have advanced notice being part of the military.

We need to make sure these kids survive. They are the ones who will rebuild in time. Mankind has run out of second chances. The Doomsday clock has hit midnight.

Any questions?"

Lake   Doomsday Clock 11:59:59

Epilogue

Now what?

Originally this story was the beginning of a seven-part series.

Let's start a dialogue. How do we address the problems facing America?

Social injustice, lack of survival skills, nuclear weapons, over-population, immigration, pollution, and the list goes on and on.

I don't want to write the second story, the day after a global meltdown.

That piece of trash you see on the ground, pick it up. End the day leaving your neighborhood, your school, your house, better than it was when you woke up.

Improve yourself. Think globally, act locally. Don't focus on telling others how to act, take care of yourself. Be the best version of you possible. It will lead to success.

We are all in this together. I win, you win. I lose, you lose, we all lose.

Dan

Printed in Great Britain
by Amazon

43576551R00179